Nemesis

THE CORPSE PRINCESS

JAYCE CARTER

The Corpse Princess
ISBN # 978-1-83943-780-9
©Copyright Jayce Carter 2022
Cover Art by Kelly Martin ©Copyright March 2022
Interior text design by Claire Siemaszkiewicz
Totally Bound Publishing

THE CORPSE
PRINCESS

Dedication

To my mom, who keeps trying to sell my books to
people she meets in the sauna.
Thank you for always supporting me!

Chapter One

Nem

Revenge is a fire that burns everything, including the person who sets it.

That was fine by me—I'd happily turn to ash if I could take a few others with me.

I glanced around the busy room, at the people who moved around with no idea about the monster among them, the one with the face of a girl.

"You want a drink?" The man who asked wore a suit, and I had no idea who he was. There were people worth knowing, people important enough for me to identify and acknowledge, and there was everybody else.

I wasn't there for fun, to make friends—those things were far outside my life. If they weren't people I could use to get to my goal, I didn't give a fuck about them.

However, that wasn't the plan tonight. Every game had its rules, its roles, and I knew exactly how to play.

Tonight? I was trying to blend in, to be just another person in a sea of people who didn't matter.

That was the plan. I needed to move through the space but not draw too much attention. It was a line — stay hidden but close enough to get the information I needed.

And what I needed was the man across the room in the white tank top, the one with the tattoos on his left arm and a shot glass in his hand.

"Thank you," I told the other man, the unimportant one who had decided to try his luck. "But I'm okay."

"I haven't seen you here before," he said, apparently not the type to take no for an answer. "I would have remembered this hair of yours." He reached out, taking a strand of the bright and completely unnatural red between his fingers.

The audacity. I kept myself still and pulled my lips into a smile. I could bury a knife between his ribs, but keeping my eyes on the goal was more important. I'd come too far to give up what I wanted most for what sounded good in the moment.

"I'm new." I shifted enough so he lost his grasp on my hair.

"Oh yeah? How'd you find your way here, little rabbit?"

Little rabbit? I struggled not to roll my eyes at the stupid nickname, at how little it resembled me at all. It was like so many other things — some man trying to put me in my place for no good reason, him judging me because it made him feel more important.

"I met someone at a party and he invited me."

The man paused and furrowed his eyebrows. *That's right. Think it through.* This world was all about who a person knew, about the connections they had. I could watch it all run through his head.

Who was this man who'd invited me? Could I already be claimed by someone else, someone he didn't want to screw with? The level of unease told me where this particular man sat when it came to power.

The more fear, the more uncertainty, the farther down he was, and the more people he had to worry about. The last thing he'd want was to piss off someone who would take the offense personally.

This guy was basement-level, judging by the way he took off with hardly a goodbye.

Good riddance. I needed to focus.

The man I'd been watching tossed back his shot. He rested against the bar, his attention on a woman beside him. Her smile was tight at the corners, a sign so subtle few would have noticed it. It told me what I could have guessed already.

A whore.

I didn't say that with any censure. Everyone sold themselves in one way or another. Muscle sold their strength, wives sold their youth and mob bosses sold their souls. Women who sold sex weren't a bit different, other than they were often more talented.

It also made it easier to watch the man, since the professional would keep his attention.

I sipped the drink I'd ordered, the whiskey sharp on my tongue. I wouldn't overindulge — I needed all my wits about me — but not drinking would make me stand out.

The club was louder than it had any right to be. It was full of people who thought they could move up in life, the ones who hadn't accepted their place in the world, which was fine by me.

Hope gave me a foot in the door.

I brought my glass to my lips again, sipping more of the burning liquid, taking in the man across the room.

Herold 'Lucky' Hanson. His parents had been idiots to give him such an absurd name, which was one reason I didn't think his nickname fit him well. He didn't seem all that Lucky to me.

He sure won't be soon...

I drank one more time before approaching the bar. Voices filtered through the music, tiny bits of information I filed away as I crossed the space.

A woman flirted while admitting she was there behind her husband's back. A man trying to put one over on his boss. Two women, sisters, who cheered while a bodyguard watched over them.

That was how it worked, though. Everyone had their own shit going on. Even though what *I* had going on was all I cared about, it was amazing how damned busy the world was. Everyone moved around continuously, always striving for something, running from things, toward other things, and all with a million plans.

It was the best puzzle in the world, one with parts that never stopped.

As I neared the bar, I closed in on the only conversation that mattered—that between Lucky and the woman who'd need to find a new mark for the night.

"That's a lot," Lucky said. "I don't normally pay for it, you know."

Liar. Everyone paid for sex in one way or another.

"That's the same thing people like to say about most jobs, but the reality is that there's a difference between a professional and an amateur. Any old person can scribble out a stick figure, but that's not the same as the skills of an artist. A quick lay, that's one thing, but what I can offer?" She dragged her fingers down his arm. "Well, that is an entirely different thing."

She's good. I filed that away, noting her black hair, her painted red lips, for when I might need information. A person could never have enough sources, and I'd learned those could be the difference between success and failure.

And failure carried a hefty price in my world.

Lucky moved his gaze over the woman, a slow, lingering perusal that made my skin crawl. "Well, that sounds fun. Might just be worth it."

The woman smiled and reached out, setting her palm on Lucky's forearm. "We have rooms here, upstairs."

Lucky shook his head. "No. I don't like having a potential audience or recording."

The woman's smile slipped, a hesitancy there. "It's dangerous for girls in my line of work to follow men home."

Lucky let out a dark chuckle. "Girls in your line of work oughta read people well enough to know which guys want to fuck you and which ones want to kill you. If I wanted to hurt you, I wouldn't be offering to pay you."

Even still, the woman didn't look convinced.

Lucky must have realized he was losing her, because he leaned in closer, lowering his voice until I could only just catch it. "You think I don't know how people are dealt with who fuck with this place? With you girls? I ain't stupid—I wouldn't put myself in the crosshairs here. I'll pay your boss personally, in advance, for the whole night. Be a fucking idiot to do anything after that, and I ain't no idiot."

The woman's smile faded, as if it took all her attention to consider Lucky, to judge the truth of his words. After a moment, she nodded. "Okay. Let me go get my boss and send her over."

I stayed behind Lucky, out of his line of sight. Another woman came up after the first left, this woman with hair so blonde it was white, the confident steps of someone who had no fear walking through the crowded club full of the sort of men no one wanted to cross.

They spoke, the woman's voice strong and sure. They agreed on a price, a time, and the woman offered a not-so-subtle threat along with the rest. Lucky paid the price—five thousand—in cash on the spot. It seemed, despite his previous objections, he'd gone there looking for sex. There wasn't any other reason for him to carry that much cash.

Lucky took off after writing down his address on a card and handing it over to the woman.

The woman didn't rise, though. Even when alone, dressed in a suit with no shirt beneath the jacket, that dipped low to show off the valley of space between her breasts, she remained.

At least, until she lifted her eyes to me. "You seem awfully interested in this," she said.

I met her gaze, surprised by her bright blue eyes. They stood out against her pale hair, making her striking in a way few people were.

I could lie, try to pretend I was just anyone there. The way to react always depended on the person I was talking to. I had to measure them up, decide the best way to manipulate them. This woman? She was too smart, too calculating for me to act as if she had it all wrong.

Recalling what Lucky had said, though, gave me my way in.

Everyone had a weakness, something they feared, something they wanted. Know what that was, and I could get whatever I wanted from them.

"I think it would be a good idea if your employee missed that appointment," I answered.

"Oh, really? Wouldn't that be bad for business?"

I shook my head. "The thing is, Lucky there won't be all that lucky tonight. That's the way the night will go no matter what, and your girl already got paid, so it'd be safest if she just wasn't there at all."

The woman narrowed her eyes. "Does he deserve it?"

I thought back, remembering Lucky when he was younger, able to picture the way the red light had bounced off his white teeth. Did anyone deserve it?

"He deserves it and more."

The woman didn't react with surprise. Instead, those red lips of hers pulled to the side in a cold grin, one that screamed of a camaraderie between us, as if we were cut from the same cloth. "Do you know why I named this place the way I did? People hear the name, Diamond's Edge, and they think it has something to do with women being gems."

"If that's not it, what is it?"

"Diamonds are the hardest naturally occurring substance on earth. Despite this, they're bought and protected and valued as something pretty while most of us ignore their reality." The woman set her elbow on the counter, her eyes unnerving in their intensity. "That's what I named it after. The girls here, they're seen as pretty, as something to be hoarded and owned. I named this club because the women here have that same edge when they need it. It's something people forget too often." She held her hand out. "My name is Valeria Preston."

I shook her hand. "Nem Syler."

"Nem?" She paused. "Odd name."

"And Valeria isn't?"

She lifted her eyebrow, then smiled again, as if she had to concede the point. "You know, I see a lot of new people walk in here, people who say a lot, make a lot of promises. Usually, they mean very little. You, however, might be the first I've fully believed. I'll ensure you're not disturbed by any of my people this evening." She rose, motions smooth and lovely. "And do make sure he doesn't get off too easily for whatever he did that put that fire in your eyes."

That was a promise I didn't mind making at all.

Chapter Two

Nem

The evening was cool, since when it hit October, the temperature tended to drop fast. It meant I'd paired my tank top with a faded leather jacket I loved, one too heavy for most of the year in Southern California. It showed wear spots, scratches — proof of the hard life it had lived.

Just as Valeria had promised, no one showed up at Lucky's at midnight, the time the girl had been scheduled to arrive. I didn't mind casualties, not if the prize was good enough, but I avoided them when I could.

Casualties drew too much attention.

Lucky's house was large, but not on the best plot of land. Then again, any property this close to the beach didn't come cheap. However, it seemed to me he'd bought the land and built the most ridiculous house possible on it. It was all about the show, and I couldn't believe code enforcement hadn't complained that he'd built to nearly the fence line.

Though, my sense of Lucky said he cared more about what it looked like than what it was, and a peek in through the large windows from across the street screamed the same. Inside was décor that would match a mansion, not the thousand-square-foot house crammed onto the tiny parcel of land.

Lucky stood by the bar, pouring drinks into two glasses as if it were a date. He was probably pretending it was, that he was the type of man that caliber of woman would be with by choice rather than for money.

He wasn't, of course.

I moved my gaze across the gutters of the house, the corners, searching for cameras. *None.* Then again, Lucky was old school. Many of them never got with the new technology, with the advancements, too stuck in their ways.

It made my job easier if I didn't have to avoid or disable any cameras.

I crept forward, my steps soft and silent. A quick hop put me over the side gate, into the backyard, before I slid the hood from beneath my leather jacket up to hide my hair, then pulled on the gloves from my pocket.

The huge windows continued in the back, and as I moved past them, I checked for sensors.

Nothing.

It was as if Lucky were begging for someone to come for him, for someone to take what he wouldn't do the least bit of work to make a challenge. Not that I wanted a challenge, not from him.

Lucky was just one name on a list for me, and he was all the way at the bottom. He had a part to play, but I didn't give a shit if it was easy or difficult. I wasn't a man who needed to prove my skill to anyone.

Near the southwest corner of the house, in the backyard, I found his bedroom — complete with hooks on his bedframe.

Only an idiot would let a man like that tie them up. Hell, I wouldn't let *any* man tie me up. In my experience people — and men in particular — hadn't proven themselves all that trustworthy. Being entirely at the mercy of one?

Fucking stupid.

I opened the window to Lucky's bedroom — slowly to avoid noise — and slid into the darkened room. He had no desk, no computer, no sign of filing cabinets. Hell, I was shocked he had a cell phone. He didn't seem a details sort of man.

The white plush carpet beneath my feet helped muffle any sound my steps made, without the groaning of wood to alert him.

Down the short hallway, I spotted him, his back to me, his gaze moving between the door and his watch as if realizing for the first time the girl might not show.

Well, a girl would, just not the one who planned to fuck him in the way he'd enjoy.

On the large bar that stretched the length of one side of his living room, I grasped the neck of a vodka bottle. It was heavy, showing it had been made with good quality, thick glass. *Perfect.*

I didn't bother with a quip, with something clever. Life wasn't about clever — it wasn't about the right little saying — it was about doing what needed to be done. About getting through the shit the world threw, about clawing to the top no matter how many times a person fell.

So grasping the neck of that bottle, I swung it at the back of his head, and the crunch of it against his skull was better than all the music at Diamond's Edge.

* * * *

It took over an hour for Lucky to come to, and by the time he did, I'd tied him to one of his precious expensive leather bar stools, the sort with a backrest.

He blinked, though each eye did so at a different time, telling me he had a concussion at least.

Was I supposed to feel guilty about that? Fuck guilt. What had that ever gotten anyone? We did what we had to do, and I didn't give a damn about what it took to get where I needed to be.

"Who the fuck are you?" he asked, wincing as if even the sound of his own voice grated on his nerves.

I pulled out another stool, away from the bar, until it was just before him. I'd bound his wrists together and his legs to the base of the stool, both with zip ties. Lastly, I used a short chain of three zip ties to connect his wrists to the binds of his feet, behind the stool, making it impossible for him to wiggle free.

A smart person never fucked with binds. People who got tied up weren't all that forgiving if they got free.

"That doesn't really matter," I told him before taking a seat on the stool and leaning forward, my hood still on. He could see my face, but if anyone glanced in—I'd pulled the blinds but being careful was important—I didn't want anything easily identifiable, like my hair.

"Oh, it does. Who sent you? Who was dumb enough to send some little girl after Lucky?"

"Talking about yourself in the third person is pretentious, and you don't look nearly smart enough to pull that off. Also, no one sent me."

He snorted, an ugly sound that came out nasally. "Right. So, what did I do to you? Fuck you and never call you again? Because even after the wallop you gave me, I can still give you what you were missing, baby."

I lowered my eyes to his groin, not the smallest amount of lust there. Not that there ever was.

Sometimes I wondered if I was broken in that way. I mean, I didn't think some old killer like Lucky, a man past his prime and who, even *in* his prime, hadn't been all that good, would spark any real lust, but it had been so long since I'd felt that sort of thing.

The need for revenge had strangled passion from me until it was buried beside mercy.

It meant even if he were the sort I might want, even if he were the hottest man I'd ever seen with a cock that could make a porn star drool, I felt *nothing*.

And I made sure that showed on my face. If he had been hard, no doubt all the 'I don't give a fuck' I gave him would have shriveled away any erection he'd managed.

"Bitch," he muttered as if that gave him some imagined upper hand.

I ignored the insult. It didn't matter at all, just the last vestige of a drowning man. One last swipe as the ocean swallowed him up.

"Do you still work for Kyler Williams?"

That got his attention, as if the name made him realize this was bigger than him or his dick. "Is that who you're after?" He let out a sharp laugh. "Only a fucking moron would go after Kyler."

"In that case, you won't mind answering my questions."

"I sure as fuck mind. Kyler ain't the sort of enemy a smart man wants."

"Neither am I, and it seems I'm the bigger threat to you at the moment." I didn't pull my knife, didn't play with it like amateurs did. Scaring a person into talking was a matter of showing them what they wanted.

Lucky had been threatened many times in his life, no doubt. He knew damn well what I *could* do if I wanted to. Showing him a knife, that wouldn't tell him anything he didn't already know.

So instead, I had to give him a glimmer of something better, something to strive for.

He snorted, though the sound came after a moment of hesitation, as if he realized…maybe he was in more trouble than he'd thought. "I once saw a man betray Kyler, and he was found the next day flayed alive. I heard Kyler started at his toes and the man didn't die till he reached his chest. Sorry, but you ain't got shit on him, little girl."

I leaned backward, giving him space, letting him stew in his own sense of certainty. "If we're talking about stories, about things Kyler has done, I feel like that's the exact topic I'd like to stay on." I moved my gaze to his hand, to a mangled patch of skin there between the tattoos. "That's some burn you have."

He made a dismissive sound, one that implied it was nothing. "A memento from a favor I did for him."

"A favor? Was it worth that?"

"Fuck yeah, it was. Kyler is a mean son of a bitch, but he pays up what he owes."

I glanced around the place, making sure to look just as impressed with it as I had been with his dick. "*This* is his gratitude? A cracker box filled with cheap, shiny shit while he lives up in the hills in a mansion? Yeah, he pays up real well."

Lucky's face went red, a rush of anger that accompanied him twisting his arms as if he could break free and get me for my insults.

Good luck.

"Yeah, he paid me well. And before you want to open your fucking trap and talk shit, you should know I got that burn dealing with another uppity bitch who thought she was more than she was. She talked shit to him, didn't understand her fucking place, and Kyler? He put her in the goddamned ground for it, and me? I lit the match."

Perfect. "Thank you," I said as I rose from my seat. "That's exactly what I needed."

He furrowed his eyebrows, a look of absolute confusion. Poor guy—I almost pitied him. Living life with hardly more than two brain cells to rub together had to make everything more difficult. "What?"

"I needed to ensure I was right. I don't do anything until I'm sure, until I know for absolute certainty. I was pretty sure it was you, but I needed you to admit it. I don't like fuck-ups or mistakes, you know. Now, let me be clear, you get one chance to answer me—just the one."

"And you'll let me go?"

"Not a chance. You answer me? I slit your throat. You don't answer me? I won't."

"What kind of deal is that?"

I leaned in close, whispering my question to him, right into his ear, as if it needed to be hidden from everyone else.

When I pulled back, his eyes widened, staring at me as if it made no sense. I didn't ask again, just waited for him.

He'd heard me.

He shook his head, a quick jerk. I figured as much. It would have all been too easy if he could have answered me, and things this important were never easy.

So, I moved backward, ignoring the way the carpet squished beneath my boots and the scent of the gasoline I'd poured all over the tiny garish house.

He didn't call after me, as if he had finally realized how fucked he really was, that there wasn't a damn thing he could do. We all paid for our mistakes eventually, and tonight was his night.

When I reached the front door, I pulled two matches from my pocket and dragged them down the doorframe, the scent of sulfur as they lit so damned familiar.

I didn't look back when I tossed them, when they caught the accelerant on fire, when those flames exploded around the living room, when Lucky screamed out.

What was there to see? We'd all died ten fucking years ago—we'd just been too stupid to lie down.

So here I was, putting shit right, finishing the botched job and finally burying the past.

Chapter Three

Nem

I was dreaming.

I knew it, the way I always knew it. I never had this nightmare without being fully aware I was just reliving it all, that the synapses in my brain were just recycling trauma in some stupid attempt to come to terms with it all.

Knowing that it wasn't real didn't change anything, though. I couldn't stop it, couldn't get off the track that I'd walked too many times. As it all played out before me, it felt like I was right back there.

I choked on the thick smoke that filled the house, the fire already consuming all the evidence. It would be so easy to close my eyes, to give in to the pain, the anger, the reality that the life I'd thought was solid wasn't, that the people I'd trusted could betray me like this.

My mother had stopped moving, her life slipping away before my eyes as the crackle of the fire neared. The pain in my chest and side melted together and made it so tempting to close my eyes and give in to what felt inevitable.

Everything I thought I had, the life, the family, it had been torn away in the span of a few gunshots. What was the point in doing anything at all? What did I have if I survived? If I lived through any of this?

Something inside me stirred, like an old whisper. A voice from the men I'd cared about, the ones who hadn't been there that day when I'd needed them came to me—*Nothing matters but survival.*

I thought about Kyler, about the father who had betrayed me, the one who had set up the murder of my mother and me. The sight of my sister's face, who now would be alone with that monster, hit me.

I wasn't sure what it was that made me move, that forced my broken body into motion. Maybe it was all of it, all the things I wasn't ready to let go. A sister I loved, a father who needed to pay for what he'd done, a mother who lay dead and four men who were supposed to protect me but hadn't.

Whatever it was gave me a strength I hadn't had before, one I'd never thought I'd possessed. I dragged my body over the flooring, away from the flames, and toward the hidden room inside my closet, the one those men had shown me. I cried out when I had to reach up, had to press the panel to get it to open. Every move I made spread agony through me, but something stronger than that pressed me onward.

The hidden room wasn't large, just enough for a single person to huddle inside. However, on the other side of it, a grate rested to allow in air. I pulled at it, slicing my fingers on the sharp edges, and I had no idea how exactly I got it free. The metal groaned, giving way, making an escape route.

I was even slower in the backyard, hauling my damn near useless body through the grass, leaving a red trail behind me.

A small line of shrubs rested only a few feet away, yet the distance stretched out. When I got myself there, when whatever strength I had left vanished, when the world drifted away and dimmed, I saw one last thing before darkness took me.

A pair of eyes, the same unique silver color as my own, the eyes I'd never seen in any of my family, staring down at me.

I bolted upright in bed, those eyes burned into my memory, the nightmare loosening its grip on me.

I reminded myself Lucky was dead, that I'd left him to burn just like he'd done to me, eased myself with the fact that I'd gotten the last laugh. The flames of the dream died down, the fear from the nightmare lessoning beneath the empty coldness that consumed me.

Breath by breath, it all went away. The anger, the shock...none of it could gain a hold now that I was awake.

The girl who had dragged herself out of that house, whose heart had stopped in the grass of that backyard, she was gone. The dreams were just echoes.

I wasn't her. When I woke, when I remembered that, the frozen waters of whatever I was now came back, filling me, drowning the memory of her suffering.

She'd died in that backyard, and I'd taken her place.

Just a corpse with unfinished business.

* * * *

I sipped my whiskey surrounded by the noise and chaos of Diamond's Edge.

The music helped to wash away the memory of my dream, to remind myself I wasn't there anymore. It let me pretend for a moment that I was just like everyone else. Not that being like everyone else was a goal of mine. Even if I wanted that—and it sounded dreadful—it wasn't possible. The fact that a week before I'd walked away as a man screamed and burned to death set up that fact pretty clearly.

And that night? When I'd crawled into the bed in my hotel room? Oh, I'd never slept so well. I didn't suffer from accusatory eyes staring at me, from recalling Lucky's frightened, pained screaming. Those things were, if anything, a lullaby. They were my reward for a job well done.

I turned on the stool, away from the bar, to take in the club. The place hadn't been open when I'd lived here.

The people inside behaved themselves. I'd seen Valeria make the rounds once or twice, intervene when needed, and the way the men listened made me take notice.

Who was she?

I'd dug up little on her, telling me she kept a low profile for a good reason. No one who lived in our world was that clean.

The rules became clear, as well.

Behave yourself.

Don't fuck with Valeria.

A central stage sat at the far end of the largest room, and a man performed up there, dressed in a black thong. He moved along with the music, motions fluid but strong. It reminded me of the times I saw gymnastic competitions, how the men could move with such confidence and somehow not look weak. It had shocked me, given my life had revolved around the sort of men who saw strength as a synonym to bulk, who killed without a second thought.

The man on stage captivated me, and judging by the others drawn to the sight, I wasn't alone.

I forced myself to look away, to take in the rest of the space. Tables were set in front of the stage, and staircases to the sides led up to private rooms that overlooked the performance areas. There were other stages, other sitting areas away from that one large space, places where people could gather, where there was more dancing and mingling.

The last area of the club was darker, a room with a few pool tables where the music wasn't as loud.

And that was exactly where I was headed.

I took my drink and passed through the hallway to the billiards area. It felt more like a dive bar and less like an ecstasy-fueled nightclub. I was only twenty-seven years old, but I already felt far too jaded for the main club.

The strike of pool balls was like home. I took a seat at one of the tall bar tables, looking over the room. The clientele was older here, less interested in dancers and more interested in getting drunk in the dark.

My sort of people.

A man shook hands with another, passing a fold of bills between them before the one who had paid walked away. The other man turned his gaze to mine, his lips curling into a smirk. "You up for a game, sugar?"

I couldn't come up with a good reason why not, so I took another drink of my whiskey, then came over, setting the glass on the edge of the table. "Sure."

"Don't worry—I'll go easy on you," he promised before he held out a cue to me.

While I'd have preferred to use my own, this wouldn't be the first time I'd wasted hours unexpectedly at a bar, when my own stick was nowhere near me because a job took me somewhere new. All real pool players knew how to make the best out of shitty bar cues. I took it and chalked the tip as he racked the balls.

"Eight-ball," he explained and hung the rack on the wall. "Normally, I expect folks to call their shots, but I think you can get away with just about anything you want, sugar."

I gave him a smile before leaning over, falling into the practiced motions of the game, the heft of the cue, the slide of polished wood against my thumb all wonderfully familiar.

The smack of the cue ball into the racked ones was like a music all its own. A solid fell into the corner pocket—the three-ball—so I focused there. The man's smile fell away as he watched me run the table, as I called each shot before taking it. *Two-ball in the side pocket. Four in the corner.* When the eight-ball fell, the man let out a curse, never getting to take a single shot.

"Well, fuck," he muttered, the end of his stick tapping against the floor. "Guess I didn't need to give you a handicap, did I?"

I picked my glass up again, taking another sip, before leaning a hip against the edge of the pool table. "I might have let you play if you hadn't called me sugar."

"That name sure doesn't fit you, does it? Not so sweet."

"I don't know about that." A new voice stopped me in my tracks, made me hang my drink in the air a breath before the edge touched my lip.

It can't be…

"I had this coffee drink one time called The Desert Dog, and it had a mix of brown sugar and cayenne pepper — sweet as hell but with a kick. What I learned was that pussies need sugar without the spice — for the rest of us, we're just fine with a bit of heat," the new man finished, his lips pulled into a smile that twisted my stomach.

The man who hadn't gotten to take a single shot during the game didn't even mutter at the not-very-subtle insult before taking off. Then again, this new man, he wasn't the sort anyone with brains fucked with.

I pressed the glass to my lips and sipped my whiskey as a way to hide my reaction while I stared at Dane, who looked so much the same even after ten years. His hair was still short and messy, and he had that five-o'clock shadow that always made him appear disheveled.

And his silver tongue was every bit as talented, if his little pick-up line said anything.

"So, looks like you need a partner," Dane said.

I set my glass down. "I'm just fine playing by myself."

"Come on, everything's more fun when you play with others." Dane didn't bother to hide the innuendo, and I had no doubt he knew *exactly* what he was saying. He was too damned smart not to. With Dane, everything was a game, a plan, something he picked to get the exact reaction he wanted. He was forever six moves ahead of everyone else.

"What I just learned from my last game is that partners don't often live up to expectation." I glanced meaningfully at his groin. "You tend to overestimate your abilities."

His smiled widened, as if he was getting off more on this exchange than he would have if we were actually naked. Then again, a battle of wits was exactly what Dane would want. "Maybe you were just picking the wrong playmates. I can assure you, my skills are every bit what I promise them to be. Let me sink a few balls and I'll show you."

The wordplay went straight through me, made me picture what neither of us had come right out to say. I wondered how it would feel when he scratched his stubble across my throat, when he dug his fingers into my thigh to wrap it around him, when he wrapped his hand around the front of my throat and yanked me toward him for a kiss.

Warmth spread through me, the exact type I'd thought was dead.

Didn't it just figure that a man I should have nothing to do with could bring it out in me?

I should tell him no. I should tell him to fuck off and walk right out of this club. I'm not stupid, and I don't make stupid choices.

And yet, no matter how many times I assured myself of that, I still nodded toward the pool cues on the wall instead of telling him where he could shove it.

It seemed I *was* stupid, that I was willing to risk everything just because some asshole in a bar could make my panties wet.

Except he wasn't just some asshole, even if I wanted him to be.

I felt like a parody of myself, like the exact sort of girl I would have laughed at. Then again…Dane had always managed to bring this out in me.

I racked the balls, since not running the table would feel like a loss after my last game. He didn't bother to hide the way he stared at my ass when I bent forward, how his gaze lingered on the arch of my back. He rubbed his fingers over his jaw as if he couldn't quite believe the sight.

Just another ploy — another game for him.

I knew his tricks, had spent years watching them. I knew how he could turn a girl mindless, could convince the most hardened, suspicious criminal that he was their one and only true friend. Dane could make an atheist believe they'd seen god if he wanted to.

But I'd learned plenty as well, tricks he'd never see coming...

He took the first shot, and I didn't resist the urge to check out his ass — turnabout was fair play. His jeans hugged the curves of his ass, and it seemed the years had been kind to him.

Which was unfair. It had been a decade — he should have been a shriveled-up old man with a flat and flabby ass.

He turned his head without standing up from a shot, his eyebrow lifted as if he caught me and it had amused the hell out of him.

I shrugged, then let out a very obvious yawn.

"There's that cayenne," he said and took the shot. He downed the first three balls before he missed, but it didn't shock me.

Dane had been good, but he'd never managed to hit those corner banks worth a damn. I used that to my advantage, sinking two of the stripes, and when I knew I didn't have a shot afterward, I set him up for another bank.

"So, do you have a name?" he asked as he eyed his options for a shot.

"Nem."

"Last name?"

"Not for you."

He huffed a soft sound before trying for the bank and missing it. "My name is Dane."

"I didn't ask."

"I noticed."

I made sure he saw me roll my eyes before I sank another two balls. "Do you always talk this much, or is it only when you're losing?"

"I talk this much no matter what. Besides, I'm not losing."

I sank one more ball before missing the last one. "Yeah, you are. I'm ahead."

"Maybe I let you get ahead to keep the conversation going."

"Men don't risk losing just to flirt."

He laughed and lined up his next shot. "Sure they do if the prize is good enough." He sank the next two balls, before missing on the eight-ball.

Which meant if he could hit that, if he could get it in on his next turn, he'd win.

"I'm not a prize, and there won't be any winning," I told him as I took my next shot. I sunk everything except the eight-ball, leaving us even, which wasn't at all what I'd prefer.

Annoyance picked at me because I *never* missed shots like this. What the hell? Was it Dane there that distracted me, that threw off my game?

It had to be, and that frustrated me more than anything else. Even after a decade, him meaning anything to me made it feel like I was still the same young girl who had met him so long ago, when I'd been hopelessly smitten, before I'd learned the truth about him and the world.

"Oh, nice try," Dane said with a mocking tone, as if he'd already won.

"Don't add the notch on your belt until you get inside the girl," I responded. "You're shit at bank shots and that's exactly what you've got in front of you."

In all the years we'd played before, Dane had *never* managed to sink a shot like this. He'd over-correct, never hitting the right spot.

I'd as good as already won.

He came closer, standing just in front of me, so close I could smell him. He smelled the same, just as he had before, like cloves and cinnamon, something deceptively sweet.

I lifted my head, struggling with the difference between then and now, between the past and the present. I felt a little like the girl I'd been before, when I'd chased behind him, behind the others, looking for their attention. How badly I'd wanted this, wanted him to look at me with this sort of passion, and he'd always denied me that.

He leaned down, then dragged his tongue over my bottom lip. It wasn't a kiss, not really, but managed to light a fire inside me larger than the one at Lucky's house. That tiny spark roared to life, consuming me, and he pulled back far too fast.

Dane gave me a smirk full of confidence. "Well, you pick your whiskey well, at least."

Before I could say anything, he bent forward next to me, aimed and took the shot. The eight-ball rolled into the pocket he'd nodded at, sinking the shot he'd never been able to do.

"I win," he said, then crossed his arms, staring down at me, *far* too pleased with himself.

I muttered something like 'good game' before rushing off, leaving him there, his smirk mocking me.

It seemed Dane had learned some tricks in the years since I'd last seen him, and I needed to make sure not to underestimate him again…

The last time I had, I'd died.

I wasn't going to make the same mistake again, because I doubted I'd come back to life a second time.

Chapter Four

Nem

When I caught sight of familiar silver eyes, I had the same moment of uncertainty I always did. Seeing a set of eyes identical to my own reflected in someone else's face unnerved me.

I still remembered the first time I saw Jarrod—drugged by pain and almost dead as I'd been—and how a world that had made no sense suddenly fit when I saw his eyes.

I had always looked a lot like my mother, with her dark hair, pale skin and spattering of freckles, but my eyes had stood out in every family photo we took. Caroline and Kenz had matched with their deep brown. Kyler's eyes were a bright blue, but I had a grayish-blue so light they appeared silver.

After meeting Jarrod, at least I'd known where they'd come from...

"Is it done?" I asked him.

He nodded, then turned his focus back to the device he worked on. I knew better than to ask what it was — even if he told me, I probably wouldn't understand. I'd taken a lot from his lessons, but he had a way with tech I'd never managed.

I guess we all have our skills.

"He won't survive the week," Jarrod said.

I didn't bother to wait and see if guilt would hit me — it never did. If it hadn't in the last decade, I doubted some criminal real estate expert would do it.

"Did you have to plant much?"

He shook his head. "Didn't need to plant anything. He was already double-crossing Kyler, just quietly enough no one noticed. All I had to do was make it a little louder." He set the device down, then turned toward me. "I saw the news story on Lucky."

I sat on the edge of the kitchen table, my hands wrapped around the edge as I swung my feet. The house was a short-term rental — strictly off the books — but gave Jarrod all the space he needed.

He liked to harp on my usage of hotels, but I preferred the benefit of living closer to other people. Befriend, threaten or pay the right ones, and I had myself an extra set of eyes.

Then again, I'd learned to use people, where Jarrod preferred tech and the environment. Despite the shared blood, we weren't exactly alike.

I preferred to set up a storage unit close by where I could store everything I needed that would raise eyebrows if found in my room. Guns, blades, medical supplies, explosives, fake documents and anything else I might need were tucked away only a few minutes' drive away, leaving my hotel room appearing entirely normal.

"Did he tell you anything?"

"No. I didn't really expect him to."

"Because he wasn't going to or because he didn't know?"

That was always the question, wasn't it?

I thought back to the fear on his face, to the tremble of his bottom lip. "I don't think he knew. If he had, I'm pretty sure he would have sung it to the rafters. I doubt he had any contact with Kyler after he got paid."

"Fire's a bad way to go," Jarrod said.

"Is it?" I thought back to the heat, to the way flames had crept toward me, to how I'd clawed at the floor to drag myself away from it before it could consume me. "There's something nice about fire."

"What the fuck is nice about burning to death?"

"It all goes away."

He furrowed his eyebrows at me, the same way he always did when I said something he didn't understand. "What goes away?"

"You understand as well as anyone how messy death is. Fuck, how messy life is. Someone shoots someone else, there's blood and damage and bodies and wounds. Fire, though? Let it rage long enough and it turns everything to dust." My voice took on a dreamy quality, as if I could already see some promised land full of nothing but peaceful ashes.

Jarrod shook his head. "You're fucked up, you know that?"

"Yeah, I know," I answered. "Any word about the reaction to Lucky's untimely death?"

He didn't respond right away, staring at me as if he could figure me out. Then again, it had been ten years together, and he hadn't yet, so what were the chances that today would be that magical day? As if he realized that as well, he let out a slow sigh. "Police looked the other way, wrote it off as an accident. I don't think anyone told 'em to do it. Pretty sure they just knew Lucky was tangled up with people they didn't want to fuck with. Easier and safer to just wash their hands of it."

"Anyone else looking closely?"

"Lucky was an idiot who never made enough of a name for himself for anyone to care about his death. Couple people came by the next day, dug around a bit—probably just low-lives hoping to score some safe that had been missed. I'd bet it'll take a few more days before news gets to Kyler."

"Even when it does, it won't mean anything. One dead body to him is nothing—just a coincidence."

"So when are you going to add the next coincidence?"

I thought about it, pressing my lips together as I considered my options. "Not for another week. I want to leave us enough time between targets to make it feel like it's on purpose, that it's coming."

Jarrod huffed, setting his foot on the crossbar of the stool. "You like your games, don't you?"

"Coming from you? You taught me to play these games."

"I taught you how to win. You prefer the game to the prize. I worry."

I tore my gaze away, choosing to stare instead at an ugly painting of wild horses in a field, the sort of art a person bought from a chain store because they thought it made their place seem fancy.

He was wrong. I didn't find pleasure killing Lucky. Planning my next kill didn't make me happy. They were all bullet points on a plan I'd been developing for ten years—nothing more.

I didn't enjoy anything anymore.

I thought back to the touch of Dane's tongue against my lip, the way it had heated my blood and made me crave more.

I guess that isn't entirely true... Clearly, I enjoy something.

Not that I'd say that out loud. Some things were far better left in the safety of my head, and that was just one of them.

"I heard you saw Dane."

And there is another one...

Leave it to Jarrod to know what I didn't have to tell him. It made me thankful I hadn't had a normal upbringing, one where he'd acted like a father to me. The thought of trying to get away with anything behind his back was a joke.

"He was at Diamond's Edge."

"Was he now?" He used that tone that told me that he knew damn well there was more to the story than that. Jarrod never brought up a subject he didn't already have a grasp on.

"We both knew I'd run into the Quad eventually. They're basically a staple in this city. I wasn't going to be able to work here and avoid them."

"Sure, but you didn't just run into one of them. I figured you'd see them when you got closer to Kyler, but I didn't expect you'd let one of them *lick* you. That's commitment." His dry words didn't disguise his annoyance.

"Give it a rest—they're here and I'll have to deal with them. This doesn't change our plan at all."

"You sure about that? You sure you can keep your head on straight?"

"Can you?"

"Yeah, I can. All I want is for the fucker who killed the love of my life to die a slow, painful death, so them being around means jack shit to me. You, on the other hand, you've got some more complicated feelings."

"They aren't feelings," I snapped.

What was between the men and me — or what had been between us — had burned away in the flames the night I had died. They hadn't been there when I'd needed them, which meant they'd either been involved or they'd failed me.

Either way, it was all in the past. Sure, Dane might rev my engine a bit — it turned out I was still human no matter all the evidence to the contrary — but that didn't mean anything.

"I'm the last person to talk to you about feelings," Jarrod said, his voice dropping its 'here, have a lecture' tone. I had no idea if it was because he really understood, or if he was just manipulating me. It was funny that the only person in my life I could lean on, I still couldn't trust. "Keep your head in the game, though. Get distracted, let them get their claws into you again, and you'll end up right where you were when I found you — dead. I doubt you've got another miracle in you."

I remembered the way Dane had tasted the whiskey from my lips, then gave Jarrod the best lie I could.

"They won't be a problem."

* * * *

The windows of the tall office building reflected sunlight, but the large round sunglasses perched on my nose kept me from squinting.

The people who entered and exited the building were all dressed well, the entire place looking far more mainstream than what I had grown used to. It had the signs of a legit business, which usually offered criminals the best camouflage.

I pulled in a breath then ran my palms down the front of my suit. I'd paired the jacket with slacks that I knew made my ass look amazing, and the thin white pinstripes stood out against the black fabric. It was one of my favorites, the sort that always made me feel like a badass bitch who could handle anything that was thrown my way.

The large security desk on the ground floor had my full attention as I entered.

I walked up to the desk, a man behind it in a security guard outfit — the standard dark gray with a patch that was just close enough to make people react as they would to real law enforcement. He offered me a dismissive look, one that said he probably dealt with a never-ending wave of people who all wanted something.

"Yes?" he asked.

I offered a smile, because honey greased more than a few doors. "My name is Nem Syler, and I'm here for a four-thirty meeting with Wilkinson Properties." I rattled off the name I'd been given, the cover company I knew damn well was run by Kyler.

Jarrod had been right — it had only taken a few days before the old real estate expert had gone missing. Whether he'd run or been killed, I didn't know.

I really didn't care, either. So long as he was out of my way, he could go wherever the fuck he wanted.

His absence created a vacuum. Kyler would need a new expert, a new magician to help him with the properties every business had to have and the legal ramifications that came with owning them. The reality was that an empire, even one from the criminal underworld, required real land. Everyone needed to sleep somewhere, to meet somewhere, to hide their shit somewhere, which made real estate experts the unsung heroes.

That was exactly why I'd worked for the last five years getting my name out there as someone who could do that. Add to that Jarrod dropping it when needed, and I had been a shoo-in when Kyler's favorite man had turned out dirty, when he'd needed a new expert and — lucky him — I'd happened to move to town recently.

The security guard ran his finger along the screen in front of him, the one I couldn't read, then went still.

Had he just realized I was there to see people who were rarely disturbed?

"Of course, ma'am," he said, his voice far more respectful than it had been. "To the left is a private elevator. Here's a keycard to operate it. It will take you directly to the fifth floor, and the waiting room will be just past the doors." He handed over that card as if he couldn't get me out of there fast enough.

Fine by me.

I took the key card and followed his directions, the strap of my briefcase digging into my shoulder. I didn't walk through the security gates, through the metal detectors or pat downs. People coming to see Kyler weren't subjected to those things, especially not out in public like that.

Then again, if they realized who I was and the reason I was there, they wouldn't just kick me out. In our world, things were done in private because they were too horrific for public view.

The elevator was quick, and the single button said it was used only for Wilkinson guests. When it came to a stop, when the doors opened, I found myself before an open waiting room.

Judging from the lines of the building, I doubted they had the entire floor. Rather than that, it seemed they had perhaps half a floor but a dedicated elevator. It was a good system, an ability to come and go without any outside interference.

I doubted they often used the space, and I would bet they had similar offices throughout the city. Moving around was the best way to avoid detection, and separating properties based on how illegal they were could help keep a lower profile.

No receptionist sat waiting for guests, again telling me they rarely had visitors. I paused for a moment, wondering if I should take a seat or just try one of the doors at the far end of the room.

They had to know I was there… the guard would have called up as soon as I left his desk.

"Ms. Syler?" The rough voice caught me off guard, like a call from the past, threatening to pull me back to years ago.

Wasn't that just my luck? Of anyone, it had to be *them* to meet me.

I turned to find Rune standing there, his long blond hair pulled back, two braids along the top, then secured into a loose bun. He was larger than life, like he always had been, with black tribal tattoos covering both arms.

His eyes were a green that was soft, almost pale, and totally at odds with the aggressiveness of his physique.

It took a moment to realize I hadn't answered, so I forced myself back into the role I'd molded myself into for this job. "Yes. I was contacted about a job."

He nodded, then gestured to follow him.

Except…it also looked a lot like a gesture to come closer, and that took me back.

I remembered when I had been sixteen, when he'd brought a necklace back from a job he'd done in South America. He'd made that motion, drawing me closer, before showing me the prize. His hands had been warm as he'd lifted my hair, moving it out of the way so he could fasten the gift around my throat.

He made a noise, drawing me back to the present, away from the fond memories tarnished by the reality of time.

That was a different man, and you were a different girl. Get distracted and you'll get your throat slit.

The reminder was what it took to get my feet moving. I hadn't expected to see these men — my men — so soon. I hadn't been kidding when I told Jarrod I knew I would run into them, but I sure as fuck hadn't expected it to be so soon. Maybe it had been stupid, for me to think I could have avoided them when they all but ran this city, but I'd held out hope. Seeing Dane had been a surprise, but I'd thought I'd have more time before confronting them all. One on one they were difficult, but as a group? Damn near impossible to trick.

Why were they doing errands like *this* for Kyler, though? These men were trained to deal with shit that had gone seriously wrong. A smart person called in the Quad, as the four men were known, when they needed something done no one else could do. They handled security for people who had serious enemies, took out targets no one else could reach and otherwise did the impossible.

So why was Kyler using them for simple business meet and greets? *Talk about wasting a good resource...*

I passed Rune, careful to keep my gaze anywhere except him. I didn't need to get sucked into the past again, to forget for even a second that the fond little memories I had of these men were fairy tales—nothing more. They were the things people kept from their childhood, things that weren't realistic, that weren't accurate depictions of what had happened.

I was much too old to believe in fairy tales anymore.

Past him, inside a rather large office, were the other three. Of course, they were there...they were almost always together. People talked about soulmates or twin flames or codependent relationships, but they had nothing on these four.

The Quad lived and breathed one another, had ever since I'd known them. They were more than brothers, more than blood.

Bray sat to the side of the large oak desk, his laptop open before him. He glanced up, pausing as he did, those dark eyes of his locking on me through his glasses. Honestly, that was more attention than he gave to ninety-eight percent of people. His hair was still buzzed to his scalp, and he wore small silver loops in his left ear and another in his septum. His scowl was as ever-present as it had been before.

Colton sat in the corner, his elbow on a bookcase, his hair longer than it had been. It meant the slight curls in it showed, and his beard was shaggier than it used to be. Maybe that was age or laziness, as if shaving had become too troublesome so he'd forgone the entire thing. He studied me, silent, as if looking for weaknesses already. No doubt he was figuring out the best way to deal with me if he needed to.

Maybe that should have frightened me.

It didn't, though. I'd rather see a threat coming. I'd prefer knowing he might kill me to thinking someone else was safe only to be stabbed in the back.

Or shot in the chest.

At the center of the desk was Dane, who gave me the biggest shit-eating grin ever, as if this couldn't have worked out any better. He was surprisingly deep, but impossible to read, to peek beneath the surface and figure out what was really happening with him.

The memory of Dane's tongue threatened to sneak up on me again, to tease me just as he had, but I shoved it away.

I needed to focus on the task at hand and *not* on Dane's tongue.

"Well, isn't this a pleasant little surprise?" Dane leaned back in his chair, appearing *far* too pleased with himself and the turn of events.

"You called me," I pressed, acting as if I had no idea what he was talking about. "It shouldn't be a surprise."

"Sure, but how could I know you'd be my little pool shark?"

I frowned, dropping my gaze as if thinking. "Oh, the other night? That was you?"

His smile didn't falter—if anything, it spread. Then again, that was one hell of a whopper I'd just told, pretending I didn't remember it.

"Besides," I said before he could continue to talk, before he could draw us off topic anymore. Each time we talked about anything else, I risked them seeing through the cracks of my story. "I doubt I'm here because of that. Don't waste my time—it's expensive."

Bray narrowed his eyes farther, until he peeked through the slits, as though he could read me like the lines of code on his computer. "You aren't going to ask who you're working for?"

"In my business, it's best not to ask. I don't need to have a relationship with my clients to complete the job they hired me to do. I just need to know what they want and how much they'll pay me to get it for them."

Bray let out a small huff, as if my answer was the right one and that annoyed him. He dropped his gaze to his computer screen, and the clicking of keys said he had finished talking to me.

Dane took over. "The client will be revealed after you complete one task."

"I don't work for free. Do you think you're the first person to try and offer me some little *task* to prove my skills, when really you're just trying to get a favor?"

"You've got it all wrong. You'll be well paid for the task no matter if we hire you for anything else or not. Think of it like a probation period—you do what we need you to, prove you can handle the work, that you can be trusted, then you'll turn official. We just don't share sensitive information until we're sure a person can deliver."

I pressed my lips into a thin line. That wasn't ideal...what if the little task required weeks or months of work? What if, during that time, I managed to get outed? The more time each step took, the harder it would be to keep the ducks all in a line.

Those fuckers liked to waddle off...

Still, I didn't have much of a choice. This was the smart move even if I didn't care for it... I was new, an unknown element to them. Despite my well-documented history, I'd been working in Northern California until now. None of these people knew me — at least, they didn't think they did — so them handing over all their real estate and financial records to some newbie probably hadn't been a realistic hope.

When I could spot no other choice, I nodded. "Fair enough, as long as the price is right."

"Oh, we pay our debts, don't worry." Colton's words had an edge that told me he didn't mean them to be reassuring.

"So what's the task?"

Rune grabbed a file from a shelf behind him, then set it on the desk before me. It let me catch a whiff of him, and for one moment, I was a lovestruck teenager again. I wanted to bury my nose in his throat, to breathe him in, to lose myself in the way he always made me feel safe, as if the world would be kept away by his presence alone.

Instead, I opened the file and flipped through the pages.

A printout of a large venue rested inside — a winery that sat on thirty acres. It was pretty, with sprawling hillsides surrounding it and a huge barn out back, the exact sort of property people rented out for parties and wine-tasting tours.

Behind those papers were sales histories, then a page with financial information.

"You want to purchase this?" I asked.

Dane nodded. "The account information shows the company the property will be purchased under and the amount you are authorized to pay for it."

"So why do you need me? This seems a straightforward transaction."

"The individual who owns it isn't keen on selling. If you're officially hired, you'll often need to *convince* people to do what our employer requires, making this a good test. The money in the account is more than enough to cover the fair market value and a bit extra as incentive, so it should be an easy job. We want to see that you can make the deal work, that you're clean in what you do, that you're as good as we've been led to believe."

I closed the file and slid it into the briefcase slung over my shoulder. "I trust there's contact information in there for when I finish?"

"That quick to be rid of us?" Dane asked.

"I don't like downtime, and I want to get this done as soon as possible. Coming south was a risk for me, a change of scenery to branch out. If I find this job isn't a good fit, I'll need to find something else."

"You seemed to enjoy your downtime the other night."

"I did, until someone thought licking my lips was an appropriate thing to do."

"Would you prefer I lick you elsewhere? I'm a man open to taking suggestions."

That damn heat came again, roaring to life inside my veins, inside the parts of me that hadn't craved anything in so long. The bastard knew, too. He was too smart not to know, not to realize his words instantly made me consider how that tongue of his would feel on my cunt.

I tried to remain impassive, as if his comments didn't rattle me. "It figures you would need directions. Men rarely know where to lick."

And just like before, the more I hissed, the more I put him in his place, the more he looked like a dog just waiting to pounce. It was as if each insult from me revved him up more, made him more excited to play.

"Well, Ms. Syler, unfortunately for you, we're going to be working with you on this."

"I work alone."

"Not this time," Bray said, his tone sharp and suspicious. "This isn't just about the final result. If you torch the place down, kill the occupants, then buy the ashes from the estate, that won't work for us. So, we need to see not only that you can do it but how you manage it."

I wanted to argue, to tell them to shove that idea up their admittedly nice asses. Jarrod's words came back to me, when he'd laughed at me saying they didn't matter, that they wouldn't cause me a problem.

Go figure—here they were, causing me one hell of a problem.

But I couldn't back down. I couldn't turn around and give in. I'd spent ten years of my life getting here and things were far too important for me to just walk away from.

So I peered across the office, taking in each of the men who I'd once been hopelessly infatuated with, who I had once trusted with everything, who had very likely betrayed me, and gave them a smile as sharp as my eyeliner. "Deal. Just try to stay out of my way."

And if lust were a living, breathing thing, if the predatory look in their eyes at that challenge and the fact their cocks were no doubt more than a little interested were beasts, I'd have been mauled right then.

Fair was fair, though. At least we'd *all* have to deal with each other while being turned on.

Let the games begin.

Chapter Five

Nem

It was funny how things could change so much, yet still feel the same.

Shelia was a perfect example of that.

The last ten years had been bad for her but good for her plastic surgeon's bank account, judging by her lack of expression and huge lips. She sat in the beauty salon, her hand on the table as the other woman worked.

And Shelia *never* shut up, as though she'd paid for someone to endure her running monologue rather than her nails.

"So, then I was going to just walk away — I mean, there's only so much a girl can be expected to put up with, right?"

The technician nodded dutifully, but even a cursory glance her way showed she had no interest in the long and self-involved story.

Jayce Carter

"But then he sent me flowers. My mother always told me men are stupid, so we have to give them a lot of grace."

And that nearly had me gagging. *What bullshit.* Men were idiots when they chose to be, not because it was hard-wired into them. They grew up being told they were visual creatures, that boys would be boys, that they weren't responsible for any of the shit they did. It was all a big scam, though.

If I could keep it in my pants, so could any man.

"What kind of flowers?" I asked—not because I cared but because I needed to broach a conversation.

Shelia glanced my way, but the injections made it hard to read her expression. "Roses, of course. If a man sends anything less, they aren't really sorry."

I nodded, as if the information were the secret to life I'd been waiting for instead of the inane tripe it actually was. "I had a guy send me daisies one time," I said with all the mock horror I could manage. "It was after I caught him with my best friend—you know how it happens."

"Daisies, hmm? I'm sorry to say he was still screwing her, then."

I shifted my hand so the woman doing my nails could reach the thumb. "That was exactly what I thought. I told my so-called friend I never wanted to see her again."

"Good bet," Shelia told me. "People like to say men are the dangerous ones, but women? I've dealt with jealous and malicious women far more. Worse, they're harder to see coming."

The words almost made me laugh, especially from her. I kept that too myself, though, slid into the same mindset—a woman who wanted to claw her way to the top and didn't give a damn who she scratched on her way up. A woman willing to make herself the victim so she didn't have to bear the weight of her actions.

"That's exactly it," I said, adding just the right amount of somber to my voice. "The girl, we were best friends for *years*. She was going to be at my wedding, all of it. I had no idea she would do something like sleep with my boyfriend until I walked in on them."

Shelia pointed at one of the colors to tell the nail technician which to use—a garish red that was far too bright for her—before turning her head back toward me. "I completely understand."

I needed more, so I pressed. "I doubt it. I mean, *look* at you. I doubt any man has ever gone with someone else instead of you."

The praise did what I wanted, soaked into her and loosened her tongue. "Well, some women are tricky. There was this man—he and I knew each other for years—but this other woman got pregnant and trapped him. I don't think the kid was even his, but she got what she wanted." The story poured from her, twisted piece after twisted piece. It was like a badly translated sentence—individual words right but the context all wrong. Shelia had changed it to fit her own narrative, to make her the wronged party instead of the villain.

"What happened to the man?" I asked.

"He wised up eventually, but I think she'd already ruined things too much between him and me."

"And her?"

"People always get what's coming to them. You remember that with your friend, that karma gets everyone in the end. The woman reaped what she sowed—she got exactly what she deserved."

I met her gaze head on, hardly able to connect this woman with the one I'd grown up around, the one I'd considered an aunt for so many years before realizing that had all been a lie. "I think you're right. People get what they deserve in the end."

Mostly right, at least. It wouldn't be karma that was about to fuck her over.

I got that honor.

* * * *

If I lived a different life, if I were a different person, this sort of house might have been the type of place I'd want to live.

The pictures hadn't done the winery justice. They'd made it look cold and modern and far too large. Granted, that was what people liked, but it wasn't the truth.

It missed the beautiful carved details in the trim above the front door and the worn patch on the patio where a rocking chair had once sat. It might get rented out for fancy parties, but showed the signs of a place someone lived and loved.

"I don't like parking where it isn't easy to leave," Rune said, forcing me to remember he'd met me there, no matter how much I'd have preferred to visit the winery by myself. He hadn't given me any way out, but at least I'd been able to drive myself.

"Well, you're welcome to leave." I didn't bother to soften the jab with a smile or laugh. He could choke on it for all I cared.

He made a soft, disgruntled noise before knocking on the door.

An older woman opened the door, her hair black with streaks of gray that went from root to tip, telling me she hadn't dyed her hair in many years. She wore a long maxi dress of red and yellow and had silver bracelets that jingled as she moved. "Yes?" she asked.

I stuck my hand out. "Hello, Mrs. Kellon. My name is Nem Syler. We spoke on the phone."

"Call me Tammy." She shook my hand and stepped out of the house. "Well, I don't want to waste your time, so let me be upfront and let you know that I'm not going to be selling. I've lived in this house all my life, and I don't see that changing anytime soon. Lots of folks have come and offered me all sorts of numbers, but life isn't just about money, you know?"

I smiled, playing the game of best friend. "Of course. I completely understand. I had to come out, for my boss, you know. I told him you weren't interested, but he wanted me to try. Maybe I can talk him into just renting it for an event—I'll get to come back, he won't be mad, you'll get paid and everyone wins."

Tammy nodded. "I understand that—bosses don't tend to listen, do they? Sure, we'll do a tour. I have a tasting coming in another hour, so we'll have to be done by then."

She gestured away from the small, cozy house. "I don't bring people into my home," she explained. "This was the original house on the property, but back in the fifties, my great-grandpa built the big house." She pointed toward what could only be described as a mansion. "We use that for events, for many of the tastings, for more personal settings. It has a full kitchen set up, six bathroom, ten bedrooms and lots of space on the main floor for gatherings."

I nodded, pretending as if I cared a bit about how it was all set up. I didn't, at least beyond how I might be able to use it. I paid attention to when she mentioned her children, to how one was in college—money problems could convince a person to be reasonable— and how another lived in Arizona with children— maybe make her realize how important family was? Each thing she said was another piece for me to twist, to use to my advantage.

Tammy talked about the history of the property, how her parents had run it and her father's parents before them. The way she spoke, I could almost see her as a kid, running around, playing out between the grapevines in the field.

I'd had plenty of room growing up, of course, but I'd never had a real connection to anywhere I'd slept. I'd never had a place that meant something to me, one that built me up as this place had Tammy. Homes had been buildings to me, just places we lived, and they had changed often.

It wasn't safe to get comfortable for long, because all that did was give enemies a way in.

Maybe that was one reason I still didn't have a place to live, at least not for long, because it always felt like tempting fate. Instead, I moved constantly. I stayed at short-term rentals or hotel rooms—wherever I could to keep myself off the radar.

Tammy took us around the grounds on a golf cart. I rode up front, while Rune sat on the back seat. She showed us the large outdoor event space, perfect for weddings or photo shoots, according to her. It could fit more people than I knew well, let alone would want to come to a wedding, but I guess I wasn't like most, normal people.

"And this is the barn," she said as she stopped the golf cart in front of a huge rustic wooden building. The front doors were pulled open, showing the massive space inside. "I love this for big receptions or parties where people want to mingle a lot. Because it's one room, unlike the house, it's great for casual get-togethers."

I walked into the barn, arching my neck to take in the tall ceiling, trying to picture the sort of get-together a person would have here. I'd been to plenty of parties, both in my old life and my new one, but they hadn't been at places like this.

Instead, they were places in high-rises, in fancy penthouses or million-dollar estates. I tried to picture Kyler at a barn like this, his shiny loafers in the hay.

It made no sense.

Which again made me wonder what he wanted the place for. It would make a good profit and might work for laundering some amount of money. He could pour money into the vineyard and claim to earn any amount he wanted from the tours and events.

Even still, it was farther out of town than he normally went, at least with how he used to work.

So, what was the plan?

I hated not being sure, having to move around blind. There was no more dangerous step than one I couldn't see.

"I've got to go meet that wine tour I mentioned," Tammy said before shaking my hand again. "I really am sorry, too. You seem like a nice girl, and if I were going to sell, I'd sell to you."

Another detail to file away.

"Thank you. Your home is beautiful, and I'll make sure to talk to my boss about renting it for an event." I offered her a conspiratorial grin, cementing this ploy of a friendship. "I mean, if I do that, I can come back and try your wines on his dollar."

She laughed, then let me know that Rune and I could walk the short distance back to the parking lot when we were done.

After she left, I turned around to find Rune staring at me. I'd tried hard to ignore him during the tour, to work and pretend he wasn't there. If I looked at him, if I thought about him, I risked distraction—I couldn't afford that. If he wanted to be a shadow on my ass, well, it was his time to waste.

Of course, now I was left alone with Rune, in a barn that had a far more romantic vibe than the place ought to. One of the men I'd been desperately in love with before, who I would have given anything for, and he was staring at me with those light green eyes, as if no time at all had changed.

My life really wasn't going to get any easier, was it?

Rune

The girl made no damn sense to me. She was a tiny thing, with absurd red hair and black eyeliner that made her eyes look sharp.

Which seemed dumb because her words were more than sharp enough.

I'd tried to make sense of her during the tour, when she looked around, when she asked questions. I got the sense she was a good eight moves ahead of me in a game I didn't even know we were playing.

Which wasn't a new feeling for me. I'd reached my age and finally got comfortable enough to know what I was good at and what I wasn't. I could fuck up near anybody's day in close quarters, could shake off most hits, but hand me a puzzle and I was fucking useless.

And this girl was one hell of a puzzle.

"She doesn't seem like she's gonna sell," I said when the silence got to me, when only the tap of her heels against the wooden floor filled it.

Nem turned, one dark eyebrow lifted as if my statement was obvious and unneeded. "We knew that before we came."

"Yeah, and you didn't get her any closer to agreeing."

"Of course not. You saw her — she isn't going to sell just because I bat my lashes at her. The more head-on we hit her, the more she'll dig her heels in."

"So what's your plan?"

She turned away and walked farther into the large barn, toward a back room Tammy had said was for waitstaff who were working parties. Nem studied every detail of the barn, just as she had Tammy, as she did everything.

It was almost interesting enough for me to ignore just how good she looked in that suit...

Not even close.

Nem filled out the suit in a way I sure as hell didn't. A white shirt beneath it hid her cleavage but was open enough for a tease, as if promising there was better beneath it. She had on a pair of slacks — similar to when we'd seen her at the office — but this outfit was pure black — no stripes.

Her red hair stood out against the black, loose and full and with just enough curl to look wild.

She was a dichotomy that drew me closer. Cold as fuck but with that wild red hair. Sharp wits, but Dane said she'd downright *moaned* at one little lick. Fucking tiny and yet seemingly made of steel. Every second I spent around her, she confused me more, as if each detail made less sense.

A glance around the area for staff after following her into the back room made me pause.

Maybe the right way to deal with this was to bend her forward, pull down those slacks and see if she was nearly as cold as her attitude let on. One good fuck and maybe I'd understand her.

People didn't lie during sex — or at least they couldn't do it well. Fuck someone to a far enough state of bliss and I could uncover all those things they were hiding, the dark places in their psyche they covered up with stories and civility.

Dane might like to play around with people's minds, to twist them up, but I'd found nothing got to the core of an issue better than a well-placed cock.

Nem ran her fingers over a shelf near the far wall, her gaze studying items that rested there — pictures and awards and other bullshit.

I went up, crowded her from behind, pressed against the curves that had taunted me since I'd met her.

She went rigid for only a breath before melting.

Yeah, hotter than she lets on.

"I'm not a prostitute," she said, a threat in her tone like the warning of a rattlesnake. "Fucking me doesn't come with the service."

"Course you're not a hooker," I responded, bringing my lips to her throat, drawing in the intoxicating scent of something wild from her hair. "I ain't offering to pay you."

"So what's this?"

"Fun."

It wasn't a lie, not really. Sure, I'd love to figure out what she was really after — everyone wanted something, especially people as focused as her — but there was no doubt getting inside her would be damn enjoyable, too.

"Fun for you, maybe." The little snort she let out felt like a challenge, like a fucking gauntlet thrown. It was a kick right to my abilities, and I didn't much care for having them questioned. I might not have been the smartest man, but I sure as fuck knew how to please a woman.

"Oh, you'd have fun, too," I promised her, sliding my hand around her front, stroking over her stomach, dipping beneath the bottom hem of her shirt.

Her skin was on fire, and so much softer than it had any right to be.

She let out a breathy sound — not a moan, as if the stubborn bitch wouldn't dare give me that. Instead, it was an exhalation, long and drawn out and teasing.

"I can get you to make other, even better sounds," I swore, rocking my hips against her, letting her feel every inch of my hard cock.

It would be so easy to be inside her in a few seconds. While there were things I wanted to do to her that would take hours, a quickie here would quiet the roar in my head, would help me remember she was just a woman.

Why the fuck I couldn't stop thinking about her, I didn't get. I fucked women all the time, most whose names I never cared to learn. There weren't many things better than a willing body to waste a few hours with, than to take all that unmet aggression out on.

This was different though. It wasn't an itch but a need, a craving so deep I'd woken up hard and sweating the night before with *her* red hair in my dreams.

She pressed backward, grinding her ass against me in a blatant offer that made me worry for a second I wouldn't last long enough to get inside her.

Nope, fuck that. I'm not about to get shown up by her. That bitch will take the upper hand and slap me with it.

"This is where we have tastings," came Tammy's voice from the entry of the barn.

I dropped my forehead to Nem's shoulder at my bad luck. "We could ignore them."

"Until they walk in?"

"Fuck 'em. If they want a look, they're welcome to it. As long as I get a taste of your cunt, I don't mind an audience. Trust me."

She went still, as if just reminded of something. Maybe she'd woken from that way lust can make a person forget the whole fucking world, maybe she'd realized she wasn't the type to fuck a stranger in a barn. *What a pity.*

I backed up when she stood straight, when the hard lines of her body said the chances of her spreading those thighs were roughly fuck all.

"Your loss," I snapped, my aching cock turning my mood foul.

"I doubt that," she answered, giving me that perfect ice princess look, the one that could shrivel a man's dick right up.

Or it could, if a man wasn't sure about his abilities. *I am.*

"I'll get together the files and send them over tomorrow with the next step." She didn't wait to see if that was okay, to ask my opinion, nothing. She spoke then turned and walked out, looking calm and collected and entirely in control.

And me? I felt like a feral animal watching what I wanted most stroll away, my cock hard and my brain in fucking chaos.

What the fuck was wrong with me?

Chapter Six

Nem

People in gags still managed to make an amazing amount of noise. It was one of those things I never knew, not until I gained firsthand experience. Movies always made it seem like a little bit of fabric in someone's mouth would silence them, but that just wasn't true.

They sure as hell could still scream, unless someone knew to cover the entire mouth with duct tape.

I could have walked Shelia down the outdoor stairs that led to the basement, but what was the point of that? Instead, with her ankles tied, I'd let her tumble down.

At the bottom, I kneeled before her and pulled the hood off, then yanked the duct tape free from her fake-as-fuck lips.

When her gaze landed on me, her eyes widened. I'd gotten her into the car with the threat of a gun to the back of her head — that tended to make most people compliant. It meant she hadn't gotten a look at me before.

"*You?*" she asked, as if she couldn't pull the pieces of information to something that made sense.

I nodded, glancing around the basement. I didn't own the place, of course. Instead, I'd checked out the owner and knew they wouldn't return for another six months, since they only used it during the summer.

It meant we had as much time as we needed, and I highly doubted it would take nearly that long. I intended to do what needed to be done and get the hell out.

"Yeah, me." I hopped onto the long workbench against one wall, enjoying the higher position compared to Shelia, who couldn't manage to stand, not with her ankles bound and her wrists tied behind her back.

"What do you want?"

"To discuss history."

She frowned, as if the answer were crazy, as if I didn't make a bit of sense. "Whatever you want, I can get it for you."

I let out a soft laugh. "Can you change the past? Can you go back ten years and fix what you did?"

Shelia didn't show any understanding on her face.

"You really have no idea what I'm talking about, do you? That means you've either done so many horrible things that I could mean anything or what you did mattered so little to you, you can't even recall it. I'm not sure which is worse."

She twisted, as if trying to free her wrists. "You have the wrong person."

"No, I don't. Even ten years isn't enough to forget. Come on, now, Shelia, think really hard. A house in downtown LA? A fire?"

She went entirely still, the way a person did when they were hoping they could lie their way out of their mess if they just came up with the right story. The thing was, to lie effectively, someone had to know the topic. Shelia had just figured out our subject. "I had a friend who was murdered ten years ago."

At least she had the decency to feign sorrow.

"What you mean is you helped murder your friend ten years ago," I pressed.

She shook her head, fake tears springing to her eyes. "What? No! I loved Caroline—"

I pointed my finger at her, my voice soft but firm. "Don't you dare utter her name."

She gulped, then tried to speak again, her tone more cautious. "I'm not sure what you think you know, but that night, it didn't happen the way you think."

"I know exactly how it happened." I didn't look away, didn't give her an inch of space to avoid my words, to try to weasel out of what I damn well remembered. "You took Caroline's phone when you stopped in to visit that morning. You did it so when the three men came in, when they started killing the guards, Caroline couldn't call anyone for help. Then, when they came in, when Caroline realized what was really happening, you laughed at her. You told her Kyler had asked you to do it, how glad you were to finally get her out of the way, how she was getting what she deserved."

Shelia shook her head again, an immediate denial tinged in fear. "I don't know who told you that, but it's not true."

"Do you really think you can still talk your way out of this? That you can convince me I'm wrong? If so, you're not paying attention."

"I wasn't there," she pressed. "And neither were you. Everyone who was at that house died in the fire."

"I watched you smile as you held the phone up, as Caroline realized you'd helped set her up." I leaned forward, wanting her to see the truth of it in my face. "You told me not to worry, that everything would be fine. The worst part? I believed you."

Shelia sat straighter, all the pieces falling into place as her brain caught up and made sense of the details.

"Kelsey?" She whispered that old name, the one that didn't fit anymore, the one who had burned away in that house, just like Caroline. Fake happiness took over her expression, even past all the fillers in her, as if it could mask the surprise. "I'm so glad you're okay! I've been so worried about you! God, do you know what it means to realize I didn't lose you that night, too?"

The platitudes burned. Was she hoping they'd save her? That she'd be able to play the part of the grieving friend who was so grateful to find I'd survived? How did she think she could make me doubt what I'd seen with my own eyes?

It was bullshit. I remembered the nail salon, the way Shelia had all but gloated her story about how that woman had gotten what was coming to her. Shelia didn't give a fuck about me, about Caroline, about anything but herself and what she wanted. It was no different than now, when she'd been using Caroline to try to get her out of this.

I'd watched her betray my mother, betray me, and had felt the bullets someone had put through me, choked on the smoke that had filled the house. Nothing she had to say could convince me of a word that left her deceitful lips.

I hopped off the table, then opened the bag I'd brought and left on the floor. I pulled out another set of zip ties, using them to hook her hands to the large pipe that reached down through the ceiling and into the foundation. Shelia kept talking, kept telling me how thankful she was to have found me, but she didn't struggle or fight me.

Then again, Shelia wasn't stupid. I had the upper hand, which meant she had to use those words of hers to get out of this.

Fat chance.

"Save your breath." I crouched in front of her, staring right into those familiar eyes. "I know exactly what happened. You're responsible for what happened that night. You helped Kyler kill Caroline, helped him try to kill me. Too bad you didn't succeed with me."

The false sorrow melted away, as though she'd realized she needed a new path. "It wasn't my fault— Kyler threatened me. He said I had to help him. I didn't know what he was going to do, though."

"You didn't know when men showed up and started killing the loyal guards what would happen?"

"No. I thought Kyler was just going to scare Caroline. She didn't listen to him, was always doing what she wanted—he said he just needed to make it clear she needed to follow his lead. I mean, *I* didn't kill her. I didn't know what was going to happen. You can't blame me for what *he* did."

I would have been angry if anger was something I felt much of. I waited for it, almost expecting her lying to be enough to bring it back, but nothing. It was as dead as the rest of my feelings. It seemed only the Quad could spark that to life.

Instead, I pulled the knife from the bag. "You know, I've had a lot of time to think about this. A whole damned decade of time, in fact. The others, Lucky, the triggermen, they did what they did because of money or favors or whatever else Kyler promised them, but they didn't know us. I mean, what were we to them? Nothing. You, though, *you* knew us."

"I wasn't there when it happened! You can't blame me for what they did after I left."

"Exactly. You walked away. At least if you'd pulled the trigger, I'd have more respect for you for doing your own dirty work. Instead, you turned away, you left Caroline alone, you walked out and let someone else do it like the coward you are. She bled out, on the floor, *alone*, because you wanted what she had, and you wanted her to suffer."

Shelia shook her head, even though she couldn't deny anything I said. The words she did manage were broken and quick and useless. They were nothing more than pleading, than a last-ditch effort to save her worthless life.

"I thought a lot about this, wanted to know what the best way to deal with you was. Lucky, the man who burned the house down, I left him in a burning house. I believe that the punishment should fit the crime, that people should suffer based on what they did. You, though? How to deal with a coward who set up a woman who thought of you as a sister?"

"Please," she whispered, when she seemed to come up with nothing else to say.

I reached past her, my knife in hand, and ran it across her forearm, over her wrist. She cried out, but I made the cut deep and quick. I repeated it on the other arm, ignoring her whimpering. It was a *lot* less painful than what Caroline had gone through.

"You get one chance," I told her. "Answer my question, and I'll make this quick for you. Don't tell me what I want to know, and I'll walk out of here. You'll bleed out alone, because no one will get close enough to hear you no matter how much or how loud you scream. It'll take twenty minutes, tops, but you'll have to sit here and wait for it, knowing it's coming, just like Caroline had to suffer through."

"Please don't do this," she begged.

I leaned in and asked her the same question I'd asked Lucky, the one that drove me, the reason I'd come back. "Where is my sister?"

"I don't know," she pleaded. "Kyler moved her after that, and he's kept her hidden since then. I'd tell you where she was if I knew, I swear."

I rose to my feet, because I doubted she was lying. Kyler wasn't besties with her, having no doubt tossed her aside the second she wasn't useful anymore. He'd never loved her, never given a damn about her. Shelia had created this bond in her own mind, and he'd been too happy to use it to his own ends. She knew that, too. It was there in her eyes, the knowledge that no matter how much she pretended that she mattered to him, she hadn't.

"This is what happened to Caroline," I told her. "It's what you tried to do to me. Except, I clawed my way out, bleeding and hurting and half-fucking-dead to escape the flames. You won't be crawling anywhere, though." I picked up the bag, pausing at the door to look over my shoulder at her. "You were right, though. Karma gets everyone, eventually, and I make damned sure of it. This is you getting exactly what you deserve.

The only reassurance you get is that you aren't alone. I'll take down every last person who tried to kill me."

Her yelling followed me as I locked the door, then closed and locked the entry that covered the stairs, leaving her there with the consequences of her own actions, alone, just as she'd done to my mother.

Karma was a bitch, but then again, so was I.

Chapter Seven

Nem

Red circled the drain of the shower, stark against the white tile, following the flow of the water.

It wasn't blood, not this time, but rather came from the dye of my hair. It was something I'd had to accept when it came to wearing such a bright shade — it bled. There was something almost poetic about it, how it would leak that color each time I bathed, as if I had a wound that never coagulated or healed.

I closed my eyes, tipping my head back so the water ran through my long hair, letting the even pattering of sprinkles ease me.

There was always this tension inside me after a job. They took so much prep, so much planning and watching and time. The actual act, though?

Quick.

Then, after that, after the nerves and adrenaline, all I could do was shower, wash away the blood or the memories or the regrets.

It wasn't that I regretted killing Shelia, but rather those moments afterward when I wondered if I couldn't have done something different. If I'd waited and found her last, would she have talked? Could I have used her first, have blackmailed her or threatened her into helping me?

That was the thing—I could only make one choice but there were a shit ton of options and in the end, a person had to pick one and go with that.

Mine had left Shelia dead, out in some cabin where no one would find her for months and months—I could live with that ending.

I turned off the water, then wrang my hair out best I could. A quick rub with a towel helped to remove whatever other water I could from it, then I braided it loosely and piled it into a bun on top of my head. Drying it like that would give it waves when I undid it the next day.

The hotel was quiet, with the walls insulated enough so I couldn't hear any neighbors. It let me almost feel as if I were alone, as if nothing else could touch me. I thought back to the times when I'd gone to a place in the mountains Jarrod owned, something far off the beaten path where the snow would pile high and nothing could plow the roads.

I spent a few weeks a year there, in the solitude, during the winter months when even random hikers wouldn't venture by. It was peaceful in a way I wasn't used to, a time when I didn't have to read into every little thing said, when I didn't have to second guess the meaning of everything, when I didn't have to worry about who might want to do me harm.

I picked up a tank top, one with a neckline high enough to hide my scars. Thankfully, they hadn't had to do open heart surgery to save me, meaning the scars from surgery were on my back rather than over my sternum. Not that it mattered — I was still a mess, it was just easier to hide.

Then, I took a deep breath and looked in the mirror. *Fuck.*

No matter how many times I did this, it never got easier. The scars stood out like signposts on my pale skin. Two were on my left side, below my breast, the ones left there from when I'd collapsed and the man who had shot me put two more through my back as I had hunched forward. The one from surgery ran across my left side, below my arm and curved around my back. The one that really hit me, though, the one I always focused on rested on the left side of my chest. It had missed my heart but hit my lung. I still remembered how it had felt to cough up blood, the way I couldn't seem to get enough air, the way each inhalation hurt.

They marred my body, but they reminded me what the world really was.

I was okay with being broken, with carrying scars. It didn't bother me that someone might see them, that they'd think less of me. The scars were part of what made me who I was, what propelled me on this course, what drove me.

They were the proof that I had died that night, even if Jarrod had managed to bring me back. The part of me that had been innocent and naive and stupid had bled out there beside my mother. That part had burned away in the fire, in the grave that the house had turned into. The new part, the new me, had clawed my way through the pain, toward the closet, toward the hidden saferoom tucked behind the false door there.

So before I slid on my shirt, I stared into the mirror, let myself absorb the proof of what I'd suffered to become who I was, now.

And what I wouldn't allow to happen to my sister, Kenz, the reason I had to be here no matter how dangerous it became.

I pulled on the shirt, forgoing a bra. My plans for the night included a few drinks and poring over plans for how best to obtain the winery. I didn't need extra support for that. I slipped on a pair of boy shorts underwear, then hung the towel back up on the rack.

The air drew goosebumps up on my skin when I walked out of the bathroom, when I left the heat and steam from the shower.

Or, maybe it wasn't the change in temperature so much as the sight of Colton standing in my hotel room that put me on edge.

Finding a hitman in her bedroom will do that to a girl.

Colton

Rune had been right. When he'd come back after following Nem out to the winery, he'd bitched and moaned about the pull of the young woman, about how something with her wasn't right.

Of course, something wasn't right. I knew that much without having to grind up against her.

She was lying through her teeth. She was good at it, too, which made everything that much more difficult.

It was like having a lioness lounging around, pretending to be docile and sweet, but knowing damn well she might just bare her teeth at any time.

And yet, seeing her like this—half naked—made it hard to remember what I'd come here for. She wore two scraps of thin fabric masquerading as clothes—a thin tank top that her nipples showed through and a pair of decidedly unsexy panties that covered far too much.

Yet, even though they weren't lace and bows, I couldn't pull my eyes away from the sight, from the strip of skin that peeked between them, from the way, turned slightly as she was, the bottom curve of her ass just barely showed.

She wasn't all that busty, if I had to be honest. She had a B cup at best. However, judging from what I could see—which was plenty—she made up for it with an ass and thighs that could change a man's religion.

Nem didn't scream when she saw me, didn't yelp or even flinch—funny that excited me more than her lack of clothing. She moved her gaze over me as if it didn't matter to her a bit that I was there—neither due to fear nor that I'd seen her damn near undressed.

She glanced past me to the clock on the nightstand. "Is there some real estate emergency you need solved at two in the morning?"

I crossed my arms, content with knowing she couldn't have hidden a weapon, not while wearing so little. "No."

"So you're here to kill me?"

"Why would you think that?"

"Because that's your job, isn't it? The Quad aren't unknown, and you're the assassin."

I narrowed my eyes, unwilling to confirm or deny it. Of course, many people knew some of what I'd done—

a reputation was a funny thing. People had to know what a person could do or they wouldn't fear them. What struck me as suspicious was the unconcerned way in which she discussed it. "Why would I be here to kill you?"

"From what I heard, the last person who held my job disappeared. It isn't a far guess to think I might meet the same fate."

"If you're that worried, why are you still here?"

"Who said I was worried?" She moved past me, giving me a full view of her ass, one that once again distracted me enough it took a minute before her words hit me, before I realized she'd asked me something. She kept talking, thankfully. "Anyone who gets into bed with people like you, like your boss, knows the risks. I'm not worried because I know I haven't done anything wrong. If I get killed anyway, then it wasn't something I could have controlled. I keep my nose clean, and the rest? Well, people get killed crossing the street all the time." She opened the fridge, bending forward in a way that made my cock perk up.

The things I want to do to that ass...

She took out two water bottles and tossed one my way. Reflexes had me catching it rather than decision-making, since my focus was firmly placed elsewhere.

"So, for the last time, are you here to kill me?"

"Not today," I admitted. Maybe if she knew that, she'd let down her guard.

"Then what is it you want? I have plans."

"Dressed like that?"

She slid onto one of the stools at the kitchen bar, her back to the counter and front toward me. "I have plans with myself, ones that don't concern you, so my outfit isn't your business, either."

Her easy dismissal of me burned. I was feared by so many, and there she was, talking to me as though I were a pizza boy who wouldn't leave even after receiving a tip.

"I came for answers."

"I was taught to never ask a question you don't already know the answer to."

"How would you ever get any information then?"

She laughed softly before unscrewing the top of the water bottle and taking a drink. With her head tipped backward, I could see how her throat worked, the way it moved, teasing me. When she finished, she set the water on the counter. "Questions are dangerous, because answers are dangerous. Sometimes we find out things we didn't really want to know."

"Answers are reality, even when they're bad. Any person afraid of answers is a fool and a coward."

"Maybe," she said softly. "Ask your questions so you can get out."

I walked forward, wanting to study her as she answered, as she heard the questions. Communication was so much more than just words, and I wanted to read her. I wasn't Dane, I couldn't read the truth the way he did, couldn't pick up a lie with such ease, but I had enough skill to be decent.

"Why are you really here?"

"Because of the job."

"Why did you leave San Francisco?"

She didn't show any surprise at my knowing her past, but then again, she was probably used to people checking up on her. Background checks were part of life for us. "It got crowded there. I'm sure you understand how working in one place too long can create hard feelings. It was time to move on, and since I'm partial to sun, LA seemed a good option."

Her words were lies, but not entirely? It was hard to place it, as if maybe she'd repeated them enough to believe them. Or as though she knew there was more to the story than she let on.

Wasn't there always, though?

"You're not here just for the job."

"You seem awfully sure of that."

"Because no person who was here to just do a job would be as evasive as you have been—or as suspicious." I came closer, drawn in by her smirk, by her nonchalance, as if she knew this would go her way.

Which was stupid. I'd said I wasn't there to kill her, and I wasn't, but that could change at any time.

I had no problem putting a bullet in her if the situation warranted it, if it was the right choice. I had people to protect, a job to do, and if Nem wanted to be in the way, I'd remove her without hesitation. I didn't kill when I didn't have to, but when someone became my enemy? When they put me or those I'd sworn to protect in danger? I'd end any life I needed to.

"You're paranoid," she countered. "You've done this too long. You see ghosts and enemies everywhere."

"I see a lot of things," I admitted, coming even closer until I could wrap my hand around the front of her throat. I didn't squeeze, leaving it there as a threat instead. "For example, I saw you talking to Shelia Tawinn last week, and guess who no one has seen since yesterday?"

Her eyes didn't widen, and no fear played across her features. Was that because she was innocent? Because the two women just happened to go to the same nail place at the same time? Or because she had something to do with the disappearance and was prepared for the accusation?

Fuck, I don't know.

"Who?" she asked, tone flat.

"Shelia, the woman you talked to at the nail place."

"Oh, was that her name? I talk to a lot of people. I'm very friendly, you know."

"Right," I muttered, then leaned in closer, my lips at her ear, my voice low. "And the knife in your car, the one you dropped off at a dumpster, that wasn't Shelia's blood on it?"

"A knife? I wouldn't know anything about that."

Well, that cleared up something while answering fuck all of my questions. Clearly, she knew what happened to Shelia, was involved with it, but why?

What game was she playing?

Shelia was a nobody—an old friend of Caroline Williams, of Kyler's late wife. She wasn't anything important, had access to nothing vital, couldn't have any secrets because the status climber would have spilled them long ago.

So why would anyone want her gone enough to be willing to make it happen?

I made a low sound in my throat, full of frustration. "I don't know what you're involved in, but you need to back off. There are things going on that you don't know anything about. You're likely to get yourself killed." I tightened my grip on her throat, begging her with the action to take some good advice.

I'd kill her and I wouldn't think twice about it, but I really didn't want to…

Why that was, I had no damn idea and didn't want to look all that closely at. There weren't many people I gave a damn about.

"So bury me," she whispered, tilting her head back like an offering.

When I tightened my hand again, she let out the sexiest moan I'd ever heard, her thighs falling open to make room for me between them.

There wasn't a doubt anymore...

This girl was going to kill me one way or another.

Nem

My moan seemed to flip a switch in Colton, as if all that aggression inside him transformed into lust.

His lips crashed against mine, rough and domineering and way too much to be sweet. This wasn't about sweet, though. It wasn't love making or dating or anything so normal and trivial

It wasn't the times I'd thought about it when I'd still been a stupid kid, when I'd thought of Colton as some all-powerful protector of mine.

This was the real us — it was the person he'd hidden when I'd been younger, and the woman I'd turned into.

I didn't need sweetness and gentle touches and reassurance. I didn't need him holding my hand and telling me I was pretty. I didn't need romance or love, and I sure as fuck didn't want either. What I needed was his teeth in my skin, his hand around my throat, and his cock *deep* inside me.

Thankfully, those were things I was pretty sure he could handle.

He didn't let go of my throat, but he loosened enough that he didn't obstruct my breathing. He bit down on my bottom lip, hard enough it would be swollen come tomorrow.

He groped my breast through my shirt with his free hand, but when he reached for the hemline, I knocked his hand away.

I might not be sorry about my scars, but I couldn't risk him seeing them. They were too personal, might tell too much. They were mine, and he didn't deserve to see them.

He let out a sound of frustration against my lips. "Afraid of me now?"

"Fuck you," I muttered before biting his bottom lip back hard enough that the tang of copper touched my tongue. "This isn't a date where you're going to get me naked. Get your cock out or leave—I have toys that can finish your job if you're unable to."

He pulled back and touched his lip with his tongue, tasting the blood I'd drawn. Fuck, that blood was something.

It was life for me, the thing that connected everything else, that strung the mess of my life together. The blood I'd lost that night, the blood I'd seen shed, the blood I'd spilled in the years since— figured that it'd be part of this, too.

Colton stared at me for a split second, his hand still around my throat, his dark eyes narrowed, his hair falling forward to cast shadows over his face. It all made him look like the monster others saw in him.

I never saw a monster, though. Or, maybe it was better put that I was the same kind of monster, so it wasn't something that frightened me. Zebras might see a lion and flee, but another lion doesn't see them as a predator.

Colton was a monster, but then, so was I.

He reached his free hand down to his jeans and flicked the button open, though he never released my throat. Was it that he didn't trust me? Did he just want that power? Did he want to remind me he was in charge?

I let him have it, basked in it. There was nothing better than someone who thought they had the upper hand but didn't really. It was delicious to watch them gloat, to see them relax into that false belief until I was ready to spring the trap.

I didn't have one set with Colton, not yet, but that didn't mean he had the upper hand. No one *ever* got that with me anymore.

"I don't know what you're up to," he said, the sound of his zipper accompanying the words. "But if you even think about betraying Kyler or my brothers, I'll put you down."

"Are you afraid of little ol' me?"

He reached between us and rubbed his fingers against my cunt, through the thin fabric of my underwear. It wasn't a teasing motion, not romantic or careful. It was almost as if he already knew I was as turned on as he was, that I didn't need much in the way of foreplay, but he needed to feel me anyway.

The rough stroke ran right through me, lighting me up just like Dane's almost-kiss had, like Rune grinding against me had.

For the past ten years, I'd thought I couldn't feel a damn thing anymore. I'd been ready to do what I needed to, to save my sister and kill Kyler, but I hadn't thought I'd feel a fucking thing about any of it. I hadn't felt anything when seeing Lucky, when seeing Shelia, just the barest memory of emotions, like a ghost to remind me of what I'd lost. When I'd died, I figured everything human inside me had died at the same time.

So what was it about these men that they could do this to me? That they could flip on switches I'd thought ripped out entirely?

I moaned openly against the roughness of his fingers, against the grip he had on my throat. It all clouded my mind as I let my head fall back, as I gave myself over to the moment and to him.

If he wanted to kill me, well, there were a hell of a lot worse ways to go.

Colton pressed forward, leaning me back against the counter. The edge jammed into my back but fuck it — nothing mattered right then except chasing this high, except having this spark of feeling I'd thought dead.

"I'm not afraid of you," Colton said, as if our conversation had been going the whole time. Maybe he was just as consumed by this as I was. "I just don't want to have to kill you for no good reason."

"I didn't think that would bother you."

"It wouldn't," he countered as he grabbed the waist of my underwear and yanked them down. The snapping of thread said they were probably ruined, but what did that matter? I'd happily sacrifice my panties for this. With the fabric gone, he brought his fingers back to my cunt and pressed two into me with a hard thrust that filled me in the perfect way. "But just because I'll do it doesn't mean I *want* to."

I spread my thighs more, an offering for whatever he wanted. His fingers made me feel so damn full, making me laugh at how sure I'd been about my toys before.

As it turned out, they were a poor substitute. The nights when I'd used them, picturing men who I had, at the time, refused to admit were *these* four, I'd thought they worked fine. I'd thought that they could replace them — be better than them, if anything.

How wrong I was.

The reality was that masturbation before had been more about releasing tension and less about enjoyment, about passion or desire.

Colton twisted his agile fingers inside of me, making me shudder at the overwhelming sparks of pleasure. "You're really tight," he growled. "For all your talk, do you not get as much attention as you pretend?"

None. I wouldn't dare tell him that, though. He'd look at me with pity, or worse, he'd think me naive and innocent.

I was neither of those things, and he didn't deserve to think for even a moment he mattered to me, that I'd think about him again after tonight.

"Do you talk this much because you know you can't perform?" I asked. "I understand in older men it's a problem — "

I would have kept going, egging him on, trying to push him over the edge so we didn't have to talk, so I didn't risk saying anything I shouldn't, but I didn't get the chance.

Instead, the blunt head of his cock pressed against my pussy for a split second.

He stared at me, his eyes intense and both familiar and foreign in a way that played tricks with my mind. "Are you on birth control?"

Right. The real world hit me, the risks, the reality. "I have an IUD," I said. I hadn't shown up expecting to sleep with anyone, but I was smart enough to know children weren't in my future. I didn't have a nurturing gene anywhere in my DNA.

"I tested a month ago, and I'm clean. You?"

The question took me a moment to understand, especially because of just how distracting his cock was, nestled against my cunt like some warning. When I realized what he meant, I nodded. Given that I hadn't *ever* had sex with anyone before, I knew I wasn't carrying anything.

"Good, because I need to feel all of you," he said before he jerked his hips forward and plunged his thick length into me.

I heard women talk about seeing stars before and I had assumed it was all bullshit. It was nothing more than people trying to pretty up the dirty reality of sex. Sex was sweat and bodily fluids and people reduced to their bases. Saying people saw stars or any other poetic nonsense was just them trying to feel better about themselves and the animalistic truth of sex.

That was what I would have said, at least, until Colton slamming into me did just that. Bright sparks appeared on my eyelids, as if the sensations were so overwhelming that my body had no idea how to process them.

He was thicker than my toys—longer, too. A deliciously sharp pain went through me as my body tried to accommodate, tried to make sense of this new feeling. That was part of what made it so much better, though.

If I had been alone in my bed with a toy, I'd have backed off. I'd have gone slow or decided I needed to scale back. Because Colton was in charge and not me, however, it was exciting and new and he filled me with every inch before I could even think about denying him.

I reached out, unable to help it, and grasped his sides, over his ribs. I dug my nails into him, almost like a punishment for the past, for him being gone for so damned long, for not being there when I'd needed him.

Leave it to me to be difficult enough that I wanted to secretly punish him for my own choice...

He didn't complain about the nails — he actually groaned, a masculine, sexy sound that teased my senses. Instead, he pulled back — the stroke of his cock against my cunt amazing — then sank back in.

It all overwhelmed me, crashing in on itself, too much for me to sort through and pay attention to.

His hand was still on my throat, pinning me to the counter, his body large and hard against mine, his thick cock deep inside me, having me in a way no one ever had before.

"Nothing smart to say?" he challenged, a strained humor in his voice.

If it were anyone else, I might have let that go. I might have ignored his attempts to goad me in favor of just basking in the new feelings, but the idea of letting him truly get the best of me chafed too much.

"If I tried, you wouldn't understand it."

He huffed, then set a hard pace, taking me with such reckless abandon, I knew I'd have bruising on my back from the counter. Still, the wild passion, the pain, it was perfect. It was everything I wanted and needed.

If we'd been in bed, if it had been some weird, sweet moment, I might just have thrown up. That wasn't him and it sure as fuck wasn't me. I wasn't the girl I'd been before, lovestruck and stupid and following at his heels like an idiot puppy. I wasn't the person I'd been when I'd tried to get a kiss from him, when he'd rejected me for being too young.

I was a badass who was fucking him because I *wanted* to. This wasn't me being an idiot, or Colton taking advantage.

If anything, I was taking advantage of him. I knew exactly who he was, knew our history, and I was fucking him because I'd dreamed of it for ten goddamned years.

He grabbed my thigh, yanking it up around his hip, changing his angle so his cock dragged against a new and *far* better place inside me. It also meant his body ground against my clit when he bottomed out, driving me closer to release.

And what a release it was shaping up to be… Already my body was on edge, all my muscles twitching with a need to let go, to experience a moment of absolute bliss where I couldn't think about anything, remember anything, worry about anything. It was like my whole last decade had been ramping up for this moment.

"You're going to listen to me." Colton's words were broken by his heavy panting. "Whatever stupid thing you're involved in, you're going to stop. You're going to let whatever this is go."

"Not a chance," I answered, the words cut off when I cried out as he rolled his hips. I was so close, striving for the orgasm that had dangled in front of me since I'd seen Dane at that club.

Hell, since I'd been a teenager, since Colton and the others had spawned to life a desire inside of me, since they'd made me feel this want for the first time ever. It was fitting that they were the ones to let me truly taste it, too. They owed me at least that much.

He pressed his forehead to mine, his hand sliding around so it cupped the back of my neck, a controlling touch but one that wasn't quite so threatening. A deep sound left him, a groan that screamed of relief, and at the same time, he sank in as deep as possible to my cunt.

The action ground him against my clit as well, and it was enough for me to follow him, to sink into the intense snap as I came. I arched against him, but he was too large, too strong to bend. He was a solid force I could hit as much as I wanted and he wouldn't give an inch.

I breathed hard, my body worn out and overworked, my cunt squeezing down even as his softening cock remained inside me.

It was uncomfortable and close and way too intimate.

He pulled back enough to stare into my eyes. "These are people you don't want to fuck with."

"I have no idea what you're talking about," I answered. "So unless you can get it up for round two — get out."

Colton narrowed his eyes.

What was he expecting? Cuddling? For me to break down in tears and tell him everything because of a little dick?

Little? Who's lying now?

He pulled away, the sudden emptiness of my drenched cunt almost shocking. Worse, it dragged a broken cry from me when it set off another wave of pleasure, my body still sensitive.

He tucked his cock back into his pants, then zipped and buttoned them. The sweat on his forehead and wild look in his eyes made him look less like the unflappable assassin others saw. He pointed his finger at me, but instead of it scaring me, it distracted me — I knew exactly how talented those fingers were, now. "You're playing with fire, Nem."

I offered him a smile, not bothering to cover up—I refused to be sorry or embarrassed about finally getting laid. "I'm not afraid of getting burned."

Chapter Eight

Nem

When women talked about being sore after sex, I hadn't ever really understood. I figured it was nonsense, a rumor spread by men who thought their cocks were far more impressive than they really were.

Boy, was I wrong.

A subtle ache in my lower stomach had persisted all day, a reminder of what Colton and I had done the night before. Even as I sat in the reception area of the law firm, waiting for Sasha, that gnawing pain was like a sticky-note about how I'd spent my night.

As if I needed any sort of reminder. It wasn't every day I lost my virginity to a killer who had broken into my room and threatened me. That wasn't something I was likely to forget.

Ever.

Still, I couldn't dwell on it. I needed to focus, to keep my mind on the task at hand. I could just imagine

Jarrod standing there, giving me that disappointed look he offered me when I failed to live up to his expectations.

While I hadn't exactly asked his opinion, I would guess that sleeping with the enemy counted as things he wouldn't approve of.

Too bad. I wasn't a child, and we were so far beyond the point where I needed a father to tell me about the birds and the bees or to tell me that boys only wanted one thing.

And more than that, Colton was hardly a boy.

It meant who I screwed wasn't any of Jarrod's business.

"Nem?" I lifted my gaze to the voice, realizing I'd been so distracted that I'd failed to notice the person I was waiting for had arrived.

Sasha stood there, an effortless smile on her lips. I liked Sasha even though she was an almost complete opposite to me. Or maybe that was the exact reason why I liked her. Where I was guarded and suspicious, she was friendly and sweet.

I had to work hard to read people, to twist them, but Sasha somehow managed to get people to do what she wanted just by asking. It was damn near a magic trick, and one I'd never learned to mimic.

"Hey," I said, the same old nerves hitting me. Sasha never failed to make me feel like someone who had no idea how to actually interact with humans. Maybe it was because, while I could manipulate people, while I could read them, she reminded me that I didn't know how to actually talk to them.

She also was the only person who could make me wish I knew that, who made me crave that.

"Come on." She waved for me to follow her. We went back, through the hallways of the large law firm. Sasha smiled at people, offering mindless pleasantries and seeming to enjoy the back and forth.

That threw me, something I didn't understand. I talked to people when I needed to, when I wanted something from them, but I got no pleasure from small talk with strangers. I could fake it, but Sasha always had seemed to relish it.

She opened the door to her office, her name on a plague there. I took a seat in front of the large desk as she closed us in, and took her seat behind the desk. "It's been far too long since I've seen you," she said.

"It's hard to make it down here," I answered, shifting in the seat.

"Of course. I mean, who wouldn't enjoy San Francisco? What are you doing back?"

"I have business."

She paused, her smile slipping free. "Business?"

I nodded.

"Is this about how I met you?"

I thought back to how she'd come to Jarrod's house to treat my wounds. She hadn't been the one who had actually saved me in the hospital, not the one who had done surgery and patched me up. Instead, she'd been a nurse Jarrod had found, one he'd paid well to care for me after he'd abducted me from the hospital. She'd all but lived with us for a few months as I'd recovered.

Hospitals were too dangerous, and doctors asked too many questions.

It had always thrown me that Sasha had agreed to help. She was a good person, the type for whom money rarely swayed. How Jarrod had convinced her to do anything for me, I didn't understand.

"Yeah," I told her. If she hadn't ratted me out yet, she wouldn't. "I'm going to deal with them."

She pressed her lips together. "You know, revenge never really helps."

"The only people who say that either don't have anything to avenge or they've already gotten theirs. It's never the ones who are still in the trenches."

Sasha sighed, setting her hands on the desk. "You were almost killed once. Do you really want to wade back into that mess again? I remember patching you back up, seeing every day as you cling to life. One time, when I was a kid, I was caught up by a riptide at the beach. It almost killed me. I didn't go back in to try and teach it a lesson—I was just grateful I made it out alive."

"You don't understand. This isn't just about me."

"Are you sure about that?"

I wasn't—not even a little. Still, I went with that. "My sister is still there, and how do I know she won't suffer the same fate? The man who did that to me, he is a monster. I can't risk that he could do it to her, too."

She let out a long sigh before meeting my gaze, that steel in her eyes one that always surprised me. "How can I help?"

That was the thing—she seemed fragile, but somehow, she showed more bravery than I'd ever have expected. She'd done it when she'd taken care of me, when she'd not fled at Jarrod—the man wasn't exactly friendly or reassuring—when she'd stood up to him at the times when he'd pushed me beyond what she felt was safe. I still recalled how they'd faced off, how she hadn't wilted even though the fear in her face said she knew exactly how dangerous he was.

I shook off my reaction, then set a file on the desk. "I need some results faked."

She opened the file and went through the pages, scanning them slowly. "Why? How does this help?"

"I need access to his files to find where he is hiding my sister, and to do that, I need him to trust me. To prove they can all trust me, I need this person to sell her property to me."

Sasha's eyes twitched, and I could just about see how she worked through it. "How does making this woman think she has cancer help you? It sounds like ruining her life, stealing her home, and for what? I know you don't like to tell me things, but I won't help you if I don't believe it really is for the best. I know you and Jarrod do a lot of questionable things, but I can't be a part of this without more information."

I would have rather kept it all to myself—more because I didn't want her to have to carry that guilt—but I needed Sasha's help. "The person who wants that house is going to get it. He's the one who put those bullets in me. If I don't find a way to get her to sell, he'll find another way to get what he wants, and he won't mind spilling blood to do it. She has family and grandkids across the country."

Sasha sighed. "You want to scare her, to make her think she's really sick, so she realizes she wants to be closer to her family. If she does that, she'll agree to sell."

"If I don't do this, if I can't get her to agree, she may not survive the next attempt to get that property." I would have sworn I didn't give a damn about whether or not Tammy lived. She was a stranger, and that didn't make her any concern of mine. She should have been an obstacle—nothing more.

Except, as I spoke, I realized it wasn't entirely true. I really didn't want to open the newspaper and find out

Tammy had died. It felt as if the world might be a bit poorer if she weren't in it anymore.

Looking at Sasha reminded me of how much danger she was in, as well. She had no idea how to hide her feelings, how to keep things to herself. Everything she thought played across her face, and anyone who wanted to take advantage of it could.

It meant I knew exactly when she agreed, when she decided she would do as I wanted before she had to say a word.

She'd given up nursing after taking care of me and moved to a medical malpractice law firm that dealt with hospitals who purposely mishandled clients. The bleeding heart was always wanting to help people. Still, it gave her the reach to do what I needed, and I wasn't above using her.

I'd already made a fake call to Tammy, posing as her doctor's office, telling her she needed bloodwork run. Sasha would handle the order at the lab and switch the results when they came back.

"Okay," she said softly, and I damn near felt guilty at putting her in that position. "I'll do it. I just hope you know what you're doing, because that riptide I talked about, when I breathed that water into my lungs, it was horrible. Be careful, Nem. I don't want to see you drown."

I didn't either, but I'd been honest before, with Colton. Dying didn't scare me. I'd already been there, done that. Dying wasn't so bad—what sucked was all the shit we had to go through before.

Chapter Nine

Nem

Ten years of planning, ten years of blood — mine as well as others — of dreaming and hoping and fighting to get me *here*.

Jarrod had told me once that the life of normal people was hurry up and wait. For us, it was the opposite. We spent forever preparing, shocked to find ourselves finally where we'd been headed.

Which, for me, was in that same office I'd met the Quad in before, where they'd given me the files and hired me.

I'd done what I needed to, the deed having been sent over the day before. Having it had turned my stomach, almost like guilt, but this meant too much to back out now.

Tammy would go off to her family, would get to spend her twilight years with grandkids pulling at her and grateful for her health after such a scare.

Or so I told myself to get rid of that horrible feeling in my gut.

I'd done what they'd wanted—*spectacularly*. They had to be calling me in to hire me, to congratulate me.

Right? I couldn't shake the worry that they'd figured me out.

Colton knew I was lying, though about what, he had no idea. Still, I'd fallen asleep each night since having sex with him wondering if I'd wake to find his pistol in my face.

And not in a sexy repeat of last time way...

If they wanted to kill me, they wouldn't need to go through this charade.

Dane opened the door to the office, the same one I'd been in before, and waved me over.

I followed him, grateful he didn't mention anything—no doubt Colton had told him, since they'd never been the kind to keep secrets. The men were closer than brothers and shared everything. Not just stories, but women as well.

Inside the office were the other three, in the same seats as before, and somehow they looked even less friendly than the last time.

Which seemed unfair. Sure, maybe I was lying about a few things, but I'd done the job they wanted.

As I took the open seat, I had a flash of years ago, back when I'd snuck out one night with a boy because I'd been sixteen and stupid. Dane had hauled me back, annoyance on his features, and they'd sat me down just like this.

They'd lectured me about safety concerns, about how boys that age weren't to be trusted, about how I needed to be more careful.

The funniest part of it all was that I hadn't cared a bit about that boy. I'd done it because they'd ignored me, because they'd treated me like I was a child, and I'd wanted them jealous. I'd wanted to push their buttons, to force them to pay attention to me.

I had that same undercurrent of excitement this time, as if pissing them off pleased me. I wanted to see what happened when I got beneath their skin.

"I did the job," I said to break the ice and put us on track. They didn't need a chance to start in on anything personal and irrelevant.

"You did," Bray said, his voice smooth and careful. "How is it that you bought it at almost half the market value?"

"It wasn't hard. I gave the owner a story about how I fell in love with the property, how I talked my boss out of it so I could buy it, but I couldn't afford that much. She'd prefer it go to someone who would love it over someone who could pay more, especially since she still made out with everything she'd need."

Again, that ugly feeling gnawed at me.

I kept a glare from appearing on my face when I wanted to blame the men for it. I'd felt nothing for ten years and now guilt? Lust? Anger?

It was all their fault, like a dam they'd put cracks in.

"So, do I have the job?"

Colton let out a soft snort, as if my bluntness amused him. Bray looked far less pleased, however.

"We'll see."

"What do you mean, 'we'll see'?" I tapped my fingers on my knee to work off the energy surging through me. "You asked me to complete a task, and I did so, following every one of your rules. I exceeded the parameters you gave me, so what exactly is your problem?"

"Your trustworthiness," Colton said from his spot near the back.

"If anyone is in our line of work, they aren't trustworthy. Secrets are what keep us alive. If anyone understands that, you should."

"Do you really think we're going to let someone who we know is lying anywhere near Kyler? That I'm going to completely ignore my suspicion that you had something to do with Shelia missing, that you're lying to us, that you aren't being honest about your reasons for being here?"

I tapped quicker, trying to spur my brain forward, to force it to come up with what I needed to say to convince them. It was a make it or break it moment, a time when if I fumbled, I wouldn't get a second chance.

Or much longer to live.

"I'm here to get the job," I pressed. "Does anything else matter?"

"Yes, it does. Betrayal isn't something I forgive," Bray answered.

"We have that in common, then. Neither do I." At least that didn't require any lying.

"So what do you really want? Why are you really here?" Dane asked, leaning forward, his gaze sharp. The bastard was a human lie detector, so I needed to tread carefully.

"I'm here to bury the past," I said. "We all have things we'd like to forget, that we wish we could just stop thinking about, but that isn't always possible. So I moved here to be done with it. I didn't want to keep thinking about it every damned day." I held his gaze, making sure my words were true.

They were. They just didn't mean what I implied. I didn't come there to run away from my past but to confront it.

"And Shelia?" Colton asked.

"That is my business," I said, not giving him any room. "While I'll tell you I'm not here to do you harm, I don't trust you nearly enough to tell you my private business. Kyler isn't my only client, you know, the only person I'm dealing with. I have plenty of things outside of you or your boss."

Dane sat backward and placed his hand on the desk. The tapping of his fingers matched mine, though I doubted he did it on purpose. It seemed like he followed it without meaning to. "And Kyler? What are your plans for him? Are you here to hurt him?"

Yes. I couldn't exactly say that, though.

"Kyler came to me, not the other way around. There are far easier ways to get to a person."

Dane nodded, as if it were a fair point. "I'm going to let you know, I don't like this. If it were up to me, I'd toss you out on your ass. Unfortunately, Kyler disagrees." He threw a set of keys to me. "These will get you into your office. It's on Kent Street, fifth floor. Rosie, the receptionist there, will show you around."

I frowned. "If you already had the okay, what was with the interrogation?"

"It's our job to keep Kyler safe, even when he doesn't know he needs it."

Something hit me, something that had bothered me for years. "Why?" At Dane's look of confusion, I pressed. "Why keep him safe? From what I've heard, you all don't need the paychecks. There are others who can pay you more, who can give you more, so why are you still watching Kyler's back?"

Dane didn't respond, tilting his head as if the question surprised him.

Colton answered, instead. "We're bound to him."

"How? He isn't the kind of person who would do anything to earn that."

"No, he didn't."

The answer gave me nothing beyond a general sense of unease from Colton, a distaste as if he didn't care for protecting Kyler any more than I did.

So why?

They'd never explained it to me as a kid, never said why they'd shown up one day when I'd been thirteen and turned into shadows. In fact, Kyler hadn't even seemed to *like* them most of the time when I was younger.

When it became clear they wouldn't give me any better an answer, I rose. The longer I waited, the more I spoke with them, the better the chance that I'd say something that would get me into trouble. It was like playing with tigers — do it long enough and they'll bite.

"Be careful, Nem," Bray said.

I looked over my shoulder, the sight of all four of them as ground-shaking as it always was. "I didn't think you care if anything happened to me."

"I don't." *Ouch.* "But I don't need you fucking up our plans because you think you're smart."

"I *am* smart," I countered, then looked over at Colton. "And stay out of my room."

Colton huffed, shaking his head, no doubt knowing how much I'd enjoyed it if he showed up again.

"Don't worry, we won't sneak into your room again," Dane said. Just as I was ready to leave, he added, "We won't need to sneak in anywhere. You'll *beg* us to fuck you the next time."

* * * *

Papers covered the surface of the desk in the office Kyler had given me. It was in a busier location than where I'd met the men, a more polished and respectable building.

The reason was obvious. The other was for back-alley sort of meetings. This was the public face. This was the place a person went to conduct actual business, to appear legit.

Which meant Kyler trusted me enough to place me here. Then again, he'd gone against the Quad's opinions on hiring me, which meant I must have impressed him.

The other employees were nice enough, though I got the sense not all of them lived in the same world I did. Some were underworld through and through—the lawyer who scowled, the security in black suits who checked people when they walked in. Others might have known something was up, but not exactly what. They were the employees who didn't look too closely at anyone else, who kept their heads down. They probably suspected there was something less than on the up and up but were paid too well to ask questions. Plus, if they never knew anything concrete, they couldn't get in trouble.

Lastly, there were the totally clueless. The young man who ran errands and got coffee, one of the managers who handled the tenants for the short-term rental company used as a false front.

It was a smart way to funnel money. They could buy property for whatever they wanted, and the price of such places were highly variable. It made it easy to hide money and create income that looked legit.

It also made my job impossibly more difficult, since Kyler's company owned far more property than I would have assumed, and this was just one of his many businesses.

The task of finding Kenz felt insurmountable.

It had seemed so simple before, or at least it had seemed like it. First, set up a background that would prove useful to Kyler. Second, show up in town prior to meeting, to bolster the story. Third, get rid of the person whose job I needed. Fourth, get hired and close to Kyler. Fifth, use access to find Kenz. Sixth, get Kenz the hell out of there and, lastly, kill anyone who had crossed me, including Kyler.

I'd spent ten years setting up the plan, preparing, getting ready, learning and waiting for the right time, and now that I was in it, everything had become so much more complicated.

I didn't know how to find Kenz, the Quad knew I was lying even if they didn't know about what, and I couldn't seem to keep my mind on the task.

My quick in-and-out job had transformed into something frustrating, and for the first time, I really started to doubt myself.

It made me sit back in my office chair and close my eyes. I'd done the few tasks my *official* job had required of me. None were all that difficult or worthy of my skills, which gave me time to doubt myself instead of focusing on what I could do.

The hum of the air conditioner eased me, the rhythmic tone of it like whale songs to those of us who lived in apartment buildings, hotels and busy cities. I didn't fall asleep, but I let my mind drift.

I went back to the last time I'd seen Kenz, the morning before it had all gone wrong. She had looked so much like our mother, with the same dark hair, the dark eyes.

She hadn't acted much like her, though. Mom had been smart and serious, quiet in a way that could trick anyone into speaking just to make the silence stop. Kenz didn't have that — at least she hadn't back then — but she was amazingly smart.

That morning, I'd made her breakfast. We'd had people to do it, but I had always enjoyed the job. Kenz had been eight, and my abilities for breakfast didn't go beyond instant oatmeal. That morning, she'd worn a dress with sunflowers on it and had asked for maple and brown sugar oatmeal with raisins.

We'd sat at the kitchen table while she ate. She'd had a doctor appointment planned, a specialist for her diabetes, and had needed to go out of town for it.

Dane had come into the room, pulling Kenz's hair before taking a seat. The memory of how easy things had been made my chest ache as it always did. It was the only time I really felt as though I had a home... It had never been the buildings, but the people. Kenz and the Quad, mostly.

Bray had come in after Dane, grabbing an apple from the basket on the table and setting it in front of Kenz. "*Eat*," he'd said.

"*I already have food*," Kenz had argued.

"*You need healthy food.*" He had grabbed a second apple and tossed it to me. "*You as well.*"

I had stuck my tongue out at him, that petulant part of me all teens had not wanting to hear his opinion, before I set the apple on the table. He'd made a sharp, warning sound in his throat that had me picking up the apple and taking a bite.

I hadn't been as stubborn back then, more willing to do what they said, especially because I'd craved their approval. It had been foolish, but I'd always wanted to win a smile, to feel like they were proud of me.

"*Can't I come?*" I'd asked Bray after chewing and swallowing the first bite. He'd already told me no, but they'd changed their minds in the past.

He'd shaken his head. "*Not this time. We have to go farther than usual.*"

"*Why do you* all *have to go?*" I'd sighed, petulant. I hadn't had many friends—any, really—because of how tight security had to be. My entire world was made up of Kenz and the men. Kyler had always been gone— working or with other women—and Caroline hadn't been all that warm and fuzzy, busy with her own aspirations.

Dane had reached over and shoved my arm. "*Sorry, but because this is a new place, we need to be focused entirely on keeping your sister safe.*"

I had slumped forward, my elbows on the table. It wasn't uncommon when, during such outings, they went with the idea that fewer people made for fewer targets. We had other guards at the house, so my mother and I would have been safe in a controlled environment while they accompanied Kenz.

It wasn't unusual for us to separate in such a way, but I'd always hated being left behind.

"*Stop being such a baby,*" Kenz had said. "*I'll be back tonight.*"

The scolding had made me smile, that fire in her from our mom's line. The Hester family wasn't known for being quiet and easygoing, for being doormats.

The Corpse Princess

The sharp rebuke was met with a laugh from me, one that spread to Dane and Bray. It had been a nice way to spend the morning, all things considered.

I took a deep breath, doing what I did often.

Wondering.

If I'd known that would be the last time I'd see her — at least for a very long time — would I have done things differently? Would I have said something else?

No, probably not. For someone who was so good at reading people, at knowing what to say to get what I wanted, I was shit at doing it in real life, when it mattered.

In fact, the thought of what I'd say to Kenz when I found her — I refused to consider I'd fail — eluded me.

In the end, my best plan was to not tell her who I was, either. I'd get her free, kill Kyler, then let her live the life she deserved.

My point was to do what needed to be done, not to start up some sisterly relationship. All that would do was hurt her and put her at risk, especially since I doubted I'd survive the attempt.

I rubbed at the inside corners of my eyes, then got back to the files.

Kenz wasn't that little girl anymore, but she was still my sister. I'd figure out where she was no matter what.

* * * *

"He is a coward," I said as I paced Jarrod's living room.

Jarrod nodded, sitting in a chair that rested on the back two legs. He hadn't said anything, letting me talk and move as if he knew I'd hear nothing until I worked out a little of the energy that coursed through me.

"Kyler hasn't even shown his face. What sort of man does that?"

"It was probably the Quad who talked him into staying away," Jarrod pointed out.

It was a fair guess, and that only annoyed me all the more. Those men were still screwing up my life and my plans.

And my sleep, since I couldn't stop dreaming about them. No amount of masturbation or toys fixed the lust that burned inside me, the want that they'd woken, like some beast that had slumbered until they'd shaken its cage. Worse, they'd made me realize what a joke the toys really were compared to the real thing.

"Have you found anything?" I asked.

"Nothing. He hasn't seemed to move, to do anything."

I rubbed at the inner corners of my eyes, frustrated by my inability to let go of the tension, the ever-increasing anxiety.

"Relax." Jarrod's chair hit the floor, the smack of the legs against the tile loud, like an exclamation point to his demand.

"I *am* relaxed."

He lifted an eyebrow. *Right.* Yelling how I was relaxed probably didn't support that point all that well.

I forced myself to stop pacing, to pull in a deep breath and center myself.

"Better," Jarrod said. "The second you get upset, your brain shifts to fight or flight. The more rational parts shut down and you stop seeing options."

It was something he'd said, but had never needed to teach me before. I'd never gotten upset before, hadn't let things get to me.

It was yet another reminder that the Quad were throwing me off my game, and it was a game I couldn't afford to lose.

"Any luck with the files?" Jarrod asked.

I shook my head. "He owns so much property that it would take months to check each one, especially because I don't have access to things like security payments or regular financials to crosscheck. There are hundreds of options, and that's just in the US. For all I know, he has her stashed in another country or a boarding school."

"So what's next?" He stared at me, as if trying to make me think through it, to look at it logically. I knew the players better than he did. He might have taught me all he knew, but that didn't change that I understood it in a way he couldn't.

"I need to turn up the fire."

Jarrod didn't respond, letting me talk it out, waiting for me to explain.

"People move for one of two reasons—either because they're comfortable or they're uncomfortable. Kyler isn't doing anything because he thinks he's safe. He doesn't think he needs to. If we can increase the tension, he'll do something. I can't find Kenz, which means the best way to get her is to force Kyler to move her."

He nodded. "What would increase the tension? A man like him is used to threats."

"He doesn't think anyone knows about that night, about what he did. What if he realized someone knew?"

"You already offed two people connected. You don't think that tipped him off?"

"No one knows where Shelia is yet, and I doubt he keeps an eye on her. Lucky? Just a death. He'd have no idea it has anything to do with him if he even knows about them. I need to bring this home to him, make it impossible for him to think they weren't connected."

"And what will that do?"

"If he realizes this has to do with that night, he's going to know it has to do with Kenz."

"So?"

I sighed, reminded that Jarrod was good at what he did, but he'd never understood people as I did. "So, Kenz is his last big bargaining chip. If he thinks someone knows about what happened the night he killed my mother, he'll want to keep Kenz closer, to make sure she's safe. He's paranoid enough to worry that there might be a leak, that someone has talked after all these years, so if I push hard enough, he'll probably want to move her just to be safe."

"And moving her will require your help, since he trusts you and you handle real estate," Jarrod said, catching up.

"That's right. As soon as I know where Kenz is going to be moved to, I can grab her."

"And how will you make sure he moves her?"

I thought about my list, about the names on there I needed to work through, the one in my head I went over every damned day. I'd checked off two of them, but there were three more. "I wasn't kidding. I'll drop the next body on his doorstep—let him try to pretend it isn't about him, then."

Jarrod wasn't shocked, but then again, not much would shock him. He'd taught me how to kill, how to hide a body, how to get information from people who didn't want to give it. It was a strange relationship, perhaps, but I never had to question what to tell him when it came to what I'd done, what I planned to do. The reality was that no matter how bad it was, Jarrod had done far worse.

"Never ask a question you don't know the answer to—"

"And never back a person into a corner, unless you're ready for them to try to go through you. I know. But what else can he do but try to move her to a safer place? I just have to keep upping the tension until he cracks."

Jarrod said nothing, just staring at me for a minute the way he did at times, as if he didn't understand me, as if he didn't recognize me entirely.

"What?" I asked, voice harsh.

"Are you sure?"

That made me pause. "Are you getting cold feet? I never figured that from you. Kyler killed the woman you loved—how can you be unsure?"

"I'm not unsure, but a bullet in his brain can take care of the problem well enough."

"So why didn't you ever do that?"

He sighed, then tucked his hands into the pockets of his jeans. It reminded me that he wasn't a young man anymore. He hadn't been, even when I'd first met him, but the last ten years had seemed to take a toll on him. It was as if a part of him had died along with my mother, as if Caroline had held a piece of him, and when she had gone, she'd taken that with her. "I hate that fucker with all I am, but you've got claim on revenge here. I figure I didn't give you that much growing up, wasn't there, so I owe you at least that. It means I decided that first day, when I was doing CPR to get your heart going again, to give you Kyler.

Whatever you wanted to do with him, that was up to you. Doesn't matter how much I hate him—he's yours."

That made me pause. It was easy to see Jarrod a certain way, as the man who had contributed the DNA to make me but hadn't been a part of my life growing up. In a lot of ways, Kyler had been more of a father than Jarrod had ever been, but I wasn't much like either of them. Still, the way he spoke made me wonder if he didn't still hold some level of fatherly concern for me. I wasn't sure I liked it.

"I'm the last person who's going to judge you for wanting to put down an asshole who did you wrong," Jarrod continued. "I'm a man who's indulged in revenge more than a few times myself. The issue comes when you're not sure what you really want, when it gets complicated, when you make things messy. A bullet solves the problem, but something complicated? That's what'll drag you under."

"A bullet won't save Kenz."

"Are you sure she needs to be saved?"

"He's a monster," I pointed out.

"Yeah, he is, but she's his daughter. He had to know you weren't. Him taking out you and Caroline doesn't mean he'd do it to Mackenzie."

"She's trapped there, little more than a prisoner."

"So? Some people like that. Are you sure this isn't just a way to get back at Kyler? To take away everything from him before you put him in the ground?"

I gave him the respect of at least thinking about it, of considering it. The thought of Kyler living bothered me. He'd betrayed two people who he was supposed to care about, that he was supposed to watch over. He deserved everything that came to him, everything I wanted to give to him.

And, yes, the thought of taking Kenz from him thrilled me. I wanted to tear apart what he had left, to destroy his business, his name, his family and his line before I put him down.

"It's about her," I said, even if I wasn't sure.

"Lie to other people, Nem, but never lie to yourself. If you had to pick, if you could only either save your sister or kill Kyler, which would you do?"

I had no idea…

My brain seemed to short out, to pause, unable to choose. If I stood there and had to pick, if I had to either save Kenz and walk away, leaving Kyler free, or take him out but leave her in danger, which would I go with?

"She doesn't have anyone else," I said, not answering his question since I couldn't confidently say what I wanted to. "There isn't anyone else to help her."

"You aren't someone who helps," Jarrod pointed out.

"Maybe there just aren't many people I care enough about to help."

He nodded, then sat back. "I'm not going to stop you, Nem, but make sure you're clear about what you really want. Uncertainty kills faster than bullets."

Chapter Ten

Dane

Diamond's Edge always made me feel right at home. Bray and Colton preferred the quiet for their downtime, but me?

Give me the noise and the movement and the dimmed lights. I could take a spot in a corner, and no one looked my way. That was the thing—a quiet restaurant, a bar, even a coffee shop, people were looking for something to watch. Every little thing was easy to pick up on and remember. I had to be on edge, play a part for anyone who looked my way.

In a place like this?

Everyone was balls-deep in their own drinks and busy trying to get laid. It meant I could study others from my own space, where no one watched me, where I could bury myself in the actions of others, in their lives, in their heads.

Like the girl at the bar, her brown hair pulled back, her shirt with just enough cleavage to show she'd thought about it. However, the way she kept pulling it up said this wasn't her normal type of outfit. A man walked up to her, and her smile was full of nerves. The exchange was tense, with the girl bringing her fingers to the bridge of her nose as if she normally wore glasses and the motion to push them up was habit.

It only took a minute to feel like I had them both figured out. The girl had just been dumped and came to prove she was still something, that she didn't need whoever had broken her heart. The man was just a predator, the sort willing to do or say anything to trick a girl into bed. That one was easy to peg after seeing how his mannerisms changed depending on who he talked to.

"Whiskey," Rune said to a waitress, drawing my attention back to the table where I sat and away from the rest of the club.

Rune made for good company, since he didn't feel the need to fill the time with needless chatter. Normally that was my job, but some of the time, I preferred to stay quiet, when no one demanded anything from me, when I didn't have to put on a mask and be whoever the moment needed.

A waitress came back with the drink for Rune and brought another vodka for me. It was a benefit of coming here — they knew us well enough to keep us liquored and otherwise alone.

We didn't partake in the girls who worked there. I had no problem with prostitutes, but I sure as fuck didn't trust Valeria, the woman who ran the club. The last thing I needed was to risk spilling any secrets along with cum by fucking the girls who worked for that viper. She was shady as shit, and I didn't like the idea of giving anything away.

"Fuck," Rune muttered, drawing a frown from me. Cursing wasn't unusual from Rune, but that level of annoyance sure was.

When I saw the reason, however, I mirrored his statement.

Walking through the club was one redhead who was seriously fucking our shit up. She wore a black shirt with a leather jacket over it and a pair of black jeans.

"She's going to be trouble," Rune said.

"She already *is* trouble," I countered. She'd distracted us, had us questioning ourselves and her motives and how it all fit together. She'd gotten Colton—normally a man who treaded carefully—to forget all his rules and screw her when he'd gone to question her. She'd managed to get Kyler to hire her despite our best objections.

Normally, we'd remove any threat, but for some reason, she was a thorn none of us wanted to dig out.

Which made her far more dangerous than a killer with a gun.

Especially because reading her had proven impossible. Where I could pick out facts from every other damned person, I couldn't get shit from her. She was a wall, this person I got nothing from, and it both excited and frustrated me.

My ability to read others kept me alive, gave me an edge, but also made life boring. I always knew what people were going to do before they did it.

But with Nem, I had no damn idea what she wanted or what she planned.

I'd never had that before, never felt so damned unsure, never had to live moment by moment.

So why exactly did that have my cock hard the moment I saw her? Why did I react to not knowing by dreaming about those red lips? By wanting to see the cold expression of hers twisted in pleasure?

She stopped when Valeria walked up to her, the two speaking as if they knew each other. Then again, trouble tended to travel in packs, and Nem knowing Valeria only served as further proof that she was a problem.

Afterward, a waitress came up, a glass in her hand that she gave to Nem. The liquid was dark, but I wasn't sure what it was. It didn't shock me she wasn't a beer drinker — she was far too complex for that.

Nem walked off, the drink in her hand, toward the private rooms. She went up a set of stairs, disappearing, giving me a good look at her ass as she went.

"Bad idea," Rune said without me needing to say a word.

"She's right there," I pressed.

"We just spent the last five minutes talking about how she's trouble, how she's a bad bet, and you're just eager to go ahead and follow her, huh?"

"You heard Colton — *she's worth it*. I can't be the only one thinking about those thighs of hers."

Rune huffed, the sound telling me what I already knew — he was just as obsessed as I was, even if he wasn't as willing to admit it.

"What better way to figure her out or forget her?"

"If I see a rattlesnake, I don't try to fuck it as a way to get safe," Rune said.

"Didn't one bite you a few years back? Maybe you're not the best source of advice on how to deal with one."

Rune gave me a deadpan look, one I was used to. Even though I could read people, even though my skills were indispensable, it didn't mean the other men liked when I ran verbal circles around them. "This is a shit idea."

"You know better than to try and think," I told him. "That's my job. Look, I'm following her, and if you want, you can sit here or you can follow me on up." I rose from the chair, tipping back my glass to finish off the whiskey.

I wanted my hands free.

I didn't need to hear Rune's feet behind me to know he'd follow. My ability to read people was a fucking gift.

At least for everyone except the enigma up those stairs, the woman who was more dangerous to me than anyone else, the one I couldn't figure out.

And I was going to fuck her until I understood every last thing about her.

Nem

The whiskey was amazing, but it didn't hit the spot. It was like going to a frozen yogurt place when what I really wanted was ice cream.

Nothing but a poor substitute.

But what did I want? That was the thing I couldn't figure out.

I'd been steady for so long, nothing penetrating the surface for me. I didn't even feel angry, not about Kyler, not about Caroline, nothing. Those things didn't matter.

They were facts. Kyler had killed Caroline, and because of that, he needed to die. He was a threat—both to Kenz and me—so I needed to deal with him.

It was simple. It had driven me for years, guided my movements when I felt nothing.

So the hollow sensation inside of me had brought me to the club when the walls of my hotel room had closed in on me. It wasn't a feeling, exactly, more like the absence of one. It was a void I hadn't noticed before, since it had been my normal.

Now I craved that feeling again. I wanted that spark back, that experience, that moment of bliss I'd had when, for that short time, I felt alive.

"Well, look who it is."

I turned slowly to find Dane walking into the small private room Valeria had given me, Rune on his heels.

If it had been any other day, I might have turned them away. I would have told them both to fuck right the hell off and drowned myself in whiskey.

That craving roared in my head when I saw them, though, as if I recognized they could give me what I wanted.

I recalled Dane licking the whiskey from my lips, remembered Rune grinding against me, lost myself in the fire Colton had lit inside me.

That was what I wanted. I needed that back, even if just for a moment, even if it was stupid and dangerous.

Especially because Dane stared at me with those dark eyes of his, the man who lived his life behind a mask, and I knew I wanted this.

No, I need it.

It was like a gasp of air after swimming under water, an instinctual requirement hard-wired into me.

I wanted something to melt the ice around me and so far, only the damned men had done it.

That frustrated me. Why was it them? Why did it have to be these men, who I couldn't trust, who came with so much baggage I could never really unload?

Because life is a bitch.

Sounded about right. Besides, what did baggage matter? We weren't headed for a happy ending no matter what.

I could have played coy, could have acted as if I didn't want it. I could have pretended to be a woman who wasn't sure, who needed to be chased.

Fuck that. I wasn't that girl, and they wouldn't believe the act even if I tried it.

The feelings they inspired in me were the only real things in my life. Why hide them behind bullshit?

I toed my boots off, not bothering to say a word, then undid the button of my jeans.

The doorway to the private room was open, but the rope at the foot of the stairs was rarely ignored—at least by anyone except the Quad.

Besides, who cared if anyone walked in? That was so outside what mattered right then, beyond concerns of mine.

I tossed my jacket over the back of the couch then slipped my pants off, dropping them to the floor along with my boots, met with the wide eyes of Dane and Rune.

Surprised? I wouldn't have figured them for prudes. Hell, I'd bet they'd have fucked me on a table in the middle of the club if I'd wanted them too.

And now I suddenly want them to…

Quickly, Dane blinked, regaining his composure, pulling that old mask back into place, the one I couldn't glimpse beneath.

It took me back to when I'd sat beside him, back before it had all gone so wrong, when he'd read books on parrots because he'd liked them even if it had no tactical usage. I remembered how he'd smiled, this half-grin full of humor and honesty that I doubted many others ever saw.

That was gone, of course.

In his eyes, I was the bitch from out of town whom he didn't trust one bit.

No, that wasn't just who he saw — that was who I *was*.

He walked forward as if nothing could keep him from me. "You drive me fucking crazy," he said like an insult before he grabbed the back of my neck and pulled me into a kiss. He undid the buttons of his shirt with his other hand, giving me access to run my hands down his chest.

He wasn't as solid as Colton nor nearly as large as Rune. Then again, he didn't fight with his body, not the way Colton or Rune did. Instead, he used his brain, a weapon that terrified even me.

It was easy to counter a person who used bullets, one who used his fists, but dealing with someone who could predict everything a person did was damn near impossible to overcome.

Dane caught my thighs and pulled them around his waist, so I wrapped my arms around him, too.

I'd wanted this for so long, watching Dane and the others with the love-blinded eyes of a teenager. Those fantasies were childish compared to the reality.

Dane took me over, and that fire inside me, the exact feeling I'd craved, came over me again. It grew inside me, filling all those cold spaces that felt so damned empty the rest of the time.

His kiss was rough and hungry, his lips skilled. He coaxed that desire to life, letting me know Colton hadn't been the only one able to draw it from me.

Which annoyed me as much as it gave me hope. Maybe I could still find this with someone else... Maybe I'd be able to recapture this feeling, chase it with other men.

The idea of touching anyone else seemed as appetizing as cold, day-old pizza, but I clung to that idea, that I could have this feeling and not have to deal with them.

The couch pressed against my back when Dane lowered me, when he followed me down, crowding me with his heated, solid body. Since I didn't have to grasp him to hold on anymore, I ran my hands over his shoulders, then raked my nails down his chest.

His groan was deep and full of want, spilling his warm, whiskey-tinged breath over my lips. "I don't mind you making me bleed," he said.

And damn, neither did I.

He pulled away to fumble with his pants. As he stripped out of his clothing, Rune took his place, already gloriously naked.

And for fuck's sake, that man was beyond gorgeous. He wasn't a model, not some lean metrosexual with perfect hair and manicured nails. No, not Rune.

He was built like a bear—wide and heavy and solid through and through. Even his waist barely tapered in from his wide chest, and his beard and long hair made him appear wild.

I'd loved him as a kid, of course, but now, as an adult, as a woman who understood exactly what his skills could do, he awed me. What would it feel like to be that damned strong? To walk around knowing without a doubt that I could take any person who stood in my way?

The times I'd stared at him, wondering what all those muscles felt like hit me, and I realized, I finally had no reason not to find out. I closed my hand around his already hard cock, my own moan releasing at how long I'd waited for this, how long I'd been denied it.

He made a similar sound, deep in his chest. "You should have let me have you in that barn," he scolded me.

"You know, you look amazing until you open your mouth and ruin it." I stroked his length, the rough blond hair at his groin teasing my fist when I reached it.

How could a man be so perfect? How could one do this to me? And why did it have to be *him*? Why couldn't it be anyone else? Someone safer, someone smarter?

Instead, it had to be the only men who could possibly figure out who I really was, who might have just been in on the plan to kill me in the first place. It had to be the only men who were truly dangerous to me.

Then again, my life hadn't ever been simple. Why should I expect it from this?

I leaned forward, driven by a fantasy that had played in my head countless times. With me sitting on the couch and him in front of me, now seemed the perfect time.

When I dragged my tongue over the head of his cock, then circled the tip, teasing the slit at the top, I could have cried. He tasted wild, untamed and unmistakably masculine. His skin was soft on the surface, unlike the roughness of his hands, but his cock was hard beneath that.

It wasn't enough, though. None of it was. Even with the want awoken inside me, I needed more. They made me feel out of control, like some junkie who had just fallen hard for the drug they were. I wrapped my lips around his shaft, taking him into the heat of my mouth, determined to have everything I'd wanted.

If I'd waited this long, if I'd denied myself this long, sacrificed so many years of this, I'd experienced it all. I wouldn't leave wondering what anything felt like. I'd had Colton, but I still had this demand in my head to have them all, to taste them all, to sample how each was similar and yet so very different from the others.

They owed me this and more.

Rune cupped the back of my head in his large hand, a reminder of our size difference, but he didn't control my motions. Instead, he just stared down at me, the light catching his green eyes and making them glow, almost otherworldly.

It made me bold, made me wonder how other women could feel subjugated by a blow job. My being beneath him didn't matter, not when that look in his eyes said I had complete control over him.

I swirled my tongue along his cock, teasing the bottom, sliding my lips over his length. After a moment, I closed my eyes to focus on the sensation, on the way lust spread through me and took me over.

At least, until I pressed too far forward and had to pull back, my gagging reminding me that I didn't know what I was doing.

Rune let out a rare laugh, one that was deep and made my cheeks heat. "Ain't got much experience, do you?"

"You really think a girl who looks like *her* hasn't blown more than enough men?" Dane asked, his voice full of mockery.

"Judging by that? No, I really don't." Rune caught my chin, bringing my eyes to his. "Could you be more innocent than you let on?"

The words took me backward, threw me into the past, into the time I'd tried to kiss Rune back before it all went to hell. I'd been on the stairs — he'd never have bent down enough for me to reach him otherwise — and I'd pressed my lips to his in a messy, rough, *if I don't do it right now all at once, I'll lose my nerve* motion.

He hadn't kissed me back. He'd set his hands on my shoulders and moved me away, pity on his face, before telling me something I'd never forget. *"You're young, Kels, and innocent. Wouldn't be right."*

After what I'd suffered because of that innocence, because of the naivety that came from not recognizing enemies where they were, I hated the term.

Innocence was a bad thing. It was a sign above people's heads telling others to fuck them over. It was a weakness, and I'd dug out my weaknesses one at a time until I was a bleeding mess, but a strong one.

"I'm *not* innocent," I bit out through clenched teeth.

He frowned, his smile sliding free as if the words took him by surprise. Then again, society told women being innocent was good, that being a damsel was what we should aspire to.

Fuck that nonsense.

I leaned in again, putting my mind to it as I had with everything else I'd gotten — by sheer willpower. I took him past my lips again, the red smudged on his cock from my lipstick a secret claim I took more pleasure in than I should have.

I hollowed my cheeks, determined to prove him wrong, to show I wasn't some innocent little deer who needed coddling. He would probably figure that out about the time I had him coming down my throat.

I used the sounds he made as my guide, chasing the tone, the rise and fall, even the silence between his groans. I didn't need him to tell me what he liked and what he didn't, because I excelled at reading people.

I wrapped my hand around the base of his cock, using it so I didn't have to risk gagging again. Even if I did, I wouldn't pull off. *Swallow and keep going.*

I craved his release more than I did my own, as if I were getting back at him for rejecting me, for being gone so long, for thinking I was too young and too stupid to know what I wanted. Maybe if I did this well enough, he'd leave thinking about me like I had him for the past decade.

Wouldn't that be one hell of a karmic payback?

He thrust forward—not far, just a tiny rocking of his hips. It was as though he couldn't not do it, as if instinctually, his body knew he wanted to be fucking me right then, but he held back.

It meant he was close, that I almost had him exactly where I wanted him.

And for my part, that feeling I chased? It was there, scorching my insides like an inferno I couldn't contain. Was it so overwhelming because I'd felt nothing for so long? Or was it just *them*?

It didn't really matter.

A moment later, Rune grasped the back of my head and plunged his cock deeper, far enough to trigger that same gagging reflex, as if being passive only worked so far. His cock twitched in my mouth as he came.

After a long second, he pulled back, and I swallowed again to keep from coughing, from looking like the innocent he'd called me. More of his hot, thick cum was left on my tongue as he withdrew, letting me taste the bitter saltiness of his release.

Before I could try to swallow it all, he wrapped his hand around my throat and pulled me to my feet and kissed me.

It was deep and wild and he licked the remnants of his cum from my mouth, stealing it from me. To kiss me, he had to lean down, crowding me, and it made me feel small, yet enticed me all the same.

Hands slid around my waist from behind, feeling over the band of the thong I wore, then cupped my ass. "You have an amazing ass," Dane said. "If I had lube, I'd be balls-deep in it tonight. Since I don't, I'm sure your pussy will more than satisfy me." He traced my cunt, along the crotch of my thong, but didn't touch me directly.

It made me gasp, even as Rune kissed me.

If dealing with one man had overwhelmed me, it was nothing compared to two. They were everywhere, taking me over, making it impossible for me to keep track or anticipate anything they would do.

Dane grasped the waist of my thong and pulled it down my legs, leaving the cloth around my ankles as if it didn't matter anymore. He stroked his fingers along my cunt as he took the seat on the couch I'd been in before, then let out a dark chuckle before leaning in and pressing a kiss to my hip. "You are so wet, Nem. Fuck, you're a dream — or a fucking nightmare, who knows?"

"Maybe all your dreams are nightmares," I said.

"Hmm?" Dane asked as he plunged his fingers into me, forcing me to my toes with the sudden invasion. As quickly as it happened, though, my body adjusted and decided without question that I enjoyed it. "Try to pay attention."

His words drew a shiver from me as I tried to do what he said—not because he said it but because not doing it felt like losing. "I don't think monsters have sweet dreams," I said, my words drawn out with a moan when Dane thrust into me again.

"You think we're monsters?" Dane didn't sound all that offended. In fact, he came across as almost amused by it. "And yet you're still here with us? Like this? Why's that?"

I twisted so I could look over my shoulder at him, my eyes narrowed. "Because I'm a monster, too."

Dane's dark eyes stared up at me from his spot on the couch. "You know, I might have doubted that at any other time, might have even laughed at you for saying it. The more I learn about you, though, the more I think you might just be right. Guess us monsters have to stick together."

Before I had to answer or keep our banter up, he grasped my hips and guided me back another step, then held me still. He leaned in and bit softly at the left side of my waist, near my hip. "It's a good damn thing that we all get tested twice a year, because I need to feel your tight cunt without anything in the way."

His cock sank into me, causing my back to arch and a whine to leave my lips.

I didn't feel as if I were falling, not with Dane's strong hands on me. The press of his bare, heated skin against me drugged me further, drew me deeper in the madness that had consumed me.

I reached backward, leaning fully against him, so I could wrap my arms behind his neck. It stretched me out and gave me the chance to roll my hips, his cock rubbing against me in all the best ways.

Hands grasped my thighs, forcing my eyes open again, and I found Rune dropping to his knees as he spread my legs wide. He took up all the space there, seeming even more massive as he knelt. He ran his palms up my inner thighs, then brushed one thumb against my spread pussy lips—where Dane's cock filled me—his gaze locked there.

It should have been weird, right? Sex was, for the most part, a two-person sport. Maybe it didn't seem odd to me because I had no experience, because I didn't know what sex was supposed to be and who could complain about this?

Or maybe it was that my life wasn't normal in any other way. Why would this be the one place where it was like everyone else?

My first crush—my only crush—had been with the four men. That had formed my entire idea of love and lust. It being inextricably tied with what I actually experienced only made sense.

Rune kept his green eyes on mine as he leaned in, and the first touch of his tongue to my clit sent a shockwave through me. It was so much more, so much better than anything I'd felt before.

He didn't look away as he teased me. He might not be a talker, might not be great with his words, but he was really good with his tongue.

I rode Dane as Rune licked me, my motions just slow and sultry rolls of my hips. Each time Rune rubbed his tongue against my swollen clit, however, I tightened involuntarily around Dane—his heavy breathing said it was more than enough for him.

Dane reached one hand around me, trying to slide it into my shirt, but I shoved it away. Even as mindless as they made me, I knew better than to allow it.

He let out an unhappy sound in my ear before nipping me in some sort of mock-punishment, then cupped my breast through the layers of fabric.

Sure, I would have loved to feel his fingers close around my nipple, to feel the roughness of his palm against my skin, but I'd take what I could get.

And what I could get was more than enough, more than I'd ever thought I'd get from them.

From anyone.

Rune tilted his head and used a thumb above my clit to pull the hood out of the way, to expose me so he could latch his lips around it.

I curled my fingers in, still wrapped behind Dane's neck, my body starting to rebel as I neared the edge. Dane took over, lifting his hips to thrust into me, and Rune sucked hard.

"I swear, I'm going to slide into this cunt of yours every fucking chance I get," Dane threatened in my ear. "I don't plan on making it to heaven, but fuck if your pussy isn't close enough for me." He plunged into me, his breathing rapid and uneven.

He pressed his lips to my earlobe, then to my neck. He sank in deep just as a sharp pain in my neck let me know he'd bitten me. Maybe that should have bothered me, but fuck if it didn't drive my need up to a whole new level. They'd already put claims on me, so what did it matter if I wore one on my skin?

I came hard, just as he did, holding him tightly to me as that wonderful pressure snapped inside me. It was as it had been the last time, an overwhelming moment of tension that released, breaking apart and shattering me in the process. The entire world went silent, a blissful peace I never really thought possible in a world that was so loud.

Except, Rune didn't stop. He ground his tongue against my clit, making my cunt pulse again. I writhed against Dane, but he wrapped his arms around me, keeping me there, making me experience the line between pleasure and discomfort.

The next pass of Rune's tongue made Dane's cock slip free, made me acutely aware of just how wet my cunt was.

Rune released my clit and pressed three of his fingers into me. He still didn't tear his gaze away, meeting my eyes, trapping me there with that look alone. "You look good covered in cum," he said and withdrew his fingers before pressing them back in.

It took me a minute to realize he was gathering what had leaked on his fingers, then feeding it back into me, as if making sure none was lost.

"You know, you'd be fucking pretty if you were bred," he admitted before dragging his tongue up my clit again, no doubt catching some of Dane's cum as he did it.

Which was way hotter than it should have been. And his words, which should have been a red flag the size of Texas, did nothing but make me whimper. I didn't want kids, and even if I ever changed my mind, I sure as hell didn't want them with these four.

Maybe it was just the way Rune looked at me that did it, the hunger in his eyes, but right then I fell all in. The idea of falling prey to basic biological urges, to be owned in such a way, to reduce us all to nothing but the animals I felt like, it was a thought I sank into along with him.

He laughed, but it was strained. "I feel your pussy tightening. You like that? Maybe I'll tie you to a bed, spread-eagle, and let all four of us fuck your pretty little pussy all night. We'll take you over and over until you're full of our cum, until I'm sure we've bred you. You'd beg for it, wouldn't you?"

"I don't beg," I said.

"You would," he countered without hesitation. "You'd sound so good, begging us to fill you up, your pussy wet and swollen and all fucking ours." He twisted his hand, reminding me of just how thick his fingers were.

"You'd beg me." I gasped when he pulled his fingers away to drag his tongue up my slit—pressing inside as he did so—then to my clit. It stole some of the fire from my words.

At the top, he pulled away to tell me, "I've never begged for anything." He shoved two fingers into me, curling them forward as he locked his lips around my clit, sucking hard and using his tongue to make it all the more intense.

The orgasm hit me like a wall, so hard I felt as if I'd run for miles before collapsing. My gasp afterward, when I could finally draw breath, was harsh and broken and almost terrifying.

Still, as exhausted as I felt, as raw and broken, I lifted one of my legs to set my foot on Rune's shoulder. He lifted his gaze to mine, his lips so close to my pussy that his breath still tantalized me.

"There's a first time for everything," I told him despite my rough breath. "And if there's anyone who can make you beg, trust me, it'll be me."

The curl of his lips said he didn't believe me, but he looked forward to the attempt.

Chapter Eleven

Nem

I heard his voice before I saw him. It was funny that so many things escaped me over the years. It had been a decade, and details blurred with time.

I couldn't remember how my mother styled her hair, or the taste of the one dish she used to cook from scratch—a macaroni dish with cheese and tomato sauce—or what Kyler used to wear.

But when that voice passed through the door before the man, I remembered it.

Not deep but deceptively smooth. Full of arrogance and self-importance. I remembered how he'd talk, never looking at me, never looking at anyone, as if we were all below him. He never seemed to speak *to* anyone, but rather at them.

Then again, Kyler always had thought himself more important than anyone else. Or at least, that was what he liked to pretend. In the years since I'd left, I'd gotten better at understanding why people did the things they did. I'd learned people like him held seeds of doubt. The over-the-top arrogance was about convincing others of what he knew not to be true. The more a person shouted something, the less they believed it down deep and the more they prayed that their insistence would keep others from seeing beneath it.

So I was ready when a knock on the door to my office came.

"Come in," I called out, trying to prepare myself to see him.

But, as it turned out, seeing the man who had tried to kill me wasn't the sort of thing I could ever really be ready for.

The first thing that hit me—Kyler looked old. It wasn't that he was old—he'd been older then my mom when they'd married, so he was in his fifties now—but it was as if time hadn't been all that kind to him.

Then again, Kyler had always been one to worry. He liked to make plans, then back-up plans, then back-up plans for those, and that must have added years to his age.

He closed the door behind him, then looked over me as if to study me.

I didn't speak. I'd love to say it was a plan, a way to get the upper hand, but it was more that I didn't fully trust my own voice. Knowing something was going to happen and experiencing it were very different things.

I'd planned to meet Kyler—to eventually put a bullet through him—but the reality of seeing him hit me in a way that I hadn't been prepared for.

As did the desire to kill him right then. With the door shut, it would be easy. The guards checked for weapons, but the sharp letter opener on the desk would do the job just as well. A quick jab, then a quicker exit.

I could be out of the city before anyone knows what had happened.

My fingers wrapped around the letter opener before I could think about it.

"Hello, Ms. Syler. I'm Kyler Williams."

The name shocked me back to my senses. I released the opener, ready to play the game, reminded of the risks.

If I killed him now, I could kiss finding my sister goodbye. With her protection gone, she'd be at the whim of whoever found out first, whatever guards took care of her and the person they felt would pay the most for her.

"It's nice to finally meet you, Mr. Williams," I said, mock surprise in my tone.

He didn't offer to shake my hand — no doubt he saw me as beneath him — but he did pull out a chair and sit without me offering. "I don't normally come into the office, but I don't normally have people quite so impressive as you've been. I found myself intrigued enough to warrant coming down."

I shuffled the papers on the desk, as if I cared what he thought, as though I were trying to tidy up.

I didn't give a fuck about impressing him, but it would feed his ego. Full egos made for empty heads.

"Well, thank you. I'm glad you've been happy with my work so far."

He nodded, sitting back in the chair and setting his elbow on the armrest. "I've had many people do the job you're doing over the years, but none quite so well. That winery deal was a thing of beauty."

"I appreciate it, Mr. Williams —"

"Call me Kyler, please. Nem, isn't it?"

I wanted to gag at the idea of using his name, but I forced myself to. "I appreciate it, Kyler. And, yes, Nem."

"That is an odd name."

I shrugged, playing the slightly nervous woman in awe of her boss. "My mother was an eccentric woman. She said she wanted to make sure I had a name no one else did."

He didn't answer right away, his blue eyes unnerving. After a long moment, he nodded. "Unique is good. The world is full of too many copies, too many people all trying to pretend to be something they aren't. I've built my life and companies on the idea of being something different."

"What you've built is amazing. I'm so glad I'm able to be a part of it."

"I am curious—with your skills, you could easily find work that has fewer..." He paused, as if searching for the right word. "Risks. Why go this route?"

I dropped my gaze as though I had to consider it. "I did more above-the-board work for a while, but I found it boring, honestly—and constraining. When I didn't have to follow the same rules as some of the other people, it became more fun. I found I had a knack for it, for negotiation, and that I liked winning at any cost."

Kyler nodded. "I can understand that. The world has too many rules for people like us, doesn't it?"

"I once heard that if you're not cheating, you must not want to win enough. Well, I want to win really badly. This is the life that lets me do that."

He let out a soft laugh. "I think we'll get along just fine. I didn't come down here just for that, though."

"Then what? Did I make a mistake...?"

He waved me off. "Nothing like that at all. I have a special project, if you will, something I wanted to discuss with you personally."

"What sort of project?"

"I need you to find a place, out of the way, miles and miles from anything else, but within a two-to-three-hour drive of here."

"What for?"

"The exact usage doesn't matter. Consider it a private summer home for vacations. I need it large — I'm talking a minimum of twenty-thousand square feet and at least ten acres, preferably twenty. No close neighbors, and an ability to put in excellent security."

As he spoke, I struggled to keep the smile off my face.

This is it. It had to be the place he wanted to move Kenz to. Something far away, something large and able to be protected — they were all the exact things a person would want for a hideaway.

"When do you need it by?"

"The sooner the better. It won't be bought on the books for the short-term rentals business — this needs to be extremely quiet. Instead, we will use another company, one without the same ties to me. There is more than enough capital to handle the purchase without loans, making it a quick process. I'd like to look in the mountains, so it is far enough away from the city to feel like a break but close enough to travel between when needed."

Close enough to check in on Kenz but far enough to check for tails.

"Can you do it?" he asked.

I thought about how much I missed Kenz, and just how much closer I was to finding her.

"I can do it," I answered.

Then, I'll kill you.

Finally, my plans were starting to come together.

* * * *

Stalking always soothes the soul.

Maybe it was strange for me to think that, or to have done it enough to know it relaxed me, but there I was.

And *where* was watching a man across a crowded restaurant. He ate at a table with a woman — they sat on opposite sides of the table and didn't play footsie or any other cute date behaviors to make me think it was new love. Rather, this had the disinterest of a man having dinner with his wife.

She spoke and he nodded, though I'd bet a quiz afterward would prove he'd retained nothing she said. Instead, he'd lift his head every so often to stare longingly at a waitress's ass.

If the woman noticed, she said nothing. Then again, after so many years of marriage, I doubted there was much that could get to a person. In my experience, love was a fleeting thing, something that burned bright for a few years before sizzling out.

People still cared, but it changed, diminished.

Of course, it also made me wonder about him, about them.

Did she know what her husband really was? The night he'd killed my mother, had he gone home with gunpowder residue on his hands and kissed her? Had he crawled into bed with her?

Had she known?

Doubtful. Men usually kept their wives out of their business. It was safer that way, and I didn't mean for her. How many times had a man been taken down, in the end, by a scorned woman?

Still, it always fascinated me how people could live two completely different lives. I could barely manage one.

I could pretend all I wanted, be a handful of people throughout the day depending on who I spoke to, on the role I needed to play, but I didn't try to form a life around that.

How could someone who had so viciously murdered an unarmed woman be the same man having dinner over there? How could he take a life without a care on one hand, then wake his wife up with breakfast in bed the next morning?

Was one of those the real him?

If he had to tell someone who he was, without worry about consequences, what would he say? That he was a loving husband who killed people sometimes because it was his job? Or that he was a killer who had a family because it was expected of him?

Or did he think they were both him?

I tried to consider if I could ever do that in my own life. Could I live a normal life? Could I find love, create a home and still be…me?

It seemed impossible. Too many conflicting things that would only muddy everything.

Love was something I wanted fuck all to do with. Whatever I felt with the Quad was hormones and childhood trauma — nothing else.

The man was named Geoffrey Kellum. He was forty-six and a free agent, so he didn't work for any one family or group. No doubt that was why Kyler had hired him, to reduce the risk of anything tracing back to him.

Geoffrey was the type of man who didn't ask questions, from what I'd found out. He didn't care who his targets were or what they'd done. That much was clear when one of his previous jobs included killing a seven-year-old girl just because the father wanted to punish the girl's mother for leaving him.

I'd stared at the picture of the child, when it was included in a check Jarrod ran on him, at her red hair and a scratch on her nose as if she'd recently fallen. Sometimes I forgot the reality of the life I lived, of the people I knew in it. Or maybe it was better to say I sometimes was able to ignore it, able to pretend it wasn't as twisted as it was.

It was easy to cross lines, to live in that gray space between right and wrong. It was easy to put personal responsibility on others and ignore our own contributions. Selling drugs? People choose to take them. People die from overdoses? People die from cars, but we don't blame the salesman. Kill someone? Well, something would have gotten them anyway.

Times like this reminded me of the darkness, too. I'd killed—I would again, and soon.

But I didn't kill children. I didn't murder innocents just because someone paid me. The line was thin, but it *mattered*.

Even I had limits, and I wasn't any model of a good person.

It meant killing Geoffrey had been even less of an issue for me. In fact, I might have done it even if he hadn't been the one to pull the trigger, the one to end my mother's life, just because of all the other shit I saw assigned to him.

He deserved everything he was going to get.

"Fancy seeing you here."

I didn't hide my long sigh as Colton took a seat across from me, effectively blocking my view of Geoffrey. Instead, I looked at Colton. "What are you doing here?"

"Checking in on you."

"I don't need a babysitter."

He ordered a beer when the waiter came around, telling me he had no plan of leaving me alone anytime soon. Once the waiter left, he sat back, eyeing me. "You're awfully interested in the man across the room."

"I'm people watching."

He huffed, as if that could be true but he didn't quite believe it. "This isn't the sort of place to eat alone."

"Why not?"

"It's the kind of place people go for dates."

"Well, then I'm dating myself, and I'm not interested in a threesome."

He lifted a dark eyebrow. "Really? That isn't what I heard from Rune and Dane."

I didn't give him the satisfaction of looking embarrassed. I didn't look away or tuck my hair behind my ear, didn't pretend to be some woman full of shame over a hook-up. "That was a fling. I'd think you'd understand one-night stands. It was an experience not worth repeating."

He didn't respond at first, but his eyes called me a liar.

As did the way my panties dampened at the memory of how it had felt when Dane had been deep inside me and Rune's tongue had been on my clit. It had been wonderful and freeing and terrifying all at once.

Which was the exact reason I needed to not repeat it. It was far too dangerous how quickly they undid my control, how they made me feel things I craved but shouldn't.

Even now, that coldness inside me, the frozen place I'd lived with, it ached and I wanted to invite him to a closet somewhere inside that restaurant and let him thaw me.

After a long moment, he shook his head. "You know why you're so damned frustrating? Because I can't read you."

"Or maybe I'm just telling you the truth and you aren't used to that."

"No, that's not it. Dane can't read you, either. You're this enigma who walked into our lives and turned it upside down. Do you have any idea how many people we've dealt with? Ones who wanted to use us, to betray us, to kill us?"

"After meeting you, I'd guess a lot."

He nodded. "But we're still here. No matter how many people thought they were better, smarter or more lethal, we're the ones standing at the end of it. Do you know why?"

"No, but I'm sure you're going to tell me." I feigned disinterest even though I wanted him to keep talking. I wanted to peer inside his head, to get a peek at one of the men who had been such a large part of my life, one of the men I still knew so little about.

"Because we don't let threats go. We're more than willing to take out anyone who needs it, anyone who might do us harm."

"Seems like a good plan. It doesn't explain why you're here bothering me, though."

"You're an unknown quantity who showed up exactly when you were needed, with the exact qualifications we needed. I'm not a man who believes in betting, but that is good fucking timing. You're lying to us, keeping secrets, and we can't seem to find anything substantial on you. You, Nem, are one hell of a threat."

I didn't respond with words, only taking a hold of my water and sipping it as if the conversation bored me.

He went on, however, as if we were having a back and forth. "Why haven't we killed you? Why haven't we removed you and the risk you pose? I've worked with Rune, Dane and Bray for a long damn time, since we were barely teenagers, and we've never hesitated before." He paused, as if he had to consider that. "Well, once, I suppose."

I wanted to ask so much more about that, to understand them better, but I kept that to myself. Colton was too smart to not pick up on the interest, not to be suspicious about it. Besides, it wasn't like he'd give me anything personal, any useful details.

"Like I said, maybe you just are smart enough to realize I'm not a threat to you."

I definitely am.

He twisted slightly, gaze taking in the room. It reminded me of how he'd watched everything before, how he'd scan our surroundings. It was never with nerves, never made me feel unsafe or worried, as if I knew he could handle anything he found.

That was how I'd felt as a child, though, when I hadn't had a clue how dangerous the world really was. Now that I knew, I didn't trust my safety to anyone—

least of all an assassin who might have been in on the plan to murder me.

"It isn't that," he said finally.

"Well then, I don't know. I'm not a therapist, and you couldn't pay me enough to try and sort out all your hang-ups."

He offered me a smile, the dry one he had used when I'd tell him lies as a teenager that he'd known damned well were lies. "If Geoffrey over there ends up missing or dead, I'm going to know exactly who to come talk to, and I can promise you won't enjoy that conversation."

"The world is a dangerous place. I can't be blamed for what happens to people, especially those who don't exactly live safe lives."

He rose from his seat, his dark eyes serious. "The world is even more dangerous for people who betray us, so I'd suggest you tread lightly, Nem."

With that, he walked away, leaving me there way more turned on than any threat should make me.

I am seriously fucked up.

* * * *

Changing plans never pleased me.

A plan required strategy, forethought and a lot of fucking work. Changing them, especially at the last moment, was dangerous and foolish. People made mistakes when desperate, when they had to scramble to come up with something new.

However, I had a chance to deal with two problems at once, and that made it worth it.

"You're sure about this?" Jarrod asked as he stared around the mansion of a house.

"It's the best shot we have."

"I don't care for you using yourself as bait."

"Is that fatherly concern?" My tone held an edge. It wasn't bitterness or anger, but rather a reminder that Jarrod hadn't ever acted like a father.

I didn't need him to now.

"No," he admitted. "I just don't want to see you get killed before you finish your work. It would be a waste of all the time I spent training you."

"I won't be."

"Really? Because setting up a contract on your life feels like the exact way to get someone killed."

I ignored his complaints. I knew what I was doing, even if he didn't believe it. He didn't have to believe it. I didn't need his approval — only his help.

I'd spent nights awake, trying to work out a way to handle the Quad's scrutiny which I doubted I could get rid of, while still completing the tasks at hand.

If Geoffrey wound up dead, even if I had an alibi, the men would suspect me. Hell, they'd do more than just suspect. They'd assume it was me, and I doubted I'd manage to convince them otherwise.

I could have skipped him, but he *needed* to die. I needed to apply that pressure to Kyler, to make sure he moved Kenz, and I wanted to see Geoffrey bleed out for what he'd done to my mother.

Besides, after him, only one name remained before Kyler, and I wasn't ready to face that one just yet.

So, when backed into a corner, there were only a few options. Accept defeat or swipe back.

This was my swipe.

Jarrod muttered something unkind before storming out. He was setting up a spot with a good viewpoint, no doubt, to keep an eye on how things went. Using myself as bait left a good chance that things could go wrong.

Even the best of plans went to hell when it came down to it, when tested, and I had too much to finish to die just yet.

Kyler would arrive soon, with the Quad in tow, to view the new property. It was everything he'd wanted and more, and as usual, I'd gotten it for a good deal. When one had access to almost endless amounts of untraceable money and the freedom to play any filthy trick I wanted, making deals was rather easy.

No doubt he'd look at the place and praise me for capturing exactly what he wanted. He'd moved Kenz in quickly, I'd deal with the final person from that night, save Kenz, then kill Kyler.

Another few weeks and I'd be free of this all.

About thirty minutes after Jarrod left—or at least after he found a hidden place to watch from—two large SUVs pulled into the long, winding driveway. They stopped below a porte-cochere before the people inside got out.

The front car held Colton and Bray, with the other having Dane driving, Rune in the passenger seat and Kyler in the back. More than one car reduced the chances of an enemy knowing which a person drove in, and no doubt both had bulletproof glass and more than a few other defensive measures.

I was a little surprised Kyler agreed to come out himself—the place must have been important to him.

It provided the perfect spot for my plan, though.

Kyler walked up and held his hand out. The idea of touching him made my skin crawl, but I did it anyway, using that 'I'm so impressed by you' look that I knew he loved. "Thank you so much for coming."

He nodded as he looked past me and at the house. "It's hard to believe you could find exactly what I was looking for so quickly."

Colton let out a soft snort, the kind that said hard to believe was putting it mildly.

I ignored him, focusing instead on Kyler. Colton didn't matter, and neither did the others. The only person I needed to play right now was Kyler. "It has everything you wanted. Plenty of room — twenty-five-thousand square feet — a huge backyard entertaining area, an indoor theater, a guard house at the front gate, and it is already wired for cameras both inside and outside." As I ran down the list of amenities, I walked in through the massive front doors.

Kyler followed, not breaking in to ask questions or for clarification. Then again, no matter if this was all a ploy, I *was* good at what I did. I'd found him the exact place he'd wanted, with everything on his list checked off and a few he never said but I could have guessed.

"The lines of sight on the back aren't the best," Bray mentioned. "And setting up proper internet access here will cost a small fortune."

"I already spoke to a landscaping company. They can remove the trees on the south side, just outside the fence line, so that the sight lines are better. As far as internet, I didn't think money was an issue, as far as I understood."

Kyler bristled, casting Bray a sharp look as if *he'd* insulted him by implying money had any meaning. "Security is the most important issue to me. We can easily set up towers if we need for connectivity."

Bray pressed his lips together but didn't respond. At least he had some brains when it came to what he should let go.

I spoke up, not trying to defuse the tension—having enemies fighting each other took the focus off me—but staying in character. "This is everything you wanted."

"How long until it's ready?"

"Another week to finish the handover and official recording. After that, it depends on what you want done. I could get new furnishings in the following day, have it ready to live in, but if you want to upgrade security or do any renovations, well, those will take time."

Kyler nodded, then turned to look at the high ceilings and sprawling staircase. "I'll want the sight lines checked and camera blind spots identified. We'll run more if there is anything we can't see. This place will need to be entirely secure. No leaks, no weaknesses."

Because he plans to trap my sister here.

At least it helped confirm that I was right, that this place had to be for her. There was no other reason to worry about that much security, not unless he feared for her safety and planned to stash her there.

I kept my face carefully void of that information. "Do you have anyone you want to hire for that? If not, I have contacts."

"We handle security," Colton said, his voice sharp, as though I were stepping on his toes.

Kyler waved him off, as if his opinion didn't much matter. It was funny because he if actually listened to them, I'd have a very difficult time doing as I planned. It was his own ego that gave him the biggest problems. "They'll check for issues and make a list. When they do, they'll send it to you, and you can hire out for the actual work. I want it done right and fast—money isn't an issue."

"In that case, I can't imagine they couldn't finish anything in terms of wiring and alarms in two weeks at the most."

He nodded, crossing his arms as he gazed around the room. I knew I'd nailed it—he might want to put on the game that he wasn't sure, but I had no doubt it was exactly what he'd wanted.

After a moment, he turned back toward me. "Yeah, this is good."

An owl hoot came from outside and put me on notice.

Game time.

I approached Kyler as he walked toward me. Because the house hadn't officially been on the market, it still had furniture throughout. While I kept my gaze on Kyler, I listened carefully.

I'd spent time finding the best silent ways in and out of the house, all entrances and exits. The owl sound from Jarrod signaled an approach from the back door.

Not the best entry point, but not the worst, either.

I shifted to the side so Kyler would follow, putting us near the back of a large couch. At the same time, I pulled in a slow breath, trying not to tense. Anxiety could lead to a delay in reaction time, and that was the last thing I needed.

Movement in my peripheral vision told me exactly what I needed to know.

Geoffrey stepped into the room, his gaze locking on me—my red hair gave him an easily identifiable trait—and started to lift his weapon. He didn't look around, didn't worry about who else was there.

It was the sign of a man who didn't do nearly enough research, one who thought a nice gun made a killer. Hadn't I dealt with enough of those, seen enough of them? People who didn't put in the work to be great at what they did, who thought themselves far better than they were. It chafed that *this* was the man who had killed my mother, that she'd been taken out of the world by a morally bankrupt man who thought he was a hitman.

I let out a startled gasp—and boy did I hate that—before flinging myself at Kyler. I took him to the ground just as the shot rang out.

We hit the floor hard, and the sound of his pained grunt was fucking music to my ears. In fact, it was not an accident as I shifted and kneed him right in the groin.

To our left—we had fallen behind but just past the couch so I could still see Geoffrey—I watched the emotions on his face. Frustration at the miss, then recognition a split second after he'd fired.

He'd seen Kyler, realized how fucked he was.

Then came the fear as Geoffrey took in the other four in the room, all of whom reached for their own guns.

It was a thing of lethal beauty, really, how the Quad fired nearly at once. They didn't mind taking people alive, but it seemed a loosed bullet in their boss's direction was unforgivable.

Geoffrey didn't get a chance to say sorry, to say anything, before the bullets struck him. I would have rather pulled the trigger myself, but watching his body hit the floor was a pretty good second.

He opened his mouth to speak, but red escaped instead of words. Dane was beside us in a heartbeat, yanking me off Kyler. "Are you hit?"

Kyler stood with the help of a hand from Rune, then brushed his hands down his front. "No. He missed."

He paused, then turned my way. "He missed because you knocked me out of the way."

I looked toward the body, trying to tattoo the sight to my memory while putting on a 'dear god, that is a dead body? I might get sick' expression. "I just saw him start to point his gun and I panicked." I patted down my front as if checking for injuries. "He could have shot us!"

"He would have," Kyler said, coming closer and checking me, as if to make sure the bullet hadn't grazed me. "You saved me."

I wanted to force him to choke on those words.

"You were watching him the other day in a restaurant," Colton said, his eyes narrowed in my direction.

Suspicion ran across Kyler's face for only a moment before I used my well-planned-out lie. I'd lain awake at night working it all out, creating the perfect stories, the response to anything someone might ask.

"I was staring at him because he seemed familiar. I was sure I'd seen him hanging around outside the office the last few days. When I saw him there, too, it made me nervous."

"You were being followed and you didn't say anything?" Kyler asked.

"I wasn't sure. I've done this sort of work for a long time, but I've never had a problem with people following me before." I let out a nervous laugh, rubbing my hands together as though anxious. "I guess I've never worked with someone as important as you are."

Bingo. It wasn't hard to see the shift, when Kyler's ego took the bait, and he was willing to hear anything I had to say. Funny that reeling people in was so easy if I had the right bait.

Kyler nodded, then cut a look in Rune's direction. "I want to assign her a guard to ensure this doesn't happen again."

"I'm not so sure—"

Kyler pointed his finger at Rune, pure arrogance in his expression. "I tell you what to do—not the other way around. The reality is that a shooter just made it into this house, and you didn't identify the threat beforehand. You had no idea, and I would have a bullet through me if it weren't for her. I suggest you do as I ask before I start wondering what exactly your use is."

I almost felt bad about the dressing down Rune was getting and had to stop myself from defending him. The reality was that they couldn't have predicted the attack.

Jarrod had hired Geoffrey through an intermediary, and no one else knew. It meant there would have been no warning possible, no whispers they could have caught, especially since Kyler *wasn't* the target. Beyond that, I'd learned early that it was impossible to prevent someone who really wanted to kill someone else.

Why? Because if they didn't give a damn if they walked out, there were too many ways for them to win. All they needed was to slip past the defenses just once, to get lucky just one time.

That was why my skills tended to be in breaking those defenses rather than setting them. Killing people was a lot easier than keeping them alive.

The muscles of Rune's shoulders twitched, a sure sign he wanted to slug Kyler.

So why didn't he? I'd never quite understood that, never figured why they listened to him, why they did his bidding. I hadn't gotten it when I was a kid, and I still didn't.

They had the skills to disappear, to do whatever the fuck they wanted. Despite Kyler's attitude and his treatment of them, they helped him stay in power.

Why?

Rune nodded, as if he didn't trust his words.

"We'll look into this," Bray said, his voice catching me off guard as it always did, since he so rarely decided to speak.

"Do you know who he is?"

Dane nodded, crossing his arms, his gaze on me. "It's Geoffrey Kellum."

Kyler paused, a stillness in him that said he damn well knew that name. "You're sure?"

That drew Dane's focus, as if he'd caught the odd tone of Kyler's voice. "Yeah, I'm sure. He's a local hitman, usually low-profile jobs. Bray can figure out who hired him."

"No—there's no need." Kyler spoke quickly, an almost panicked tone. As fast as it happened, though, he seemed to realize he'd shown his hand. After a second, he shook his head. "I mean, don't bother. It was nothing."

"Nothing? You were almost killed," Bray pointed out.

"It wasn't that close," Kyler snapped, his easy disposition shattered. "I mean, it was clearly someone who had no idea what they were doing. We'll increase my security as well and be careful for the next few weeks."

"Of course," Dane said, speaking first as if to silence the others. Then again, he was no doubt best at keeping his voice controlled and flat. "Rune should take you back. We'll handle the body and cleanup."

"Then one of you escort Nem home as well."

Dane gave me a look that spoke volumes, his eyes sharp and full of suspicion. "Oh, trust me, she won't leave our sight."

Chapter Twelve

Nem

I sat on the edge of a table and watched as Colton spread a tarp out on the floor besides Geoffrey's body.

A man who kept a tarp and bleach in his car should have been one of those warning signs, but I actually liked it. A man who showed forethought was a hell of a turn-on.

"Are you going to just sit there and watch?" he asked.

"I don't get paid for body removal."

Dane snorted as he walked in with a mop. "You sure don't seem as upset as you did earlier. Corpses don't bother you now? Or is it just that you don't have to convince Kyler about what a docile little woman you are anymore?"

"No idea what you're talking about." I tilted my head, spotting where blood had splattered on the wall. "Don't miss the spots there."

Colton turned to give me a look so vicious, I might have been worried if I thought he'd dare to hurt me. "You won't be able to convince Kyler forever, you know."

"I'm not convincing him of anything."

"So, you just happened to be watching the man who later attacks Kyler?"

"You can think what you want, but if I was out to hurt Kyler, would I have saved him? And are you really going to tell me people wanting to kill him is all that unusual? I highly doubt this was all that unique."

Colton paused to look my way after Bray helped move the body onto the tarp. "Maybe you want something you haven't gotten yet. Trying to get closer to Kyler? Are you hoping he'll fall for you and take care of you?"

The thought of getting closer to that man made everything inside me rebel, especially the way Bray said it, the implication he'd levied.

Beyond the fact that Kyler had essentially been my father until I was a teenager, he was a horrible excuse for a human who I wouldn't let touch me if I were on fire.

"I'm tired," I said instead of addressing his guess. "I've worked all day to get this deal done, and I don't have the energy to fight with you over something so stupid. Good luck with the body disposal." I slid off the table and slid my purse over my shoulder.

"You're not going anywhere alone," Dane said. "Didn't you hear Kyler?"

"He was kidding."

"Kyler doesn't kid."

I blew out a slow breath. "Well, he didn't mean it, then. I don't need a guard."

And I really didn't need a shadow, not with the things I had planned. It was hard enough to deal with these men without worrying about someone tracing my every step.

"Too bad," Colton answered. "I'm not about to piss off Kyler, and maybe you'll behave yourself if you've got someone watching you."

Not very likely.

"I'm not having some stranger around."

"Won't be a stranger," Bray said as he stood up, brushing his hands on his pants as if he could get dead guy off his palms. "I'll watch you tonight."

That was miles worse than some random guard. "Not a chance. Nope. That is not happening. Assign me whoever you want, but *not* you," I said, giving in. While any shadow wasn't ideal, throwing one of the Quad, losing them, that would be monumentally more difficult.

"The more you resist, the more I know it's the right choice."

"Well that's some rapist bullshit," I muttered.

He shook his head, then glanced toward Dane. "I'll take the first shift."

Dane sighed, his head dropping back. "I guess that means we'll handle this body, which feels like the much less fun option. I'll have a schedule set up when you check in tomorrow."

Bray nodded, not acknowledging Dane's joke, before turning back to me. "Let's go, Nem."

And despite me wanting to argue, I gave in. Sometimes blunt force wasn't the best way to deal with a problem.

Good thing I didn't mind the underhanded method.

* * * *

Dealing with Bray hadn't been as bad as I would have expected. He was quiet, especially compared to the other three.

Dane never quit talking, Colton was blunt and would say things normal people knew to keep to themselves and Rune, while not overly friendly, didn't enjoy silence.

Bray, however, hadn't said a word to me on the trip to my hotel or once we'd gotten there. He'd checked the lobby, the layout of the building, and rented the adjacent room for himself.

After ensuring I couldn't lock the door between our rooms, he'd retreated into his own space and left me be.

Still, even without him saying anything, he managed to dominate the space. He was in his own room but I could *feel* him.

I'd showered, the action helping me to wash away my frustration at not being able to kill Geoffrey myself. It was the right choice—and as a bonus, the men had to deal with the body—but I would have preferred to pull the trigger myself.

Memories of my mother gasping for breath hit me as I sat upstairs, the hour late and sleep still so far away.

She'd been wearing loose black slacks and a white blouse, and the way that shirt had soaked up the blood haunted me. It had been my first exposure to real blood like that, to injuries. For living such a dangerous life, I'd been rather sheltered. I'd caught the men, from time to time, with blood on them, but it had rarely been their own.

She hadn't screamed, hadn't cried, hadn't begged for her life. Instead, she'd gasped for air she couldn't seem to pull in, and the blood had just kept spreading. It had pooled beneath her.

Lucky had been pouring gasoline everywhere, not worrying about us. They'd put more than a few bullets into both of us, and our guards were all dead, our phones gone, so they didn't think there was anything we could do.

When the smoke had floated into the room, after I heard Lucky's laugh and the click of the door as he walked out, my mother had let out one last shuddering gasp.

Then she was gone. It had been strange, because I'd thought there would be some big difference, like seeing her dead would be obvious.

It wasn't.

She'd still looked like her, other than the blood, like she was sleeping and could wake again.

I'd wanted to reach out for her, to crawl over to her, but something had kept me from doing it. It wasn't the pain—but fuck, there had been a lot of that.

The idea of Kyler, of my *father*, having done this had rooted me in place. He was one of the people who was supposed to love me, supposed to look out for me, and he'd planned this?

The thought of the men had hit me, too. They were always there, but not this time. It felt like a hole, like something I couldn't believe had happened.

How could they have been gone during this?

Maybe they knew about it...

The fact that they'd refused to let me come, that they'd taken Kenz only, it had hit me as I coughed, blood splattering.

The crackle of flames from the other room reminded me that it wasn't a time to just think, to ponder.

Survival is all that really matters.

Colton's words came back to me, from when he'd taught me how to shoot a gun. I'd been nervous, admitting I didn't think I could ever pull the trigger, that I couldn't kill someone else. He'd told me, *"When it comes down to it, Kels, when it's you or someone else, you damn well better pick you. Survival is all that really matters."*

That was what had gotten me moving. Whether or not Colton was behind it, whether or not he knew anything about it, his words kept ringing in my ears.

So I'd pulled myself toward the closet, toward the hidden door Bray had shown me when we'd moved in, the one that led to a small safe room, then to the backyard.

I shuddered as I came back to the present, as I tried to remind myself there wasn't any smoke, that I wasn't bleeding out on the floor, that I wasn't crawling through the unimaginable pain.

Even as I thought about it, though, I didn't feel anything. I wasn't angry or sad or anything else.

It was an event, something that pressed what I needed to do, but it felt almost like it happened to someone else — minus the pain.

Why?

It should matter to me, should make me sad, should make me feel something.

I *wanted* to feel something.

That thought had me on my feet before I even considered it, knowing the only time I felt anything and exactly where I needed to go for that.

My feet pressed against the tile as I crossed the hotel room, as I headed for the place I knew I could get what I needed.

Inside the adjacent room, Bray sat at the small kitchen table, his laptop out, his face bathed in the glow from the screen.

He looked so much like he had before, nose in his work even when he should have been sleeping. How many nights, when I had been up too late, had I ended up sitting with Bray as he'd worked? I'd fallen asleep to the sound of his typing in his room since he'd often not made it to bed until the daytime, and usually sleeping in spurts broken up into a few hours at a time.

He still had his hair buzzed off and the septum piercing that caught the light from the screen.

He'd always been cold, always difficult to read, but that had gotten worse. Why?

He turned to look over at me, his eyes red from lack of sleep, giving me *nothing* in his expression. No pleasure, no expectation, nothing.

I should have wished for Dane to be there, for Rune or Colton. They'd have stripped out of their pants and given me what I wanted without question. Sure, they'd have insulted me a bit during, but that was par for the course. They'd still have wanted me.

And I needed that.

"What do you want?" he asked me.

A glance down showed an outline of his erection in his slacks, proof that he wanted me even if he didn't admit it. I'd say it made me bold, but that would have been a lie. I was bold anyway — it just let me know he really did want me.

"I'm here to fuck you."

"Just making the rounds with the Quad? I'm not sure what you're hoping that will get you, but I can tell you, it won't be much."

I shook my head. "Believe it or not, I don't want anything from you all."

He lifted one of his dark eyebrows, as if calling me out.

I amended my statement. "I don't want anything other than to fuck you — how about that?" I slid into his lap, my silk nightgown with lace trim sliding up.

I hadn't bothered to put on underwear — they were a barrier I didn't need. I was all for heat-of-the-moment quick sex.

It was safest, after all, better to get right to it, to drown in those feelings then move on.

Bray didn't grab me, didn't pull me into a kiss as the others would have done. Instead, he just stared at me as if I were his computer, as though I were another piece of data he could work out. "I'm not as easily swayed as my brothers."

"You not already being inside me tells me that." I ran my hands down his chest, over his clothing. He was lean, less muscular than even Dane, but he lacked any fat, either. He used to run, a counter to the rest of his sedentary lifestyle, and given his thin frame, I'd guess he'd kept up the habit.

He narrowed his eyes. "You are a trap, Nem. Everything about you is bait — your hair, your body, your brain. It all seems to be made to draw us in."

"You're overthinking it. This is simple."

"Nothing about you is simple." He set his hands on my thighs as if he couldn't help it and just had to touch me somehow. It reminded me of how warm his hands were and how they lacked the callouses Rune carried. "And I know what happens when you let down your guard and shouldn't."

I leaned in and brushed my lips against his. "So don't let your guard down. I'm not asking to tie you up or for you to tell me all your secrets. I'm just asking you to take your pants off and do what we both want."

His hands flexed, tightening on my thighs, the first sign of a crack in his defenses. "Why?"

"Why what?"

"Why here? Why me? You clearly have no problem screwing strangers, so why sleep with any of us? You're not stupid — no matter how much I wish you were — there are far safer ways to get off if that's all you want."

"Are you going to just keep asking questions?"

Bray released one of my thighs and caught my chin, forcing my eyes to his. He was intense and demanding. "Answer me."

Fuck. The way he said that yanked me back again, kept me unstuck between the past and the present. Bray had never been giving, never been the type to allow anything he didn't want. I recalled when he'd demanded such things of me before — eating, sleeping, basic safety concerns — and how I'd always folded.

After the evening, it hit me harder, made it even more difficult to separate a decade ago from now.

That was probably what had me giving him the truth. "I don't feel anything," I whispered. "Life doesn't mean anything, like I'm not really alive. I feel like just a walking corpse. Nothing touches me except *this.*" I shifted, arching my back so I rubbed my bare cunt against his erection. "*You* four make me feel something, and I want to feel that right now."

Bray didn't answer at first, just stared at me as if weighing my words. They'd been far too open, too honest, but I couldn't help it. Even uttering them made me admit their truth.

I needed this from them, and the part I'd kept to myself?

I needed it from Bray. As much as the other three would have been easier, I needed him, too. He was a part of this, and without having had him as well, it felt unfinished.

So would he turn me down? Force me back to my own empty bed full of coldness? Make me spend the night in that dead state I'd spent the last decade in?

I only had to wonder for a moment before Bray used the grip on my chin to pull me forward and into a hard kiss that was full of more than a little anger.

He spoke against my lips after, his voice angry and strained. "I don't know what this is between us, why we're tied like this, but the reason doesn't change a thing. I promise you, Nem, if you're lying to us, if you are any sort of threat to us, I'll use those binds between us to strangle you."

And that threat was better than chocolates to a girl like me.

Bray

Her lips were so soft and reminded me of the muzzle of a tiger—deceptively innocent but able to kill with ease.

Not that it stopped me from kissing her. I wasn't sure anything could stop me from that.

Nem looked more casual, less made up. She had no makeup on, so instead of the bright red, her lips were a soft pink. Her eyes lacked the black liner drawn to a sharp point at the corners, the dark eyeshadow.

It let me see the bright silver, made it look more natural than it did when set off by the makeup.

She wore a black silk night gown with lace trim and straps.

Nothing underneath, of course. Then again, she didn't seem to care about tempting me. This wasn't seduction — she didn't ask if I thought she was pretty, if I cared a bit about her.

Instead, it was like some itch she had that she thought only I could scratch — well, me and the other men, it seemed.

But worse than that was the fact that I felt the same...

Even if I'd held off when she'd walked in, even though I'd tried my damn best to ignore her, there was no way for me to deny I wanted her.

I'd dreamed of her, fantasized about her, had felt the sparks of jealousy when Colton had talked about sleeping with her, when Dane and Rune had told me about just how soft and giving her body was.

Still, I'd taken over the night of watching her because I had my head on better. I'd been through this before, experienced how it felt to get a knife in the back because I'd trusted the wrong person, because I'd fallen for a pair of pretty eyes that batted just the right way.

I knew all the risks so why the fuck was I reaching between us to yank down my sweats, to free my cock which had been hard and aching since she'd walked in?

Because I couldn't not do it. I couldn't not taste her, not try to drown the feelings I knew were dangerous in her.

And, fuck, what she'd said stuck with me. *I feel like I'm a walking corpse.* I understood that. I damn well knew that feeling, when nothing in life seemed to reach me anymore, when all I could do was make a fucking list and complete it for the day while feeling nothing from it.

Maybe, if she felt something from this, maybe I would, too.

If not, at least I could give her that for a little while. I wasn't a giving man, one who cared much about anyone else, but the thought of Nem in that dark, endless place could almost make me pity her.

She reached between us, but she didn't go for my cock. Instead, she slid her fingers against her clit, a gasp on her pink lips. It shouldn't have shocked me — she seemed fully capable of getting whatever she wanted herself. She didn't need me to do it for her, to show her anything to take the lead.

And that turned me on all the more. I stroked my cock, using a tight grip as I stared down between her pale thighs, at the black pubic hair that told me her natural color was dark.

I liked the red, though. It made her look like flames, like something wild and dangerous — which she was.

She moved her hand so those fingers of hers pressed into her cunt as she let out a moan. Afterward, she shifted her hand away, and I caught her wrist, bringing her fingers to my lips.

I used my tongue, first, to gather her wetness, to taste her. I doubted I'd get a more direct chance, and I wasn't willing to try for it, anyway. I wanted to fuck her, to plunge into her cunt, to feel her tight around my cock, and waiting to do that seemed impossible. Besides, I wouldn't let my guard down enough to put my mouth on her sweet cunt, not when I was alone with her.

So I satisfied myself by licking clean her fingers, by sucking them past my lips and sliding my tongue between them so I didn't miss a spot.

Meanwhile, I grasped my cock with one hand and her hip with my other. She rose, her toes barely touching the ground, the position no doubt awkward for her, but if she cared, I couldn't tell.

It was as if the prize were worth any inconvenience. She didn't come down slowly, didn't ease into it.

Then again, I hadn't seen that sort of caution from Nem yet, so why would I expect it here?

Instead, she lowered herself in a hard motion, taking my dick all at once, the tightness of her pussy drawing a broken, almost embarrassing sound from me.

I wasn't a virgin, but fuck, this felt *different.* It felt important, like it reached beneath my skin and got to some part of me I didn't even know I had. It was like being a teenager again, when I'd thought my hand around my cock was as good as it got, then sliding inside the first girl I slept with to realize how wrong I was.

Her cunt was impossibly snug, and it tightened more around me in sexy little waves that teased me.

I put both hands on her hips, and she moved her legs so her feet didn't touch the ground anymore, so her knees pressed against my hips and her feet tucked beneath my thighs. She tensed, rising by moving her hips, and I helped her.

She was wild and rough and lost. She slid her eyes closed and let her head fall back, those red strands of hers cascading down, making her look like some goddess.

She wasn't dead, not right then, and I got it. *This* wasn't the woman I'd seen before, the one from the office, from the house. That woman had been controlled, careful, subdued. She'd watched every-thing, taking in the details, and always a million miles away.

Nem, in this moment, was different. She was alive, passionate and lost to whatever consumed us both. Was this the real woman?

As much as I liked her smarts — and I shouldn't, given the likelihood they'd be used against me — I was fucking obsessed with this woman here.

I leaned forward, capturing her nipple through the silk of her nightgown, taking it between my lips, then between my teeth. She took the pleasure and the bite of pain, her cunt doing that squeezing thing that told me she loved it no matter what her lips said.

I licked across the hardened bud, disappointed to not have better access, to not get any more of her. I could have moved, could have bent her over the desk or fucked her right on top of it.

I was going *nowhere* near the bed, though. I'd learned my lesson before with that.

This was sex — crazy, amazing, filthy sex — and I didn't need to risk making it any more complicated with things like a bed, like anything that implied permanence.

Even if I wanted more, though, even if I'd have loved to strip her naked and take her every fucking way I wanted, it wouldn't happen. It was in the way the muscles of her thighs twitched, the gasping sounds she made, the arch of her back as she gave herself over to the moment.

This was a race. It was a fucking scream of frustration to break the monotonous silence, an attempt to obliterate the world and whatever it was that made her feel like she was dead.

It was starving and being given a meal—savoring and questioning and trying to make it last were for times when it wasn't an emergency.

So I leaned back, giving me the ability to lift my hips as well, so each time she came down, when I yanked her with my grasp of her hips, I thrust up into her. I took her as hard and as deep as possible, trying to erase whatever we both were running from.

She reached between us with one hand to rub her clit and cupped her breast with the other. She closed her fingers on her nipple in a tight pinch—girl got off on the pain, huh?—and shivered as she neared her release.

And me? I fucked her through it. I kept it up, even when she cried out, when she made sounds that could have made a lesser man come right there, when her back arched impossibly more, when she would have fallen if I didn't have a hold of her so well.

I let the way her cunt gripped my cock take me with her, let it sweep me away and to the same pleasure she'd found.

It was like the whole damn world shorted out, like it all went away. I spilled into her, the muscles of my back tightening, my eyes falling closed for that moment of absolute silence that never lasted long enough.

Sure enough, far too quickly, she shoved at my chest. I realized then that she'd had her forehead against me, as if she'd collapsed forward and hadn't had the energy to move.

Those silver eyes of hers met mine and for one moment, I saw her. It was something beneath, something dangerous and broken and beautifully twisted.

As quickly as it happened, though, it disappeared. Nem came back to her senses, and everything about her grew cold.

And right then, I understood. I knew why she'd come to me, why she'd slept with the others, because I'd *watched* her sink back into that blackness, watched the passionate woman recede as if drowning beneath freezing water.

I heard before that still waters run deep — that no matter how quiet something seems on the surface, a person could never know what was beneath it.

Nem seemed the poster child for that, and it excited and terrified me.

Some things should stay dead and buried, and no matter how much I liked her, she might just be one of them.

Chapter Thirteen

Nem

Walking into Kyler's house made me realize...I didn't know the man at all. It was nothing like where we'd lived before.

The places my mother had lived in had been warm, even though we moved often. This place was cold. The house itself wasn't as large as I'd have expected, but it was modern. It appeared to have two stories and large windows on the ground floor. A gate at the driveway and mature trees afforded privacy, and the intercom outside the gate meant people couldn't get access without someone buzzing them in.

Dane drove, having come over with his own vehicle to relieve Bray. I would have rather driven myself, but Dane had reminded me that his car was better protected. He wasn't wrong, even if I didn't love the idea of being trapped. Having him drive meant I couldn't leave when I wanted, that losing him would be exceedingly more difficult.

However, I couldn't exactly say that, which meant I ended up in the passenger seat of his king cab truck while he maneuvered the vehicle up the winding driveway of Kyler's house.

"Not many people come here," Dane said as he put it in park.

"Well, I didn't ask."

Instead, Kyler had called me, inviting me in a way that couldn't be rejected. At least, not if I wanted to keep breathing.

Then again, the closer I got to him, the more information I could gather and the better my plans would be. If I could get him to let down his guard, then he might just let slip where Kenz was.

Still, the house seemed cold, and our places growing up hadn't. Was it because my mother had decorated all those places? Because Kyler, despite being who I thought was my father, hadn't really been a part of my life in the same way?

He'd always been on the outside, someone who appeared from time to time but didn't interact much. He sure as hell hadn't been the type to have movie nights or drive me to school. I'd see him at the house, and at parties where we had to attend, but not much else. At most, he'd been adjacent to the family unit. It was strange to realize I knew so little about a man who had been my father.

We got out of the truck, and I prepared myself to see Kyler. It always took a moment to school my expression and hide my revulsion upon seeing him.

"Nervous?" Dane asked.

"It's a short walk from friend to foe in this world," I reminded him. "Anyone with brains is cautious."

He inclined his head as if he couldn't argue against the point. The reality was that most people were killed by someone they'd known, someone who could get to them. It meant that even if Kyler was suddenly all ready to protect me, he could just as easily change his mind and decide to kill me for his own benefit, for imagined slights or for nothing at all.

Dane knocked on the front door, despite Kyler's assistant already having buzzed us in from the gate. It wasn't as if they didn't know we were there…

Probably just more power games, where Kyler wanted to make sure we knew where we fit in the power structure.

After a moment, a large man opened the door. He was tall and possibly even larger than Rune. His hair was buzzed so only the barest hint of the dark color was visible, and his gaze was hard. He stared between Dane and me. "No weapons."

Dane let out an unhappy huff, as if they'd had this conversation and he didn't care for it. I expected him to complain or object, but he turned around and went back to the truck. He opened the center console with a key, then punched in a code into a custom-made gun safe inside. When it popped open, he removed his pistol from its holster at his waist and placed it into the safe.

Then again, arguing wouldn't make much sense. Dane worked for Kyler, he was protecting me for Kyler, so there wasn't much reason he needed a weapon in Kyler's house.

When he returned, he held his arms out. The guard came around, onto the porch, and patted him down. It was quick, as if more cursory and the guard didn't expect to find anything.

After finishing, he looked my way.

"Really?" I asked.

The guard nodded. "No one comes in without being checked."

It wasn't as though I hadn't suspected such a thing. I'd left all my weapons at the house already. The true sign of a professional was an ability to use their environment to their advantage. Someone in my position, who had to keep a low profile, could out myself easily if I strapped up with weapons.

The guard came up to me and moved his hands over my sides, patting carefully but professionally. He didn't grope, didn't take advantage, even when he checked over the pockets of my slacks, when it would have been easy to *slip* and touch something else.

When the guard moved up the insides of my thighs, however, when he checked my back pockets, Dane's sharp voice came out as a threat.

"That's enough," he said.

The guard pulled away, though even that last touch hadn't seemed inappropriate. "You know how pat downs go."

"Yeah, well, if you want to touch her ass again, you'll need to get a new job—don't think you'll be a good guard without any fucking hands."

That made me turn to give Dane one hell of a 'are you fucking me?' look. Dane had never struck me as a jealous man, even when it came to someone he cared about.

He sure didn't care about me.

Maybe it was just a power play? Maybe he saw me as a thing and thought it would make him look weak if someone else touched me? Like a toy he wanted other kids to know belonged to him?

I bristled at that. "Knock it off."

He offered me a glare that lacked his normal humor. "If you want to be groped, I can do it for you."

"Maybe I like it better when he does it," I countered, narrowing my eyes. "And whoever touches my ass isn't any business of yours."

"You can say that all you want." He walked behind me, then leaned in closer so his voice wouldn't carry. "But I just take it as an offer to prove you wrong. That ass is *mine*, Nem."

I would have kept fighting with him, but Kyler walking into the room silenced us both. It seemed Dane didn't want Kyler in his business any more than I did.

"Nem," Kyler said, an odd fondness to his voice. Had I ever heard that from him? He'd never been fond of me, never showed any affection to my mother or to Kenz.

"Kyler," I said, forcing a smile to my lips, the lipstick I always wore feeling like both armor and camouflage. "Sorry it took a while. I'd planned to work from home, so I hadn't gotten ready."

"You didn't need to worry about dressing up, not here." He turned his gaze on Dane and the guard. "You can go to the guardhouse." The dismissal was sharp and made obvious he was used to people listening to him.

"Sir—" the guard said.

Kyler lifted an eyebrow, silencing him. "I am perfectly safe, and I don't pay you to question my orders."

The guard pressed his lips together, then nodded. Dane gave me a loaded look, as though he had things he wanted to say but kept them in.

It had been far too long to think I could read such a thing from Dane. My guess? He was unhappy about leaving us there alone, but whether that was because he was worried about Kyler or me, I had no idea.

Once alone, it was as if Kyler shifted, and changed before my eyes. Some of that arrogance slid free.

It was a strange thing to witness, like someone pulling off a mask.

"Come on," he said, nodding for me to follow. "I have food already set out."

I followed, the entire thing surreal. I was going to kill this man after I ruined him, after I took everything from him, yet here I was, following him as though we were friends.

In the large dining room sat a table with platters of fruit and pastries on them—far more than two people could ever eat—and carafes beside sugar and creamer. It felt like some friendly breakfast get-together.

Kyler pulled out a seat and waited for me to sit. After helping to push it in, he took the seat beside me, at the head of the table.

He reached out, pouring coffee from the carafe into a cup for me, then got a second for himself.

I wasn't hungry, especially with the tension of the moment. Still, when Kyler put food onto a plate for himself, I figured I didn't have a choice. I didn't need to give him any reason to be suspicious.

I didn't eat or drink any, however, until he did so first. While there wasn't much reason for him to poison or drug me, that didn't mean it wasn't possible.

"Thank you for coming," he said after taking a bite of some sort of banana bread. "I don't have many people over."

"This house isn't what I expected," I admitted. "After the other place, I thought your home would be similar."

He laughed, the sound not fitting him at all. Had I ever heard him laugh like that? "Yes, I'm not a fan of massive homes. I don't have any meetings or official parties here, so I don't need much space. I don't care for bringing work here."

"So why am I here?"

"I had time to think about what happened last night. Despite the threats against me, there haven't been many times someone has gotten lucky. Typically, my personal security and the Quad handle threats before they ever get that close."

I asked the question before he could, a way to make it seem I was concerned for him. "How did this one, then? And how did he even know where you'd be?"

"The best I can work out, he was following me. After the attack, I had Rune sweep the car for tracking devices. One had been placed behind the back tire. That SUV had been in the shop a few days before, and I have to assume it was placed then."

Wrong. Jarrod placed it the morning before to sell the story.

"And no one found it?"

He shook his head. "We don't sweep for devices very often. Clearly, that will change going forward."

I popped one of the pieces of strawberry into my mouth, then swallowed before speaking again. "I'm glad you're safe, but I'm still not sure why I'm here."

"You saved me. I don't think I've had that happen except from those who are paid to do so. Even they don't always do that well, and often not where it risks their own lives. Why did you do it?"

"I don't know. I just saw someone with a gun and reacted."

"Not many people react by trying to save someone else."

"Good people do. People like us do."

I managed to get the words out without laughing. Obviously, Kyler was *not* good people. Neither was I, though. Still, people driven by ego always liked to think they were good people. They clung to the belief they were the hero in their own tale, that if other people knew the real story, they'd support them.

So, I offered Kyler breadcrumbs of that, a chance to be seen as the good guy.

Sure enough, he took those breadcrumbs with his greedy little hands. "That's why I invited you. I'm surrounded by people who all want something from me. There aren't many real people in the world anymore. The house you found for me, that's what everyone else thinks, what they see. This place, though? This is the real me."

I sipped my coffee, taking in the information. He was ridiculous, trying to pretend he was something different, that he was somehow deep.

He wasn't. He was a petulant child who wanted what he wanted and didn't care who he stepped on to get it.

He'd stepped on Caroline, and he'd tried to step on me.

Too bad he hadn't quite gotten that one right, because I wouldn't stay down.

"So is the house for parties?" I asked. "To keep up what other people see?"

"No. It is for someone else, someone I need to ensure stays safe."

"A mistress?" I asked, making sure to sound as if I knew that was the answer.

He let out another of those laughs. "No. I learned my lesson a long time ago about women." He paused, giving me an apologetic look. "No offense intended, but in my experience, women cause problems."

"Life is awfully lonely like that."

"I didn't say I don't enjoy the company of women. I just learned not to intertwine them with my life. So, I wouldn't buy a property for a mistress, no."

"Oh," I said, dropping my gaze as if embarrassed. "I didn't mean to ask things I shouldn't."

"It's fine. I wanted to talk to you because you're more honest than other people — part of that is not being afraid to just talk to me. It's for my daughter."

"You have a daughter? She would have to be too young to live there alone."

And there was that curl of his lips again as I buttered him up. "I'm not as young as you seem to think. My daughter is eighteen, and she has plenty of staff who help look after her since her mother's death."

"Her mother died? I'm so sorry."

He tilted his head as he stared at me. "I forget that you're not from around here. For most people around, this is all a very old story."

"You don't have to say anything if you don't want to," I offered, since often pulling back was the best way to get people to chase.

He waved off my concern. "It's okay. As I said, you could ask anyone, and they'd know. My wife was Caroline Hester." He paused, as if the name should have meant something to me. When I didn't react, he huffed. "It's refreshing to have someone not know who she was, really. My wife was the last of a very powerful family here—a legacy, really. Seventeen years into our marriage, she and my oldest daughter were both murdered."

"Who would do that?"

"Enemies—another family who wanted to increase their own standing by removing us. They had assumed I'd be there, that they could wipe out my entire family in one swoop. They were dealt with afterward. However, my daughter, Mackenzie Williams, is now the only family I have left. She doesn't live with me to help keep her safe, because with her bloodlines, she's at risk from others who would want to use her."

I thought about Kenz, about how alone she had to feel, how isolated. No doubt Kyler hadn't let her have any sort of freedom. I'd been alone all these years, but with purpose.

Kenz would have been lacking even that.

Stay on topic.

I looked over at Kyler, trying to keep myself in the mindset of a stranger, of someone enamored by a person so powerful and interesting. "What's she like?"

He paused, as if he'd never considered it. After a moment, he spoke slowly. "Mackenzie looks like her mother did. When I see her, it is like looking at her mother all over again."

It was his tone that hit me. Those words from most parents in that position—when they had one child left who resembled a late spouse—they'd be with sorrow, with yearning. It would be a mixture of pleasure at seeing their love in any form and sadness of what they'd lost.

That wasn't how Kyler said it. He almost spat the words, as if the reminder of his wife enraged him.

It furthered my belief that I was doing the right thing. I needed to get Kenz away from him.

He let out a loud sigh, then looked at me. "Do you ever feel as though you're on a track? That life is really just fixing things after the choice that put you on that path?"

I thought about the night everything had changed, when the course of my life had shifted all because of Kyler. "Yeah. I know that feeling."

"What do you do, then? How do you handle knowing things are all heading in one direction? That all the choices we already made led us here?"

I met his gaze. "I decide what I really want and go after it no matter what."

He nodded and sat back, as if that made sense to him. Too bad for him he didn't know what I wanted was to watch him bleed out.

* * * *

The mansion was just as impressive as it had been the last time I'd been there.

"No blood." I gestured at the place where Geoffrey had been shot, surprised to find nothing stained on the wooden floor.

"Getting blood out is a life skill for us," Rune said. "If we had to move each time a little blood got on the floor, we'd never spend two nights in the same place."

That should have bothered me, but the practicality made sense. It was like someone in the forest knowing how to gather wood and start a fire or someone in the desert knowing how to get water and avoid the heat. It was a life skill which meant a person was well adjusted to the world they lived in.

We went farther into the house, just Rune and me. Colton had gotten out at the gate to talk to the workers there, wanting to see their progress.

Having a shadow had started to become normal. It was strange how that happened, how people could get used to anything. It was something living creatures managed that never failed to fascinate me.

No matter how horrible something was, we could adjust, grow used to it, even find joy in it.

So despite my annoyance with the situation, I'd grown accustomed to it. I recognized the prattling of Dane when silence made him uncomfortable. The clicking of Bray's laptop keyboard felt normal. Rune's furrowed brows when he was trying to keep up but didn't want to admit he didn't understand something was commonplace, and Colton's blunt comments could almost make me laugh.

It meant walking with Rune felt normal, felt like so long ago, when we'd been close.

"This is a lot of house for one person," I said.

Rune frowned and looked over at me. "One person?"

"Mackenzie."

He narrowed his eyes, the way he tended to do when unsure about my intentions. "Who said that's who'll live here?"

"Kyler. He said this was for his daughter."

Rune tore his gaze away, and I could tell by his expression he'd had no idea.

Which threw me. "You didn't know that? What did you think this place was for?"

He shrugged. "I had no idea what it was for. Kyler doesn't share much."

"But you work for him."

"So do you. Do you know everything?"

"I'm new and I just handle real estate. You're entangled in all his dealings — you're like his second."

"Not really."

"No?" That was interesting...

The Quad were capable, ruthless and well-connected. Anyone who had access to them and failed to use them was an idiot. I recalled, back as a child, how they'd been so entwined with every part of my life. They were a larger part than my own father.

Either of them.

The thought that Kyler had put them on the bench, that he used them as basic muscle or lackeys was not only crazy but absolutely stupid.

Jarrod had taught me once that the dumbest thing a person could do was not use the tools at their disposal. The Quad, no matter my personal feelings about them, were one hell of a toolbox.

Leaving them to the background made no sense, especially because they'd proven themselves loyal.

"Have you met Mackenzie?" I asked.

"Of course," Rune said, his tone sharp as if he didn't care for the question.

"Well, you didn't know she'd be living here, so why would I think you knew her?"

He pressed his lips together, then sighed. "Sorry. It's just a sore subject."

"Why?"

"Because we used to handle her security ourselves."

"What changed?" I paused, thinking back to what Kyler had said, to what I knew. "Was it when Kyler's wife and other daughter were killed?"

He nodded once, quick, as if he didn't care for the topic. "Kyler moved Mackenzie after that, and no matter how much we wanted to take care of her personally, he wouldn't allow it."

A frown touched my features. They'd wanted to keep taking care of her? It almost seemed as though they cared…

But maybe Kyler moved them because he knew they'd been willing to help him kill Caroline and me, so he felt he couldn't trust them? Or perhaps he just wanted full control over Mackenzie?

Too many variables.

"What happened that night? Kyler didn't want to talk about it."

Rune rubbed his hand on the outside of his jeans, as if his anxiety caused the action. "I wasn't there. None of us were—we were taking Mackenzie to a doctor's appointment. She's got type-one diabetes and needed to see a new specialist out of town. As best we can tell, men broke in, killed the guards stationed there then killed both Caroline and her daughter. They set a fire to cover it all up and destroy any evidence."

"How did they kill them?"

"Shot them, we think. They used an accelerant to make sure most of the evidence burned, so it's mostly a guess. Neighbors heard shots, and two of the guards on the outside didn't get burned. Shot would be a lot better a way to go than burning to death."

"Did you know them well?"

"Yes." The answer was short. After a moment, his shoulders dropped. I got the sense he wanted to talk about it, but hadn't ever been able to. That made sense—in our world, sharing things was dangerous. "We basically lived with them for years before it happened. They were…family."

"Caroline and her daughter?"

He nodded.

He still hadn't said my old name. It bothered me, that no one had said my name at all. I'd heard all about Caroline, about Kenz, but no one seemed to think I was important enough to mention.

"What were they like? What's Mackenzie like?"

Rune paused by the back door, as if he wanted to finish the conversation before seeing anyone else. "Caroline was strong. She was the tough sort of woman who could hand a man his balls with just a sharp word. She wasn't soft or sweet, but she was smart, and she'd do what needed doing. Mackenzie, well I haven't seen her much in the past ten years or so. She was sweet, though I have no idea who she got that from. She's smart, though, just like her mom was. She's grown up to look like her mom, too. Last time I saw her was about two years ago, at a party. It was weird, you know, because I remember her at about eight years old, so seeing her as a teenager threw me. She recognized me, and I didn't really expect that." He stopped, as if that was as far as he'd go.

But I wanted more. I wanted to hear about the one person he hadn't mentioned.

Me.

"And Kyler's older daughter?"

"*Her,*" Rune said with a sigh, as if that one word held a wealth of information.

I waited, wanting to hear him talk about me, needing some view into his feelings, to try to figure out where he stood about it.

Maybe it was some masochistic streak of mine, but I didn't think so. Instead, I think I just wanted to feel as if someone remembered me. I wanted proof that I hadn't been forgotten entirely.

Except, Rune shook his head. "Come on, let's get this done."

His words gave no room to try again, having shut down entirely. That meant I wasn't going to get what I really wanted—information.

Stop being sentimental. I needed to be focused on the tasks I had before me now.

The fact I'd been completely head over heels for these men back then had nothing to do with the present. I didn't need to hear anything about myself. Either I'd hear they cared or they didn't, and either way, it wouldn't help me. It wouldn't give me info that would help me find Kenz, that would help me end Kyler.

It was useless, and I wasn't stupid enough to waste my time on such things.

Or so I told myself as I watched Rune's back while he walked away, an ache in my chest as unwelcome as everything else they spawned in me.

Chapter Fourteen

Nem

The office was quiet, which was normal around nine on a Friday night. Most of the other employees had headed out hours before, leaving only myself and a handful of overachievers. Still, it was my only sense of privacy.

The men remained near me everywhere else. Even at the hotel, they checked in on rotation, every hour or so. I couldn't go a few feet without someone on my heels.

Well, everywhere except at the office. Given the security in the building, the men allowed me time in my office on my own. The one person who followed me would stay either in another area of the office or down on the ground floor with security. My shadow currently was Rune, but he'd stayed out of my way and let me work.

It meant while I generally preferred to work from home, I had taken to working at the office just for the quiet.

And the work was still easy. There wasn't much of it, really. I'd helped with the purchase of a new short-term rental property, connected with the security install team for Kenz's house and otherwise poured through the files I had for any other detail that might prove useful.

Knowing the security details of the house had allowed me access to any weaknesses. There weren't many, and a few that were there had been caught and fixed by the Quad.

This entire job would be far easier to do if it weren't for having to outsmart them.

I pushed the files away when my vision blurred, telling me I'd spent too long staring at the small print. An hour before, Rune had come in and told me to start wrapping it up.

That reminded me of how they'd cared for me before, and just like then, I'd ignored them. In fact, I might have been done about the time Rune had told me, but by him saying anything, I'd put in more time out of spite.

I rubbed my eyes, careful to keep to the inner corner so not to smear the makeup.

A sound outside made me lift my gaze. I ignored much of the noise—the movement of people walking by, the closing of filing cabinets, the clicks of locks from other offices. Working in close quarters with others meant there was noise.

This, however, broke through all that.

It was something I'd learned early, to identify things that weren't right, that didn't fit.

In this case, the creak of floorboards filtered through to alert me. Not the quick ones of someone walking past but slow and drawn out, as if trying to be quiet. There was a hesitation, then the door to an office beside mine opened.

The muffled sound of voices floated through the wall, then a bang. It wasn't a gunshot, more like something hit something else — hard.

I went for my phone, grabbing it off the desk and calling the first number there, the one at the top due to him having called me.

Dane answered, his voice cheerful. "Hello, Nem. Are you looking for a quickie? I don't mind stopping in to take care of you."

"Shut up," I said, my voice low. I took the letter opener from my desk before moving to the wall behind the entrance, so if the door opened, I'd be hidden.

His tone changed in an instant, the humor leaving it and reminding me that beneath that jovial mask was a capable killer. "What's wrong?"

"Someone's here," I said. "They went into the office next door and it sounded like they hit someone in there."

"Where's Rune?"

"Not here."

Something shifted, and more background noise came through. He had probably put me on speaker phone. "Where are you?"

"In my office."

Colton spoke from farther away, as if behind Dane. "Rune was downstairs in the security office. The elevators are offline."

"We're around the corner," Dane said. "You need to stay out of sight."

"You think?" I kept the rest of my response to myself. What did they think? That I'd walk up and introduce myself?

What inane advice.

"Just hold on," Dane said.

When the handle twisted on my office door, I hit the End button on the call. There wasn't much the men could do over the phone against an attacker who was in the room, and I didn't want my position given away by them talking too loudly. A quick press to a button on the side of the phone silenced and turned off the vibration before I slid it into my pocket.

The person came into sight, and I didn't recognize him. He was rather short, only a little taller than me, and dressed in a pair of black slacks and a tan shirt. It was the sort of outfit someone wore when they wanted to blend in, and a patch on the shoulder told me why. It was for a delivery service.

No one thought twice about delivery men—at least until they put a bullet in someone.

He came in farther, not noticing me in the small corner between the door and the wall.

"Anyone?" another male voice from the hallway called.

"I don't think so," the man in the room responded.

If they were yelling, they had to assume everyone else was dealt with. It meant they didn't think they needed to be silent anymore.

The man in the room went forward, checking behind the desk. "There's a lot of paperwork out on the desk here," he said, loud enough for the other to hear. "We should check the bathrooms, make sure no one else is here."

I held my breath, trying to drag out the moment. A holster on the man's hip said he was far better armed than I was. I never played a game if I wasn't sure I could win it, and guns won against knives every time.

I wasn't the kind who often asked for help, but I also knew that calling in the cavalry when needed was important. I couldn't go hand to hand with most full-sized men, so I never let myself get into such positions.

Then I'd gotten caught unawares here.

Yet another thing to blame the Quad for. If it wasn't for them, I'd have my gun and would have been working from my hotel room.

The man called over his shoulder without looking. "How long before Kyler hears about this?"

"He'll know by morning when the cleaning crew comes in." The man outside let out a laugh. "Wish I could see the bastard's face when he realizes we one-upped him."

"This isn't about winning."

"Course it is. Life is about winning."

"You're a fucking idiot. Go check the bathroom and breakroom." The man in the office with me shook his head, then turned.

Any hope I'd had that he'd miss me, that he'd somehow look the other way and walk out, fled when his gaze landed right on me in my hiding spot.

He didn't reach for his weapon, holding his hands up as if to reassure me. "Hey there."

I kept the letter opener hidden, the handle in my palm, the blade tucked up against my wrist. "What are you doing here?"

"Nothing," he said, as if I hadn't just overheard his conversation. "We're friends of Kyler's, checking in."

What a lie. Still, I needed to buy time. "Why are you sneaking around, then?"

He paused, then looked out through the still-open doorway, as if considering his options. Finally, when he looked back at me, the game slid away.

Worse, he didn't look like a bad man. I didn't see the signs of someone who killed happily inside him. Instead, he seemed resigned rather than eager. "This is a wrong time, wrong place sort of thing, love."

"I don't understand."

Sure I did. They were pissed at Kyler over some slight and figured the best way to get to him was to attack those close to him. It was a coward's move.

I'd take out whoever I needed to, but I didn't kill random innocents just because I was afraid of the person I was really after. A person should either boss up and go after the real villain or they should let it go.

"Kyler has done some terrible things, things he has to pay for."

He will.

"But that doesn't have anything to do with me. I'm just a real estate agent." I used a pleading tone, playing up the whole frightened-woman thing.

If I were aggressive, it might push him to act sooner. If I made him feel guilty—and the man looked like someone who that might just work on—it could prolong the interaction and give Rune and the others more time to take the stairs up.

"Life isn't always fair," he said, pity in his tone. "I can promise to make it quick, though. I don't want to make people suffer."

"What did Kyler even do?"

That made the man pause, anger slipping into his features. "He killed my daughter."

That didn't surprise me. Kyler was willing to kill his own daughter — why wouldn't he go after someone else's?

"I'm sorry that happened, but I didn't have anything to do with that."

"No, you didn't, but he has to pay for it."

"So go after *him*."

The man shook his head. "The world is a complicated place. I *can't* go after him. That would mean war, and I'd lose a lot more people."

"So you're going to kill people who are somewhat close to him? Even when I didn't do anything?"

"This is his most important office, at least of the official ones. There were ten people here, ten people who help run his little empire. None of you are innocent, not if you work for him, if you help him in any way. This won't fix what he did to my daughter, but it's something."

The man came forward, still trying to look as if he were my friend, as though this were all a horrible job that had to be done and he held no real responsibility for it.

I didn't move away, didn't want to get my back pressed to the wall, to limit my range of movement. Instead, I tightened my grip on the handle of the knife, trying to let the tension drain from my body.

The hardest part of any attack was deciding when to move. Go too soon, and I'd lose my surprise, show my hand before it could be useful.

Wait too long, and I could end up dead.

He wrapped a hand around my throat. "Close your eyes," he said, voice soft and almost reassuring. "It'll be over fast."

Yeah, it will.

I let the knife shift so I could wrap my fist around the handle, then drove it up. It wasn't a long blade, which meant hitting the right spot was the most important thing. I picked between his ribs on his left side, since his lifted arms revealed it. With him so close, I couldn't aim that well.

Maybe I'd hit his heart or lungs.

He let out a pained shout and yanked back, and I twisted the blade to do as much damage as possible.

It was something Colton had taught me. His voice in my head kept repeating—*If you're going to fight, you go for the throat.*

The meaning was clear. If it was worth fighting, if it was worth drawing blood for, don't fuck around with it.

So if I was going to bury that knife in his side, if I was going to go that way, I'd damn well play for keeps.

The man grasped his side, blood pouring from it and coating his hands. "What the fuck?"

His tone was absurd, as if he were personally offended by my stabbing him. He had been ready to strangle me. That seemed like a fair response.

The other man rushed in, no doubt called by the shout of his friend. He looked very different from his friend—taller, more muscular, more like the stereotypical bad guy I expected when it came to murdering an office full of people out of revenge.

He darted his gaze from the other man to me, as if piecing it together, his eyebrows furrowed as if it didn't make any real sense. He dropped his eyes to the knife in my hand, then let out a quick snort. "Did you really let this little girl get the best of you."

"Shut up," the first man snapped, though the words weren't as strong or kind as they'd been before. It seemed his pity for me had bled out—much like he was.

"Well, we need to get out of here," the other man said, still looking amused. "I'm sure someone heard that bitch-ass scream you let out."

The bleeding man gave me a chilling look, one I returned. I'd stabbed him—there probably wasn't much point in acting demure and scared anymore. "That was a mistake."

"You were planning on killing me anyway."

"Yeah, but it would have been quick and painless. Now? Not so much."

"Painless and quick don't matter," I countered. "Alive or dead, that's all there is. Offering a quick death is nothing but a lie, a poisoned dessert people offer."

He narrowed his eyes, and I was reminded that even if he wanted to pretend he was somehow better than Kyler, he wasn't. He was driven by the same selfishness—he just disguised it as justice. He wanted to hurt people because of his own pain, and he didn't give a damn who it was.

His friend reached for the pistol from his holster. "Let's get this done before anyone else shows up."

I moved quicker.

I'd lost my main element of surprise, but I could still use what little I had to my advantage. The world expected people like me—small, female and not all that intimidating—to cower. They didn't expect us to attack. It was like how, when a chicken charged, people ran. Despite being larger, despite knowing the chicken didn't have a chance at actually doing damage, people would run.

I used that fact to my advantage and charged the two of them.

The bleeding man backed away, cradling the wound I'd already left in his side. It seemed he didn't want a repeat introduction to my knife. The other didn't scare so easily—he wasn't bleeding, of course—and I slammed into him with my shoulder. He hadn't been able to brace, so he fell backward, striking the wall.

I kept moving, not pausing to see where they were. The bang of a gun shattered the quiet, and plaster flew from the wall beside me. It told me the men probably lacked much experience with guns.

Good news for me.

I went down the hallway, the strike of heavy footsteps behind me saying they'd given chase. A trail of blood followed me from the blade, so I tucked it against my shirt. The fabric would soak up the blood, making it harder to follow me.

The office wasn't huge, and there weren't a lot of great places to hide. The elevator at the far end was open, and a spark from inside told me that wasn't an escape route. They'd damaged it to ensure no one could follow right then.

Another gunshot rang out, and a sharp pain engulfed my shoulder. I held in a gasp at the shock as my entire brain focused on the reality that I'd just been shot. There was no way to check it, to worry about just how bad the injury might be. Even a bad shot could get lucky, and getting killed by some two-bit wannabe assassins was *not* how I planned to go down. It meant I had to tuck my arm against my side and keep moving, push through the pain and not let it stop me.

I twisted the handle to the door of the large conference room and ducked inside, twisting the shitty lock on the door as I closed it.

A heavy weight slammed against the door. It wouldn't hold for long, not against the force that hit it. These doors were made for the illusion of privacy, for people to have sex during the day and not get walked in on. They hadn't been built or installed to prevent real violence.

I set myself on the other side of the door, just behind the bookshelf. Never use the same trick twice was another lesson I'd gotten, though I couldn't recall who had taught that one to me.

The last time I'd hidden. I'd waited, hoping not to be found. This time? I grasped the knife in the hand of the arm that didn't hurt.

This time, I'd strike first.

Another slam happened along with an annoyed grunt before, finally, the door splintered, and a body charged through. At the front was the unharmed man, and on his heels, the one I'd stabbed.

I didn't wait for them to get a feel for the room, moving immediately from my spot behind them. Their gazes were locked across the room, expecting to find me hiding beneath the table or even through the door on the other side of the room.

I grasped the handle of the knife, reached around the man at the back—at least he was short—and dragged the blade across his throat. He moved, a wild flail that caught my face with his elbow.

Warmth poured from my nose, but I ignored it and him. He grasped at his throat, but there wasn't any saving him. He wasn't a threat anymore. Very few people could manage to keep their wits about them when bleeding out, and I doubted he was one.

The other man turned around, and he was quicker than his friend. Another bang from the gun, but he missed. Too much movement, too much adrenaline, too little practice. I hit his wrist with the hand that held the knife, causing the gun to sail from his grip and slide across the floor.

Not that he needed it. He caught my hand before I could sink my blade into him, and his being larger and stronger than me meant that I needed a better advantage.

Well, *any* advantage.

He shoved forward, making me hit the large table, pressing me down onto it. He hit my hand against the table, knocking the knife from it. The clatter of my makeshift weapon against the floor felt like a death knell.

He wrapped his hands around my throat, slamming me against the table so hard a pain in my head echoed through my brain. The world seemed to lose its sharp edges.

Fucking wonderful.

Just as everything started to darken, however, a shot rang out. Had the man I stabbed gotten back up? This whole thing had been a mess — it wouldn't shock me for that to go horribly wrong as well.

But, no, that wasn't it. The man choking me lost his grip, letting me suck in a deep breath of air.

As I rolled, the world still wavering in and out, a fucking dream come true happened.

Funny, since I didn't believe in dreams — never had. Even back before I'd witnessed the ugliness of life, I'd never really thought people got the things they wanted, or that dreams were anything other than the brain trying to come to terms with the shit we went through.

Except, I watched the Quad pour in. Colton had his gun up, the first to have fired, the flat expression of his face one that said killing was no issue to him. Behind him, Rune entered, Dane behind him and Bray as well.

Their expressions all said the same thing. The man who had just been shot, who was still making noises on the floor, probably wished I'd gotten to him first. If he didn't, he would soon. He'd curse me for not slitting his throat, because the look on those men's faces said he'd get worse from them.

And, as the world went black, that sounded fine to me.

* * * *

The only good thing about being in a hospital was that they had the good drugs. The better thing about being in a hospital where the staff were terrified of my bodyguards was that they gave me as much of those good drugs as I wanted.

And I wanted *plenty*.

I'd had my wounds treated by Jarrod most of the time, or by some vet or medical drop-out who was willing to take cash and not report the injuries to anyone. That worked well enough to stay under the radar, but they didn't tend to have access to the really good stuff.

One sharp look from Rune when the doctor had been hesitant about more pain meds had had him falling in line, however, and giving me exactly what I wanted.

Which seemed fair to me. I'd taken a bullet—I deserved to be drugged up enough to forget the entire thing.

"Not so fast," Dane said as he set his hand over the spoon so I stopped eating the gelatin.

"I'm hungry." I tried to pull my hand away.

"Yeah, well, you won't be so happy when you throw that all up — *again*."

I ignored him. He was right, but that didn't mean I had to give a damn. Pain meds tended to mess with my stomach, and the doctor hadn't wanted me to eat much. He'd agreed to gelatin, but after eating two containers of it, I'd thrown it all up.

This was take two at trying to keep it down.

"I'm going to get sick anyway," I told him. "I'd rather enjoy this now if it's going to happen either way. Nothing is worse than dry heaving."

He sighed and let go of my hand. The lemon of the gelatin was like a religious experience, or maybe that was due to the drugs in my system.

Either way, I enjoyed the room-temperature, sugar-filled dessert like it was the meaning of life.

Bray had his computer out on the table, working as he had most of my stay, occasionally looking up at me as if he needed to check in.

Rune was stretched out on the couch, eyes closed, a soft snore escaping from him — the jerk always had been able to sleep anywhere — and he looked terrifying, his large form dwarfing the small couch and his tattoos standing out in the bright hospital-white room. Colton sat in a chair outside the door, and I'd catch a glimpse whenever someone walked in or out.

A nurse came in, the same one who had treated me the whole time. She had a bob cut, longer in the front, shorter in the back, and blonde highlights that lightened her brunette hair.

She was also a bitch.

Not that I didn't respect that. The way she'd set up the machines, the way she'd moved said she knew exactly how to handle all of it. She was no-nonsense, sure of her own skill and more than willing to put anyone in their place over it.

She read across the screens, the machines hooked up to me all making some sort of beeping noises. After that, she peered at Bray and narrowed her blue eyes. "It's past visiting time."

"And?"

The simple one-word response made it clear that he didn't give a fuck about her rules.

The nurse didn't seem willing to take that response. "*And* that means you all need to leave. In fact, we have a limit of two visitors at a time. My patient needs to rest, and she can't do that with you clicking away on that thing and your friend snoring on the couch."

A tension filled the room, Bray's expression flat. I knew him well enough to know that wasn't a good thing, though.

"We ain't leaving," Rune said, having sat up, as if the threat alone was enough to wake him. Maybe he'd never been fully asleep, was just resting his eyes for a moment but still aware. "I don't care about your rules—we ain't going anywhere."

She squared off against them, all five-and-a-half-foot of her, in her light blue scrubs, against men who would have probably been happy to leave her in a ditch if they needed to.

A laugh bubbled out of me before I could think about it. Fuck, forget laugh, it was a *giggle*. A drug-fueled giggle that could have made any sorority sister proud.

The men all twisted their gazes my way, as if I were fucking nuts. It only made me laugh harder.

Men used to people falling at their feet in fear were being put in their place by a Karen with a stethoscope.

It wouldn't have been so funny any other time, but right then? It felt damn good to laugh.

Well, not physically, as it fucked with my shoulder, but I couldn't remember the last time I'd laughed.

After a moment, Dane let out a chuckle, the tension dissipating due to my giggles. "Why don't you go check in with Dr. Harrison. He'll okay us. Besides, she's leaving soon."

"She isn't ready—"

"Go talk to the doctor," Dane repeated.

Once the nurse scurried out, Dane offered me a wide smile. "You know, I don't think I've heard you laugh like that before."

"We've never gotten her high on pain pills either," Rune offered. "Maybe that was the trick all along."

"Do you have to drug women to get them to enjoy you?" I asked as I went back to my gelatin.

"Pretty sure you enjoyed us all just fine," Dane countered.

I swallowed another bite, then looked over at him. "How long before I can leave?"

"Doctor said another hour to get back your MRI results. Normally he'd want to keep you just to watch over you for the night, but I told him we'd have a nurse on call."

"Can it be that nurse?" I nodded at the door, toward the one who had left after facing off against each of them.

"Fuck no," Bray muttered, telling me he was paying attention even if his gaze rarely strayed from his screen. "She's trouble, and you're enough trouble as it is."

I rolled my eyes, then peered at my shoulder.

The bullet had grazed me on my right side. The nice thing was that it meant the scar wouldn't clash with the ones I already had. Another gunshot scar, another day.

It had gone through clean, so the doctor had only needed to disinfect and sew me up. X-rays showed it hadn't hit bone, that it hadn't damaged anything that would require surgery.

Just a sling, time and a lot of physical therapy down the road.

At least I wouldn't have to do that. Most likely, I'd be dead before that came up.

It was a strange silver lining, but I'd take it.

"Do you know who the men were?" I asked finally.

I hadn't asked anything about what happened — it had been a far second concern at first. Now, however, since I'd survived and was well medicated, curiosity was all I had.

Rune nodded. "Two men who worked for Kyler a few years back."

"One said Kyler killed his daughter."

"Yeah. What he probably didn't mention was that his daughter was nineteen and ran off with about four-hundred-thousand dollars' worth of Kyler's cocaine when she and her boyfriend decided it was a good idea to fuck him over. When they were caught, she pulled a gun. She probably would have been killed anyway, but if you pull a gun, you ain't going to walk away."

I sighed as I thought about the man's pain. People didn't see family the way they really were. We all saw what we wanted, and that meant the father had only seen his baby girl.

"So they're both dead?"

Dane answered that one. "You got one of them yourself, and the other one? The one who choked you?

Oh, yeah, he's dead." A darkness in Dane's tone drew a shiver through me.

I *loved* that tone. It was this bottomless insanity, something I understood. It was the casting away of all those civilities people were taught. It was the real animal beneath the masks we all wore. I was finally old enough to really understand who Dane was, who all the men were, and now I could really appreciate it.

"Good."

That drew a lifted eyebrow from Dane.

I shrugged, tightness there telling me it would have hurt if it wasn't for the pain killers. "Did you expect me to cry about the death of someone who tried to kill me?"

"A lot of women would."

"I'm not a lot of women."

"So I keep figuring out."

I shifted in the bed, the band of the sling digging into my other shoulder blade. I'd need to switch it out, get the kind with two straps and a closure that secured it around me. I'd had to deal with slings enough to know what worked, what I could sleep in. "I can't wait to crawl into my bed," I admitted. The thought felt like the filthiest fantasy, as if I could moan out loud at the mere consideration of those soft sheets, of stretching my legs out and closing my eyes.

"Not a chance," Bray said.

"What?"

"You aren't going back to your hotel."

That made me stop, as if he'd snatched away an orgasm. "Pretty sure I am."

Rune shook his head. "After this? With you still hurt? No fucking chance."

"The men are dead, and they weren't even after me. It'd be one thing if they'd come looking to put a bullet in me, but they weren't. It was about Kyler."

"Too fucking bad," Rune said. "This is *twice* that you've been far too close to a bullet you can't walk away from. You're going to need help and someone to make sure you take your meds. Besides that, you've already got one of us watching you all the time, and doing it at your hotel is a stupid waste of resources."

"I agree—it is stupid. I don't need a guard, which I've said from the start." At the unwavering look in each of their eyes, I realized I'd already lost. Whatever the plan was, whatever they intended, they'd already decided.

Digging my feet in would only get me dragged through the dirt.

It also hit me what they meant. Maybe it was the meds, but it took far too long for me to piece it all together.

"You can't be serious," I said.

"Oh, I am absolutely serious," Dane said, his smile having returned, as if my annoyance was better than excitement. "You're coming home with us, Nem."

This is not the plan.

* * * *

Talk about firsts…

I never figured I'd see the Quad's place. Part of me had wondered through the years if they had one. Back, when I'd been younger, they'd spent shifts at our house. Since they weren't always there, I had to assume they'd lived elsewhere, but I'd never seen it.

The only thing I had figured out for sure was that they lived together. It was in the passing comments back then, when one would snap at another for leaving something out, or parking in their spot. Again, it reminded me of their weird dynamic. Closer than brothers, closer than family.

What would it be like to have that?

I pushed away that idea as soon as it came to me. There were thoughts that could help a person and ones that were useless. Wondering about—or worse, craving—a connection like that was the definition of pointless.

I couldn't have it. Maybe I wasn't built for it, maybe almost dying had made it impossible for me, but none of that mattered. I couldn't have it, so wondering about it or wanting it would only cause me pain.

I wasn't a masochist.

A shower hadn't been possible, not with the bandages, so I'd use a washcloth in the bathroom to do the best I could.

Dane had offered to help, a promising grin on his lips, but I'd refused.

On top of the fact that it would have been exceedingly stupid and far too personal, I didn't plan on removing my shirt around any of them.

Still, the process took a while. It gave me time to think as I sat in the large bathroom that was off the room they'd given me.

Their house was quiet, cozy and very much a bachelor pad. It was located on the edge of a preserve, which meant it had acres of open space behind it. The furniture was all black, as if they had no idea how to match fabrics or colors so figured black went with everything. In fact, I'd guess they went to a big box store and just pointed at the black items.

The house wasn't dirty, but clutter said regular cleaning wasn't high on their list. They threw their trash away, washed their dishes, but dust sat on the shelves and television. A robotic vacuum zoomed around the one level house, a further testament to their limited domestic abilities.

They'd let me be after a short tour and giving me a run down on the rules.

Not that I gave a damn about their rules.

They were what I'd expect when forced to stay with people who worried about my safety.

Don't leave without telling us, don't give out the address here, don't tell anyone where you'll be.

I didn't need them to tell me those things—I knew them well.

Still, being told what to do almost made me want to break the rules just to be contrary. *Good thing my desire to finish my job is larger than my stubbornness.*

After my makeshift bath, when my meds had eased from my system enough that I felt like myself, I was ready to face them.

The night at the hospital had been long, and I'd managed a few hours of sleep there. Still, I was too keyed up to sleep now, with the sun up and night fresh in my mind.

I expected the men to be asleep. It had been a long night for us all, so I'd figured when I walked into the living room, I'd find it empty.

Instead, all four men were there, coffees in their hands as if they needed them.

Rune glanced my way, then rose and poured me a cup as well.

"I'd tell you that you should go back to bed," he said as he handed it over, "but you wouldn't listen."

"You aren't asleep," I pointed out.

"Yeah, but we're used to missing sleep."

"I'm not as delicate as I look." I sipped the hot black coffee, enjoying the burn of it.

"So it seems," Colton said. "You slit someone's throat."

"He was going to kill me. If you're planning on lecturing me, can you wait until I've had my coffee?"

He snorted. "No. You did a good job—stayed alive when most other people wouldn't have. Clearly, you're not just some real estate agent, as if we didn't already know that."

I blew out a breath, the steam from the top of the cup dissipating. "Is this another 'who are you really?' conversations? Because I'm tired of those."

"If you told us the truth, maybe we'd stop asking," Rune said.

"Everyone has a past," I said. "No, I wasn't always in real estate, but I am now."

"Who taught you how to slit a man's throat?" Colton asked.

"That doesn't take a lot of skill." At Colton's deadpanned look, I went on. "My father did. He said if you're going to use a knife, use it right." I remembered Jarrod's lesson that day, remembered how I'd soaked it all up. "He said hesitation will kill you as fast as a bullet, so if you go for someone, go all in."

Colton had his dark eyes locked on me, then nodded. "Smart man—that's good advice. Did he also teach you to shoot?"

"Of course."

"Good. We'll see about getting you armed."

"You trust me not to shoot you in the back?"

That time it was Bray who made a noise and seeing him without his nose in his laptop was almost weird. "Not even a little. I just trust you won't be able to shoot all four of us before we can kill you."

Fair enough.

"I'm not going to shoot you," I said, surprised by how much I meant it. Just the thought of harming any of them made me sick, like the thought of hurting Kenz. Still, I forced myself to not let the statement stand there. "I mean, I don't have any plans to shoot any of you, not unless I have to."

"Have to?" Dane asked.

"Yeah. No matter what you think about me, I'm not new to this world, to what people in it are like. People fuck one another over, betray them, take what they want and leave corpses behind. I'm not planning on killing any of you, but if you do that, if you betray me, if I think you're going to hurt or kill me, I'll put as many bullets into you as I need to."

All four men stared back at me, the moment quiet and full of so many things — questions, secrets, lies, lust.

Bray responded, the quiet one, the one who didn't trust me at all. "Well, at least we are all on the same page then."

Dane lifted his cup as if toasting with the coffee. "To strange bedfellows."

I lifted my cup as well.

Strange bedfellows indeed.

Chapter Fifteen

Dane

Taking the day off had been a good idea. After coffee, after checking in with Kyler, after making a few calls to make sure shit kept moving in my absence, I'd gone the fuck back to sleep.

Everyone had.

A good security system could help a man close his eyes and get some shut-eye. Add in a reputation as bloody as ours, and we weren't likely to be bothered.

At least, not by any person.

Dreams were another story, and mine were fucked.

They'd started out with seeing Nem there, the fucker's hands around her throat. I'd seen a lot over my life—had done a lot—so why did that bother me so much? Why did it make my chest ache and my vision blur?

Nem was just some woman. She was an enigma, a mystery, a pain in the ass, but nothing more.

You can lie to other people, but lying to yourself is stupid.

Fine—she wasn't just some woman. The fact I couldn't get her out of my fucking head was proof of that. Even her drugged-up smile, crooked and adorable, had drawn me in.

She was tough, smart, fucking gorgeous and vicious—everything I could possibly want in a woman.

And entirely off-limits.

Making relationships work in my world was almost impossible. It was why so many men ended up with wives—the appropriate woman to settle down with and have kids—and mistresses—the wild one to fuck on the downlow. One was in the fake world men created, the one where they were regular businessmen, and the other in their secret life, in the darkness and the filth.

However, neither was all that important. I'd seen it time and time again, watched men try to balance that shit and saw them miserable from it.

It wasn't the life for me.

And yet, this part of me I couldn't seem to silence kept looking at Nem and wondering…*what if?*

What if she could offer me both things? She was clearly tough enough to survive in our world, to thrive in it, and she didn't reject the uglier parts of it—or us.

What if she could bridge that gap?

Then the other part of the dream hit me, the worse part, the one I refused to speak of even after all these years.

I remembered Kelsey's face, the morning it had all gone wrong, the morning everything had changed. She'd wanted to come with us, and I'd wondered so many times since that day…what if I'd let her.

What if we'd taken her with us?

Caroline would have still died, but at least her two daughters would have lived.

What would Kelsey be like now if she'd lived? She'd be nearly thirty and probably look just like Caroline. She'd have been smart and sweet and snarky.

I remembered how she'd looked at me, at all of us. Too young to know it wasn't a good idea, but just old enough to get the idea.

I rubbed my hands over my face, trying to dispel the memory, trying to stop the connections from forming.

Kelsey had died because I hadn't been good enough. I hadn't seen the dangers to her that lurked, the ones that targeted her and her mother. It was my job to read people, to see those things, and I hadn't, and she'd paid the price for it.

Nem was smart, sure, but I didn't want to go through that again. I didn't want to feel the way this dark emptiness could swallow a person up, the way each fucking day marked another chance to regret and go over all the things I'd done wrong.

Fuck, I can't do that.

I left my room around three in the afternoon. Four hours of sleep wasn't much, but it was better than nothing. I just couldn't sit there anymore, waiting in the silence, giving me a chance to think way too much.

I needed distractions, and there was no distraction better than other people. Even the men who shared my life, the ones closer than brothers, could prove a worthwhile distraction. I could lose myself in their facial expressions, in picking apart their motivations and their meanings and their actions.

Well, everyone except for Nem—she was still a mystery.

And damn, I loved a mystery.

I went to scold myself again when I spotted her, when the world seemed to go silent in the best way.

She stood in the kitchen, her back to me, her hair piled messily on top of her head with a clip as if it was the best she could do one handed. She wore a pair of oversized sweats she'd gotten from Bray — he was the smallest, but they were still far too big for her — and a tank top that showed off the bandages of her shoulder. The sling was wrapped around her, and she stirred something in a cup, oblivious to my presence.

Fuck, she was pretty. Why, though?

Sure, she was objectively beautiful, but what was with my reaction? I'd fucked hotter girls, ones with bigger tits, a better ass, who gave better head. So why was she special?

What made her different?

I walked up, my steps silent, until I stood just behind her.

She didn't jump when I dragged my fingers across her neck, over the dark marks that discolored her pale skin.

Brave girl.

"He got you good."

She stirred the liquid in her cup — a whiff told me it was jasmine green tea. "It happens when people try to strangle someone."

I followed the bruising, worse on the sides and two spots on the front, where he'd dug his thumbs into her. "Another minute or so, and you'd have been dead."

"With how many times you've threatened to kill me, I didn't figure that would bother you."

"Me either," I admitted, softly. "But it does." I leaned in and pressed my lips to the spot on the side of her neck, leaving kisses along the marks as if that could erase them.

Which was hilarious since scars weren't a turn-off for me. Scars were proof a person had lived through something that had tried to kill them. They were badges of honor, evidence of how fucking tough a person was.

So why did the new marks on her bother me so damned much?

Nem tilted her head, a sweet surrender, so I wrapped my arm around her, careful to avoid her shoulder. I teased the neckline of her shirt, then over her breast. I could feel her nipple through the thin fabric, no bra to keep me from my prize.

The moan she left out was decadent but tired.

I wasn't a gentle-sex sort of man, but she wasn't in any condition for rough right then.

I grabbed her hips and twisted her. Seeing her face made me pause.

The hours since the attack had darkened all the bruising, which made me realize she'd gotten a black eye from it as well. She'd said the man had elbowed her — the cause of the blood that had run from her nose — and it seemed it had been enough to blacken her eye, as well.

She looked like she'd gone three rounds with a boxer, and I couldn't shake the anxiety at the realization that I could have lost her before I really knew a damn thing about her.

Two men had gone looking to end her, but she'd fought tooth and nail. She'd driven a knife into one, slit his throat, held her own. She'd given them hell to the last second like some feral cat they'd thought to tame.

And if that didn't get my cock going, nothing would.

I took her lips in a demanding kiss. Gentle, I could do that, but passive? Fuck that. I wanted to spread those thighs of hers and reacquaint myself with every inch of her body. I wanted to fuck her until I was sure she was fine, until she was too tired to get into any trouble at all.

A throat cleared behind me. In any other situation, I might have barked out some insult. *Get the fuck outta here.* Anything to make sure the moment didn't stop. I didn't care for cockblocks.

Instead, my lips curled as if my body were already on board.

Behind me stood Rune, Colton and Bray, their gazes just as ravenous as I felt.

Which had me looking back at Nem, a question in my eyes.

Would she tell us no? Would she chicken out? Or would she let the four of us fuck her, let us all drown in her like we all wanted?

There wasn't an ounce of hesitation in her face. She didn't worry, didn't second guess anything. She faced it with the same tenacity she must have had when facing down those two men.

A quick nod made me groan.

I was in so much fucking trouble with this woman.

Nem

Was it really happening?

I'd thought about this for years, since before I even knew enough to really picture it. I'd wanted these men, the ones who had been more my family than anyone else, who had been the only ones to make me feel anything, and now I was going to finally have them all.

Not one on one, but together, like it was *supposed* to be. For a woman who didn't believe in fate, I sure as hell seemed to here.

And it was something I hadn't even recognized I needed. I didn't expect to survive this job, didn't think I'd make it out the other side in one piece, but the idea of dying before I'd experienced this would have been something tragic that I hadn't even been able to consider.

It meant going into dealing with Kyler, finishing everything, was okay because I'd gotten this. If felt like a bucket list item I was able to check off.

Rune yanked his shirt off, revealing his sculpted physique, the way his tattoos covered his chest, highlighting his muscles, as mouthwatering as ever. His long hair was down and wild, more curly than usual as if still damp from a recent shower.

Everything moved so fast, I struggled to follow each piece. They stripped down as I stood there, as I watched, as I salivated over the sight.

Bray's lithe figure and hard eyes, his nose ring catching the light. The scars on Rune's chest, evidence that he liked to get in close when fighting, that he bore the results of it. The dark hair that ran down, below Colton's navel, to the thatch at his groin. Dane's shit-eating grin, as if he knew we'd end up here and loved it.

The meds were still in me, less than before, but enough to help the worries and doubts drift away. Rune walked up, grabbing my waist and hauling me against him. I clung to him, wrapping my legs around his waist and my good arm around his neck.

My lips found his, aggressive and hungry. I kissed him with the passion I'd had stored up for so long, the desire that felt as though it had simmered and reduced to this potent mixture, waiting for them, for this.

Then I bit down on his bottom lip, a punishment for the fact I wanted them, that no one else could replace this, that I couldn't get this anywhere else.

A scraping sound, then the shattering of glass. I tore from the kiss to see that Colton had swiped his arm across the kitchen table and knocked off everything. The vase sat in pieces on the floor, forgotten and unimportant.

I shifted, trying to grind against Rune, needing any friction I could get. My body burned, strung too tight and being pulled more. I didn't care that they knew, that they could see how desperate I was.

As long as they helped, as long as they could douse the flames that consumed me, my pride didn't mean shit.

The table pressed against my ass as Rune set me down. He grasped the hips of the sweats I wore and yanked them off.

Without any underwear on, it left me bare, the cool wood of the table nice against my burning skin.

Rune pulled away, stealing his lips from me, taking the kiss away and making me want to curse from the loss.

Until I looked around. While Rune stripped off his jeans, the others were all gloriously, wonderfully naked. Every inch of their skin was on display, all of it *mine*.

I wasn't a possessive or jealous woman, but maybe that was because I'd never had anything worth desiring. I'd never cared about anyone enough that the thought of someone else touching them made me crazy.

These men, ones who were so feared, were *mine*. Even if it was just for the moment, for the night, they were all mine. Every inch of them — their strong bodies, their wicked tongues, their hard cocks — it was all for me.

Colton came up first, his dark eyes full of promises. He didn't kiss me, instead leaning down to capture my nipple between his teeth. Because of the sling, he couldn't get to the other one, but he made me not care. He nipped the hardened bud through the fabric of my top, his hand cupping the breast in a demanding grope. I let my head fall back, enjoying the touch, the way he did it as if he owned me.

I wanted them to own me.

Right then, I wanted to be their plaything, wanted to surrender to the heat and the insanity and the absolute passion.

I didn't want to plan, to think, to have to figure out a damned thing. It was an exchange, how we could all belong to each other entirely.

Hands spread my thighs, and I looked down to find Bray there. He didn't look happy, as though he didn't want to be there. Then again, the hunger in his dark eyes said he did. Maybe that was it — he wanted this more than anything and boy did that piss him off.

Still, I let him spread my legs, gave him access to whatever he wanted. He didn't ease in, delivering a hard lick to my already swollen clit that said this was as much punishment as pleasure.

To my left, Dane had his hand around his cock, stroking slowly, his gaze locked on what Colton and Bray were doing. The voyeuristic bastard grinned at me, then *winked*.

Yet, that heightened it all. Being watched, being desired, it made me arch back more, offer up every single part of me to their debauchery. When I'd been younger, thinking about love, about my future, getting fucked on a table by four killers wouldn't have made the list of my guesses, but damn if it wasn't exactly right.

Bray's fingers dug into my legs, his grip almost bruising as he held me still for his assault. He plunged his tongue into my cunt, his nose grinding against my clit, as if he could swallow down every drop of me and die a happy man.

A hand caught my chin, and I lifted my gaze to Rune's green eyes. He slid his thumb along my bottom lip, then pressed it past. I wrapped my tongue around him and sucked. It wasn't the cock I wanted, but it was something.

He withdrew the thumb, then pressed two fingers in. *Better.* I toyed with his fingers as though they were his dick, letting him thrust in, hollowing my cheeks. I imagined they were his cock, that he had a hand behind me head and was feeding me inch after hot inch.

He let out a moan so deep, it was almost a growl. "You're fucking something," he said, his voice low. "Don't have a clue what exactly that is, but you make me so fucking *hungry*."

I almost laughed at that, as if he were the only one consumed by that feeling. The pain killers didn't drug me — *they did*. There were *four* of them touching and tasting and watching me and they thought they were hungry?

Bray didn't fuck around as he ate me out. He slid one hand up higher to spread my folds, to move the hood from my clit so nothing stood in his way. He took me between his lips and sucked so hard. I cried out, muffled around Rune's fingers.

Instead of easing off, Bray sucked harder, throwing me headfirst into an orgasm that tore through me. I lost track of everything as I tried to just breathe, to hold myself together through the waves of pleasure.

When I opened my eyes, I found Rune still there, his green eyes locked on mine. I'd bitten down on his fingers, but he didn't seem to give a damn. As soon as I loosened, he thrust deeper, as if he could pretend it was his cock as well.

Bray had stood, my cunt wet and pulsing and desperately empty. Dane took his spot, but instead of dropping down, he lined up his cock and sank into me.

My pussy tightened around him, the feeling overwhelming on my sensitive body. He didn't pause, though, didn't go slow. He plunged his thick cock into me, his hand on my hip to hold me still, forcing my body to take every last inch.

And I wanted that. Fuck, I wanted him, all of him, everything he could give me.

Colton moved from my nipple, using his fingers instead to pinch it, to make sure I got no rest, no chance to gain my footing. Still, it gave Dane more room to fuck me as hard as he wanted. Rune withdrew his fingers, then slid them into my hair in a tight grip.

"You could have died," Dane said, frustration in his voice. "If that bullet had been a few inches over, you could have fucking bled out and died right there."

"So?" I asked, meaning it.

"So?" He bottomed out as he asked, now grasping both my hips in his hands.

"Yeah. So. Fucking. What? Everyone dies."

His gaze was angry, as if my words pissed him off.

Too bad.

I knew better than most what death was like, knew it was the thing we were all headed for. If the men had killed me, I'd be dead.

What the fuck did I care, then?

Rune used his grip on my hair to pull me back, to stretch me out on the table. Dane moved my legs, lifting them and spreading them out, so he could grip my waist from beneath them. It exposed me, made it so he could fuck me as hard as he wanted and gave him one hell of a view.

"I don't want to find your dead body," Rune snapped.

"Too bad."

Colton leaned back in and bit harder on my nipple. He might not have anything to say in words, but that told me he didn't appreciate my opinion.

And it melted more of that resolve inside me. It brought to life everything that had sat below that calm surface of water, the parts of me that had sunk beneath years of not caring about anything.

"You're not going to get yourself killed," Rune said, his grip in my hair solid. "I won't *let* you."

"You can't control everything," I countered.

The table groaned, and I found Bray crawling on top of it. It held, though. He slid above me—careful to avoid my shoulder—and bracketed my head with his knees. It didn't take a genius to know what he planned, with his hard cock inches from my waiting lips.

Before he gave me what we both wanted, though, he stared down at me, his gaze intense. I didn't know what he was trying to say with that look, one full of anger and frustration and need. I gave him the same look back, because I had all those things, too, feelings too powerful for me to deal with, feelings *they'd* woken inside me.

He grasped my chin, holding me still as he rubbed the head of his cock against my lips. I darted my tongue out, unable to help it, to collect the pre-cum at the tip of his shaft. He groaned, then pressed his length into the warmth of my mouth.

I couldn't do anything. He had my good arm trapped and my bad arm was stuck in the sling. I had Dane fucking me to within an inch of my life, and now Bray thrust his cock past my lips, using my mouth as though it were my cunt.

Colton still abused my nipple, and each time he plucked it, each time he tugged or twisted it, I arched off the table.

It was all *too* much.

My saying yes struck me as a stupid fucking decision suddenly. I'd thought I could handle this? That I had what it took to fuck all four of them and be fine? That I wouldn't shatter beneath their experience, their demands, their talent?

And yet, I felt oddly safe. Despite knowing I'd never been in more danger — both to my life and my heart — I relaxed into it. I gave in to them, into what I'd wanted since I'd been old enough to know what it was.

I came again once, or maybe twice? Time slid together, confusing my senses, and I lost myself in the rhythm. They had to have done this together before, because they were synchronized perfectly. As soon as Dane pulled back, Bray pressed in. I was never empty, never alone, never had time to think or worry.

Dane's thrusts turned harder, wilder. He fucked me as if possessed, as if he had no idea how to stop. He set his hands on my knees, spreading me wider, and even without seeing him, I could *feel* his gaze on my cunt. "You look good all spread out," he said with panting breaths. "Your cunt's wrapped around my cock like a fist. You're going to take my cum like a good girl, aren't you?"

I couldn't nod, not with Rune's hand behind my head, not with Bray's cock deep in my mouth. Even if I could have, I wasn't sure I would have.

Part of me craved their praise, wanted to be a good girl for them.

Another part, a bigger and stronger part, wanted to tell them to fuck off. It wanted them to take me, wanted them to prove they really wanted me. Fuck being a good girl. I hadn't been a good girl in a long damn time, and I had no intention of trying to turn into one again. I wanted to be difficult and bad and make them prove themselves to me.

Dane didn't need an answer, and a sudden pinch to my exposed clit — not by Dane, since he still held my knees open — sent me over that edge again just as Dane came. I made the filthiest sounds, all muffled around Bray's cock, careful not to bite even as my brain and body were thrown into absolute chaos.

Rune pressed up on the back of my head at the same time Bray sank deeper, plunging farther into my throat to come as well.

I couldn't swallow, didn't need to, and Bray didn't stay that deep for long. When he pulled back, I gagged and sputtered, gulping in air, the residual taste of his cock and his seed coating my tongue.

Bray didn't move away at first, staring down at me. Was he trying to memorize the sight? His lips were still set in that tight line, the one that said he didn't like that we'd done this, that he'd been a part of it, and that he didn't much like me, either.

Too fucking bad. A man couldn't complain about his feelings about a woman when she could still taste him on her tongue.

His gaze softened for a moment that passed so fast, I wondered if I'd seen it at all. As quickly as it happened, however, it was gone, replaced with an even angrier glare.

"Get off me," I snapped, giving him back every bit of the hatred he'd shown.

He didn't argue, moving off me just as Dane pulled out as well. I held in the gasp at how even that set me off, at how wonderfully used my cunt felt. They had seemed to fire up every nerve inside me, turning the power up to the top, so even the air blowing across my clit was far too much.

Dane ran his hands along my thighs once more before pulling away, reluctance in the move.

I shifted, making me remember that a table had no real cushioning, and that I'd squirmed a lot against the hard surface.

Before I could complain about it—I had no problem bitching at the Quad over it—Rune gathered me against him. I wrapped my arm around him because I couldn't not do it. It was as though even now, even after so much time, I knew him and trusted him.

Stupid.

Still, my lips found his, drawn by history and want and pain. This was what I'd needed, the way they sparked things to life inside of me that I'd given up on. They weren't all good, but they were *something.* I was drowning in desire and angry at our past and so damned lonely from the years of loss.

It all overwhelmed me, but I took it out on him, on them all. I kissed him, my hand moving to the back of his head to hold him still for me, his long hair entwined between my fingers.

We dropped, but I didn't bother to break the kiss to see where we were. I didn't care, not more than everything else that took my attention. I ended up in his lap, my knees pressed against something soft. *The couch?* I just didn't care so long as it didn't keep me from this.

And the press of Rune's cock said it didn't keep me from anything. I shifted up, needing to be filled again, to experience that perfect stretch as I took him deep inside me. He didn't disappoint, either.

The burn shoved a moan from me when I lowered my hips, when I sank down on his hard cock. If he made a sound, I didn't hear it—I was too wrapped up in my own head, my body, in my reactions to each sound and taste and touch.

Hands stroked over my back, my waist, then across the curve of my ass. The touch when they spread my cheeks, however, was the one I focused on. It was enough for me to break my kiss with Rune and glance over my shoulder.

Colton stood there, locking his gaze with mine just as he pressed his very wet thumb against my ass. He lifted his eyebrow—a dare? Was he waiting for me to complain, to chicken out?

I'd wanted this, though, and that meant *all* of it. I wanted everything they could give me, to walk away knowing I hadn't missed out on anything. This would all end as soon as I found Kenz, when I faced Kyler, when it would kill me one way or another. I'd died once with so many regrets—I wouldn't let that happen again.

When I didn't stop him, he narrowed his eyes, but even that couldn't hide the want in his expression. He pressed that thumb forward, into my ass, taking me in a way no one ever had, in a way I hadn't even *considered* before.

Not that I was naive by any means. I knew about anal sex, but it wasn't the sort of thing I'd ever thought about trying myself—well, trying ever, but since I hadn't planned on having a partner, on my own had been the only option. However, when Colton looked at me like that, when the thought of being so fully taken by the men who already had so much of me, I couldn't resist.

The sensation was odd. It wasn't painful, though it wasn't particularly pleasurable either, at least at first. It was overwhelming in a new way, something I couldn't easily define or categorize, though each moment that passed woke more nerve endings inside me.

Little waves of pleasure arced through me, sparking around my body as though that were its way of coming to terms with so much new. Rune didn't move, buried deep inside my cunt, as that almost made it worse. It made me focus fully on Colton, on how his thumb tunneled into me, smoothly from what had to be lube, and my pussy squeezed down in response.

The sound that spilled from my lips said it all. It was soft yet strong, a surrender and a demand for more.

Colton read it for exactly what it was and pulled his thumb free, replacing it with two of his long, agile fingers.

I twisted back toward Rune, but I didn't kiss him. I couldn't focus enough for that. Instead, I rested my forehead against his shoulder, shuddering when that seemed all I was capable of.

It was odd, the sense of peace, the safety in Rune's wide chest, in the familiar sandalwood scent that clung to his hair, even in Colton's insistent touches and Dane's and Bray's lingering stares.

Instead of fighting it — fighting the impossible never worked out — I let myself have it. Was it stupid? Insane? Dangerous? Absolutely. That didn't change it just was.

I could try to pretend that wasn't true, I could tell myself all the reasons I needed to keep my wits about me, but that would only steal the moment from me. I'd spend the whole time in my own head instead of experiencing this, instead of savoring it.

So I gave in to it. Jarrod had taught me many things, but one was that fighting the inevitable was pointless. It was better to go with it and look for options later.

Sure, he probably hadn't mean it in *this* circumstance — as in, me getting plowed by the Quad — but it didn't make it any less true.

So I let that current take me. I could deal with the consequences later.

Colton's knuckles pressed against me, telling me he'd fed every bit of his fingers into me. He twisted that hand, stroking the joints of his fingers over the sensitive walls of my ass, and I dug my fingers against Rune as another orgasm threatened to roll through me.

My skin felt thin and electric, so even the brush of air against it was way too much.

"You feel so good," Rune whispered into my ear, his voice deep and vibrating through where I touched him as well. "Your cunt is heaven."

"Her ass is so tight," Colton said. "I swear, I don't think anyone has ever taken it. Fucking criminal with how much I can tell she likes it." He paired the words with pulling out and pressing three fingers against me, the burn enough for me to whine through my gritted teeth.

It didn't just blur the line between pleasure and pain, it removed it entirely. That fit, though, didn't it?

We weren't simple — we never could have been.

Simple, sweet sex was for simple, sweet people. It was for those who went on perfect little dates at candlelit restaurants and were headed for white picket fences.

That wasn't us. It wouldn't have been, even before it all went wrong.

Now, though?

We were rough, angry sex just to come to terms with feelings we couldn't seem to grapple with any other way. And it wasn't just me.

It was in the way Colton fucked me with his thick fingers, as if he needed to own me. It was in the way Rune whispered filth into my ear. It was in how Dane wrapped his hand around my throat when fucking me and how Bray never looked at me with anything less than confused hatred.

We were broken — shards of glass that couldn't ever fit right and just kept cutting each other up as we tried.

So Colton fucking my ass, stretching me to make room for his dick, that was right in line with the rest of our fucked up dynamic.

Rune rolled his hips, the action reminding me of his cock, of how deep inside me he was, of how he could tease my pussy with such a small motion.

I shifted as well, needing something to take my mind off how overwhelming Colton was.

Rune grabbed my hips, pulling me snuggly against him, not giving me any room to move, to gain reprieve. "Feel it," he whispered. "Feel every damn thing he does. Is he right? You never had your ass fucked before?"

I didn't shake my head, refused to give him the answer. It took me back to being that teenager again, to them seeing me as some little girl not worthy of their time. I didn't want those looks again.

He huffed, his warm breath sliding over my ear. "You don't need to answer — it's pretty damn clear. So, I want you to feel it all, not to distract you with anything else, and I want you to know that next, he's going to slide his cock into your ass, and you're going to fucking love it."

It wasn't fear that skittered through me at that, even though it should have been. Instead, I was all on for that plan. Would it hurt? Maybe. Did I care?

Not even a little.

I'd burn to nothing with them if that was what it took.

"I thought about taking your ass," Rune admitted, his words making me feel everything all the more. "You'd be such a tight fit, wouldn't you? Except, I prefer your cunt. See, there is nothing better than filling your pussy up with cum, than seeing it leak out of you, then pushing it back into you. You got any idea what a turn-on that is for me? You've got the sort of body just meant to be bred."

Bred. He'd told me that before, but I'd thought it a passing fancy.

It seemed he had a pretty specific kink, and while the idea of actual kids held zero interest from me, I couldn't deny that it turned me on when he said it like that. It wasn't about having kids, or the sweet 'trying-to-conceive' that normal, married folks did.

Instead, this was primal, animalistic. It was like giving in to instincts, into old desires to fuck, to breed, to own. It felt like a pack, where the strongest got to breed the females, and like Rune, I wanted *that*.

So no matter how weird it might have struck me at any other time, it seemed when my head was clouded by lust and orgasms, I was on board for pretty much anything Rune said.

"You think you're strong enough that I'd let you do that?" I asked, my words broken and breathless, daring him to prove his strength.

He let out a feral sound that drew a pleased shiver through me. "Yeah, Nem, I am. And if you need proof of it, I ain't got any problem showing you."

"How would you do that?" The last word came out weaker than I wanted, since that was the moment Colton removed his fingers from me.

I knew what was coming next, but I focused on my battle of wills with Rune, not wanting to tense, to work myself up about what was to come.

"I'd spread these thighs of yours and fuck your pretty little cunt until I came. I wouldn't let you come, at least not yet. Filthy girl like you might not be able to hold off for long, though." He twisted to nip my earlobe, leaving a sting that make me clench around his cock. "I wouldn't tie you down—wouldn't need to. I prefer holding you down myself, or letting my brothers help out, make it clear we're more than enough to handle little ol' you."

The images of what he said swamped me, made me have to hold in a plea for exactly that. I thought about how strong he was, how strong they all were, and how he could do exactly what he claimed.

And how he was right—I wouldn't be able to hold off long.

Colton pressed his cock against my ass, slippery enough to tell me he'd lubed himself up well, and the pressure was terrifying and exciting.

It was like sitting at the top of a roller coaster, seeing the twists and turns and the loops a moment before diving forward.

"After I had my turn, Colton would go next. He's quick, usually, and more than a little rough. We'd make sure no one touched your slutty little clit, no matter how much you begged. After that, Bray would take a turn. You'd be so wet from all our cum, that he'd slide in easily. He's damn thick, and even after so many dicks, you'd feel it. Last would be Dane, because he likes to wait, to fuck a girl after she's so tired and sensitive that it's damn near torture. You'd be crying by then, wanting to come, and fuck if that wouldn't be exactly what I like."

The first inch of Colton's cock plunged into my ass when he pushed past the tight ring of muscles, and I couldn't hide the whine I made that time.

"Fuck, I like that sound," Colton said, not giving me a moment of rest. He pulled back the tiniest amount before another sharp jerk forward seated him deeper. He wasn't gentle, didn't go slow, but fucked me with those quick, hard jabs as if to prove he owned me.

And I was pretty sure at this point he did—they all did. It was like they'd gotten inside me so deep and so early that they'd twisted me, that no other men could ever take this place or satisfy me in this way.

Rune bit my earlobe again, as if punishing me for my wandering focus. "Then, after we all had a turn? I'd hold those legs wide and fuck your messy, full cunt again. See, you are *ours*, Nem. No fucking idea what that means or why, but what better way of proving it than marking you, then breeding you like our own little bitch, hmm?"

I should have punched him for that, should have told him I was no one's little bitch. I would have shot anyone else for such a statement.

So why didn't I? Why did my pussy react with another frustrating pulse and my heart speed?

Because I'm an idiot and these men are further beneath my skin than even I realized...

I didn't need to say anything, though, my body had said more than enough. With Colton pressed against my back, telling me he'd filled me entirely, Rune lifted his hips from beneath me.

The two men didn't set a rhythm. They didn't plan, didn't work together. Instead, it was as if the two of them were so crazed with need, they fucked me exactly how each wanted, and I was trapped in the middle, between their bodies, between hate and love, between the past and the present.

I dangled on that precipice, terrified to move in either direction, pulled in both.

It was that fight which made it impossible to hold out any longer, to keep myself from falling into the ecstasy that beckoned.

The last orgasm hit me hard, more consuming than the others. I cried out against Rune's shoulder as my entire body seized, as my muscles tightened and the tension inside me drew to a painful point.

It went silent.

In that moment, sinking deeper into my release, everything drifted away. Blissful silence came over me, a sense of peace I hadn't known really existed.

Rune groaned against my ear as he came, and Colton slammed into me, as deep as he could, before shuddering in his own release.

Those things were a distant thought, to me. Instead, I embraced the quiet, the calm, the way that for just a second everything made sense.

Or maybe nothing made sense and that was enough for me.

As quickly as it happened, however, one second passed to the next and I gasped in a breath. I was exhausted, worn down to the bone and content in a way that confused and frightened me.

Rune pressed his lips to my ear, a touch far too sweet, and I discovered yet another new feeling these men could inspire in me…

Panic.

Chapter Sixteen

Nem

Good lord, as it turned out, banging four guys took a lot out of a girl. I should have expected it, but pornography made it all look so easy.

They didn't show the next day, the aches, the sore muscles, the hickeys or marks from bites.

Then again, maybe that was like romance novels not showing how a year down the road, the leading man had stopped washing his ass. People like to see the good, the exciting, and forget the rest, the reality and the aftermath.

A good night's sleep had helped me put myself back together after the huge mistake of having sex with the Quad.

I'd known it hadn't been smart, but by the end, it had become clear just how stupid the choice had been. I'd wanted to feel something and had ended up overwhelmed by it all.

Be careful what you wish for.

It hadn't really happened until the end, until that last orgasm had cracked me wide open, when I'd leaned against Rune, when I'd lifted my head to see Bray and Dane staring at me, and I'd wanted….

Something.

I hadn't dared allow myself to take that thought to its conclusion, to consider what I wanted, because it wasn't possible.

For *so* many reasons.

I doubted they wanted anything real. I couldn't trust them and I'd likely be dead soon anyway. All of it meant this was cursed from the start, and that terrifying moment of desire had made me shut down...*hard*.

At least that was my reaction to panic. It would have been far more difficult to extract myself from that loaded situation if I'd actually had some sort of panic attack, if I'd let on how deeply unsettled they'd made me.

Instead, I'd welcomed that coldness again and let it consume me, had allowed it to hide anything I felt beneath miles of solid ice.

Whether they'd noticed anything or not, I didn't know nor care. They'd served their purpose, had gotten off and gotten me off—even I couldn't lie about how much I'd enjoyed it—so I figured our little transaction was completed.

At least, that was how I played it off.

Now, I stared at the walls of the room I'd slept in, the one I'd been given, and felt as though I'd crawl out of my skin. Staying in one place hadn't been something I'd ever been good at.

It had probably started from moving around so much as a child, and had continued in my life with

Jarrod. It was made worse because this wasn't *my* space. It was theirs.

They were everywhere in the house. Each had left their marks in the décor, the colors, the furniture. It had Bray's minimalism, Dane's humor, Colton's weapons and Rune's masculine edge.

Finally, I gave up and left the room.

It was Saturday, and I had talked the men — and Kyler by extension — into allowing me back into the office on Monday. It meant I had an entire weekend to kill, and I couldn't very well do that sitting in the room by myself.

Besides, I'd spotted a library in an office through one of the doorways when I'd come in the day before, and if nothing else, I could steal something to read.

I heard nothing through the house. They hadn't all left me — there was no way I could have gotten that lucky. I figured they were either hiding out somewhere, or possibly outside.

Either way, I savored my moment of privacy. I went down the hallway to the kitchen, finding a pot of coffee already brewed. I poured a cup, then added two cubes of sugar from the bowl beside it.

The coffee was stronger than I normally made, the sort of brewing method that said they'd gotten used to drinking bad coffee from a lot of places.

Still, bad caffeine was monumentally better than no caffeine at all.

I took the cup with me to the left, toward the office I remembered. I found it, the door cracked open. It had a large oak desk in the center, though it didn't seem it got much use. That meant it wasn't Bray's office. No doubt, he had monitors and cords strewn about his.

Behind the desk, which faced the door, was a full wall bookshelf. The books lined the shelves nicely, though there didn't appear to be room for new ones. Had they filled it and started using space elsewhere?

I ran my finger along the spines, tilting my head to read the titles. *Body Language for Beginners. The Human Lie Detector. The Mind in Chaos – How to Read People Under Stress. How to Move Through Grief and Loss.*

That last one made me pause, my fingers stilling over the writing. For a moment, I wondered…

No, that's absurd. They probably just have it to fill the shelf so they look smarter.

However, since nearly all the books were on behavior, on body language and communication, I was clued in to whose office I'd stumbled into.

It belonged to Dane.

Knowing that didn't change anything, though, so I tried to look for something he had that wouldn't bore me further. I understood body language fairly well and had no desire to waste my time nose-deep in a book about psychology.

"You know, going through people's stuff is rude."

I turned to find the devil himself leaning against the doorframe.

"You know, shoving people into a room with no source of entertainment is also rude. Maybe we should call it even?"

"I think we entertained you enough last night."

I gave him a smile intended to belittle him. "Turns out that didn't last all that long."

"Such sharp words for a girl who probably is still wincing when she sits." He smirked, then walked into the room and beside me, so he was looking at the bookshelf, too. "I don't have a lot of fun reading here."

"So I've seen. Do you do anything but work?"

"Sure, but I don't read much unless it serves a purpose. Otherwise, I prefer other interests."

I could have asked him about those other interests, but judging by the way he grinned, I knew the answer would be a joke — and filthy.

I turned to give him a flat look, one that said I didn't find him funny, when my gaze landed on something that stopped me in my tracks.

A silver frame sat there with three pictures inside it. One of my mother, one of Kenz — from when she was a child — and one of me.

I hadn't seen pictures of myself from then, because I hadn't had access to any. Seeing it made me freeze.

My hair had been chin-length and dark. I recalled how I had fought with my mother about cutting it above my shoulders, how Colton had broken up the argument before I'd gotten myself into trouble by escorting me out of the room.

I never knew why she'd changed her mind afterward. Maybe she'd realized she were being unreasonable. Maybe I'd just worn her down. Either way, she'd agreed to let me cut it to the length in the photo a week later.

I looked so different in that picture, though, so young. So naive. My stomach churned in response, unable to help it when I came face to face with the girl I had been, the one who had died that night.

I hated that girl in so many ways, hated how stupid she'd been, how she'd let Kyler fool her into believing she was safe, into letting them *all* convince her she was safe.

I bore the scars, the proof of her stupidity.

Dane turned, following my gaze, and his smirk left his lips. After a moment, he nodded at it. "Caroline, Mackenzie and Kelsey."

My old name on his lips *hurt*. It was a pain that laced through me, like he'd torn off a scab.

I kept my face blank. "Caroline was beautiful."

"She was," Dane admitted. "But she was more than that. She was smart and tough in a world that doesn't always like to recognize that in women."

The remark threw me, made me frown. It was more honest than I'd expected. "I'm sorry she's gone."

He nodded, then reached for the picture.

No, not that one, but *my* photo. He stared down, his expression impossible for me to read.

"What was she like?" I asked, no idea why I asked. It was a dangerous question, but I couldn't keep it to myself.

His knuckles had blanched as he gripped the frame. "She was smart, like her mother. Too old for her years, but I always tried to make sure she didn't have to grow up faster than she needed to."

I remembered how he had turned me down when I'd tried to kiss him, and yeah...he'd seen me as a child. "Maybe you saw her as a kid when she wasn't anymore," I pointed out.

"Maybe," he admitted softly. "It doesn't really matter anymore, does it?"

I forced myself to ask one more question, one that was far more dangerous than any before but one that had kept me up at night. "What I don't understand is how they died. You four are supposed to be the best there is. How were they killed if you all are as good as everyone says?"

He gripped the frame tighter until it groaned. "You think we had something to do with it, don't you? You wouldn't be the first to think that. It's convenient that all four of us were gone, right?"

"Well, did you have anything to do with it?"

He set the picture back down, red coating the edge. He'd sliced his thumb on the sharp edge from the pressure of his grasp. "Answering questions doesn't matter. You think we did or you don't, but nothing I say will change your mind. If you want better reading material, go look in Rune's office—three doors down. He has fiction."

With that, Dane shook his head and walked out, leaving me with more questions than answers.

Especially since he didn't actually answer my biggest one.

Were they part of the plan to kill me?

* * * *

Rune calling my name made me frown.

I sat on a swing in the backyard, and he had called as if he wasn't sure where I was. I had no doubt that they kept close tabs on me, that they always knew exactly where I was in the house.

So why was he shouting for me as though he had to search for me?

I twisted toward the door, and the reason made itself clear.

Kyler stood beside Rune.

That meant Rune had offered the odd call of my name as a warning? It had helped, since spotting Kyler out of the blue might have proven more difficult to hide a reaction to.

I rose to my feet—staying seated around Kyler felt like letting a wolf come near when I was flat on my ass. I preferred to be on my feet.

The strangest thing was when his lips curled into a smile...

Had I ever seen him have one as a child? He'd been stern, usually at least seeming slightly annoyed about something—sometimes me, but rarely did I matter enough for him to take notice of. I wasn't sure he'd ever looked pleased to see me.

"Kyler." I held the book I'd stolen from Rune's library in my grasp, giving me something for my hands to do.

He nodded, then dropped his gaze to my sling. "How is your shoulder?"

"Better," I assured him. "It isn't as bad as it looks. Just a graze, really." No need to mention the lingering pain—or how I hadn't been taking the pain pills.

The last thing I needed was a repeat of the night with the men, and pain pills led me to make stupid choices.

"Good," he said, then turned a sharp look toward Rune. "I would like some privacy."

Rune didn't respond, but I knew him well enough to read annoyance. It was in the tic of his jaw, in the way he went entirely still. No doubt, he didn't care for being ordered around in his home.

Then again, it wasn't as if he could say anything to Kyler. At the end of the day, Kyler could do whatever the hell he wanted, and for a reason I still couldn't understand, the Quad let him get away with it.

Rune nodded after meeting my gaze for a split second, then turned and walked back inside.

Being alone with Kyler was as strange as it had been each time. That hard edge of his expression slid away, as if unpeeling a mask he wore for others' sake.

He nodded at the swing again before taking his own seat on the chair across from it.

I lowered myself onto the swing, unsure what to say.

"I wanted to apologize," he said, the words taking me off guard. That might have been the last thing I'd expected him to say. Thankfully, he kept speaking. "What happened, it never should have happened."

"It's okay," I assured him. "You can't be everywhere at once."

He shook his head. "I'm supposed to be. They targeted you because they were cowards and wanted me. That makes this my fault, and for that, I apologize. You shouldn't have to fear attacks like this just for working with me."

With? The wording struck me as odd. I worked for him, not with. It was a level of familiarity that made my skin crawl.

Unsure what to say—I wasn't often caught speechless, especially with stakes so high—I sat there, silent.

Kyler let out a laugh that reeked of nerves. "I just wanted to say, I put the Quad on your protection to assure you that it won't happen again. They are the best at what they do, and after my wife…" He paused.

He almost looked sorry.

Which didn't make a damn bit of sense. "I asked Dane about that."

He lifted an eyebrow, a reminder that despite how well he played at sorrow, he was dangerous. "And?"

"And, he said a lot of people think the Quad had something to do with their deaths."

"I'd considered that, at the time. The fact they left just before, giving them a perfect alibi and excuse to not be there is more than a little suspicious."

"But?"

"But nothing." Kyler shrugged. "I have no proof either way, and I couldn't find a reason they would have done it while leaving my youngest untouched. In the years since, I've had no reason to suspect them, so that rumor has remained just that — a rumor."

"If you think they might have helped kill your wife and daughter" — boy, that word was hard to get out — "then why would you trust them with my protection?"

"Because if they did that, it was for a reason I can't figure out. Power, perhaps? They knew something they shouldn't have? No matter what, there wouldn't be such a reason to harm you." He sighed, leaning back. "You know, having to look at everyone as a potential threat is hard. It is exhausting to never be able to just relax, to feel some sort of easiness around other people."

I understood that. At least, I did now, after seeing what people were capable of. I guess seeing my mother killed in front of me, feeling the bullets meant to murder me tearing through my body, all at the order of the man who was supposedly my father, could do that to a person. It was one hell of a wakeup call.

"I understand that," I responded.

"Do you? You don't look like someone who has had to deal with that much." The edge of his voice told me to tread carefully.

Careful now, the best lies are ones with bits of the truth to make them go down easier. "Yes. I was raised up north, in the Bay Area. My father worked a lot and wasn't ever home, and we lived in a bad area of the city. It was just my mother and I, and I saw how ugly the world is, how people will take advantage whenever they can."

Kyler's gaze was solid as he stared at me, as though picking apart the story. "And that explains why you're so good at what you do."

I furrowed my brows.

He went on. "You work so hard, are so successful, because you've seen the dangers of poverty, of powerlessness, and you don't want to ever experience that again."

His words struck me in the face like a backhand.

Even with the lie I'd given him, he'd somehow picked out the truth, one I wouldn't have even been able to voice on my own.

He offered a smile that felt far more condescending than I liked, as if he found it endearing I either questioned his statement or that I hadn't expected him to understand it. "I wasn't always what I am now."

"What were you before?" I asked.

"Poor. Weak. *Useless.*" He spat each word with the hatred born of a man who had spent years loathing those things. "Most of these powerful men you see, they were born into it. They were gifted their positions from their parents in this never-ending cycle of unearned power. The oldest families aren't the strongest or the smartest—they're simply so entrenched that they're like weeds with deep roots. That wasn't me, though. My mother worked in a cheap strip club, and I grew up in the back rooms, watching what happened to the people who got walked on by everyone else. I swore I'd never let that happen to me."

His story was unexpected. He'd never told me any of this as a kid, and I wondered if my own mother had known. It couldn't have been common knowledge, could it? Kyler wasn't the sort of man who would want people to realize he came from such a low start.

"So how did you end up where you are?"

The obvious answer was marrying my mother, but I had no idea how that had happened. She'd never spoken about it, and Jarrod hadn't, either. No matter how much I had begged for more information from Jarrod, he'd remained tight-lipped.

Kyler leaned forward, his elbows coming to rest on his knees. "The thing is, people only get what they're willing to fight for. I started learning, listening, gathering everything I could. Men tend to spill a lot of secrets in those clubs. By the time I was sixteen, I already had a crew, was already a name, even if it wasn't a big one. I kept working, never willing to rest, did what others weren't willing to. When I hit twenty, I realized there was this ceiling I couldn't get past. The Williams name didn't hold the power to contend with the others, the Rodriguezes, the Romanos, the Hesters."

That last one was, of course, the most important. My mother's maiden name.

He paused, then sighed. "The Hesters," he repeated, a soft laugh in his voice. "That's what Caroline was, my wife. I won't deny that her name drew me in first, since she was the last of that family, the last of this legacy, this royalty line. It would connect me to the one thing I didn't have — a legitimate bloodline."

"You married her for her name?"

"Yes and no. I needed that name, but she fascinated me. She was tough and far too smart for her own good. Maybe we weren't in love the way people think love is supposed to feel, but that didn't make it a bad marriage."

"I can't imagine her parents were happy to have the last of their name married to someone who…" I paused when I realized there was no way to end that sentence without an insult.

At least he didn't seem offended. "Someone without any standing? No, they weren't happy about it, but Caroline was difficult to argue with, even for them. She pressed and eventually, they gave in. They didn't live long after — a car accident took them a few weeks before the wedding. Still, Caroline's name opened a lot of doors for me, gave me access to people who would have never talked to me without."

A few of the pieces I'd never quite understood came together, but not all of them. Kyler's thirst for power had always seemed odd, but it was easier to understand it after his story.

He wanted what he hadn't had, what he didn't really think himself deserving of.

"The thing is," he went on, "I thought those big names were a key, a way to unlock doorways to everything I ever wanted. I've realized since then that they're a trap. No matter what I do, I can't get away from that Hester name. It's attached to everything I do, as though I couldn't have done this all without it. It's like, my accomplishments are assigned to it instead of *me*." His voice dropped, anger seething through it.

I wanted to tell him he was right — he'd stolen that from my mother, had decided to kill her and me to own that name, to use it as he pleased, and that I'd make him pay for it. I'd rip everything he'd gotten from that family line away from him, because none of it belonged to him.

Before I could say something more in line with my game, however, he leveled me a hard look. "Be grateful you come from nothing. The old names are cursed, and the people who carry them are just walking corpses."

Well, he's right about that...

Chapter Seventeen

Nem

I might have fallen to my knees and kissed the ground if I wasn't certain Rune or Colton would have taken advantage of the position.

Returning to the office after days of being cooped up in their house felt like breaking free of prison. I wanted to throw my arms out and twirl like in an old movie, feeling the sense of freedom.

Sure, I still had shadows—two of the Quad trailed me like cock-blocking babysitters—but at least I could see something other than the walls of their house.

They'd ended up keeping me cooped up an additional three days until I'd broken down and *begged* Kyler over the phone to let me go out. I could be shameless when I wanted, and it was easier to beg when I got to pretend it wasn't me.

It was the character I was playing, and she was desperate to get back to work.

Rather than that, what I needed was enough space to finish my plan on how to get to the final person on my list—Carlos. After retiring, he had seemed to set himself up happily in a compound which he rarely left. He had a good security detail, making hitting him at his house not the best of ideas.

The best way to handle someone entrenched was to make them come out of their thick walls, then herd them in the direction I wanted until they fell into my trap. Such methods would be safest with Carlos. Give him a reason to leave, ensure a flat tire while out, then deal with him on the side of the road, when he had fewer security guards and lacked the home field advantage.

Still, having a plan and setting it into motion were different. I needed the men off my ass before I could carry it out.

It meant seeing the large office building—cleaned up and with upgraded security measures, according to Kyler—was a blessing.

At the front desk, I found Kyler hadn't been joking about the changes. Instead of the one guard, there were four. In addition, another stood before the elevator. He took one look at me and nodded, the deference given to someone they knew better than to fuck with.

What has Kyler been saying about me?

When the doors closed, Colton made a soft, telling sound.

I turned, my eyebrow lifted. His gaze was locked on my ass, a hunger there that left no room for confusion on what he was thinking about.

Like about how it had felt to fuck my ass…

He met my gaze, no apology in his expression. "Don't blame me," he said. "You're the one who has spent the last few days hiding."

"If you're expecting me to apologize for not spreading my legs whenever you want, you're going to be waiting for a very long time."

"It's funny how you talk to us compared to how you talk to Kyler. What would he think of *this* girl? Pretty sure he wouldn't be so smitten if you were this foul mouthed and contrary to him."

"I have no idea what you're talking about," I lied.

Colton snorted. "I wonder which of you is the real you. Maybe neither."

"This is the real her," Rune said, forcing me to turn fully to face both of them. "You can't hide everything, not when you're as mindless as we've gotten her. No way to pretend to be anything other than what she is — which is the best fucking pussy I've had in a long-damned time."

I should *not* have liked that. The words were vulgar and dehumanizing and yet I was drenched from them. Maybe it was the way he stared at me, or how despite his words, I knew it wasn't just what was between my thighs he was talking about.

I swallowed hard, trying not to let it all show on my face. "Maybe," I said. "Or maybe I'm just a really good actress. Faking orgasms is the first thing any smart girl learns. It throws men off their game."

Rune narrowed his eyes, the green nearly disappearing.

And that turned me on even more. It was the challenge there, the way he rose to the occasion, to my insults, to my challenge.

The ding of the elevator, a split second before the doors slid open, was my savior. No doubt he'd been considering how to shove me against that elevator wall and show me exactly how little I needed to fake *anything*. And he would have been right, because each time they'd gotten their hands on me, I'd fallen deeper into whatever we were doing, into a trap I wasn't sure how to pull myself free from.

I turned on my heel and strolled from the elevator as if we'd been talking about what we wanted to pick up for lunch rather than whether or not I'd been faking orgasms.

The receptionist smiled at me, and I was glad to see she hadn't been in the building when the attackers had been there. She was far too sweet to end with a bullet.

From what I'd heard, six others had been killed that night. A few attorneys, two members of the janitorial crew and a food delivery person who had just been in the wrong place at the wrong time. Kyler had swept it all under the rug, of course. No one wanted police sniffing around the building, given what else they could accidentally uncover.

Instead, the right palms were greased with more than a little money, and an elevator accident was staged for the employees. The delivery man was simply reported missing and the records of his stop at the office erased.

It was like it had never happened. As I walked down the hallway, even the paint colors matched from where they must have patched up the wall.

"You okay?" Rune asked.

It was then I realized I'd stopped in my tracks, staring at the spot that couldn't be distinguished from the areas around it. "I should know better by now, but it always surprises me how easily violence is washed away. Something horrible happened here, but it's like it's all gone, like it never happened. That should have stained this place, like blood on a shirt, but we manage to just bleach it all away."

The words slipped from me before I could consider them. They were foolish and too real and far too telling. They didn't just mean the place, either. I thought about what people saw when looking at me, when looking at Kyler, when seeing both the victims and perpetrators of violence, and how those things didn't stick. It was so easy to not see them.

A hand rested on my shoulder, and I turned to see it was Rune's, that he squeezed gently as if not sure how else to help.

That woke me up.

I offered a quick shake of my head, as clear a sign as I could give that I was fine, that I wouldn't break down, that we could keep moving.

That was all a person could really do, at the end of the day, was keep moving forward. The bullet holes might get patched, and the wounds might heal, but life was just about putting one foot in front of the other.

No matter what.

Three hours later, my head throbbed. Maybe it was from having taken a few days off, from the nagging pain in my shoulder that never quite went away, from how I hadn't been able to sleep worth a damn.

It turned out wearing a sling to bed didn't make for restful nights.

Whatever it was, I rubbed the corners of my eyes.

A sound on the desk had me opening my eyes to find Colton had set two blue gel capsules there.

I frowned at them. Having people do anything for me felt strange, made me stop and evaluate the reasoning, figure out what their real motivation was.

Colton giving me the pills could be him trying to curry favor. Perhaps he knew headaches were a fast way to a boring night for himself? Maybe he didn't want a headache affecting my next meeting, scheduled to start in around thirty minutes.

"I'm not poisoning you," he said, and he almost sounded...hurt?

"I didn't think you were." The fact that hadn't been on my list of maybes bothered me...

"But you were trying to figure out why I was giving them to you."

"Well, why are you?"

"Did it ever occur to you that I might just not like to see you in pain? You aren't taking the pain pills anymore, so these will take the edge off at least."

The answer seemed so obvious...so why hadn't I considered that one?

Because it was absurd. People never did anything just to help someone. There was always an ulterior motive.

"No, it didn't." I scooped the pills up and popped them into my mouth, dry swallowing them. "I'm too smart to believe that."

"And I thought I was jaded."

"I'm not jaded—just realistic. Everything a person does is for themselves. Everything has a reason, even if the person denies it, even if they don't realize it."

"So why'd you save Kyler?"

I went with a *close-enough* response. "Because if he died, my big opportunity here died with him."

"Uh-huh," he said, all the *yeah right* in his tone. "Why do parents take care of their kids?"

"Because they'll go to jail if they don't." At his look, I sighed and gave a better answer. "Because they're biologically programmed to care for them so they can pass on their genes."

He didn't respond, staring at me, drawing out more when I wanted the silence to end.

"Not all parents care for their kids, or haven't you looked around? There are plenty of shitty parents who don't give a damn about their children."

Colton tilted his head. "Those wounds of yours run deep, don't they? So much bleeding from them, I can't even call them scars — those things are still fresh."

Instead of giving him anything else — I'd given too much away today already — I tore my gaze from his and back to the paperwork before me. "Well, in that case, please stop poking at them."

Thankfully, Colton listened. He retreated from the office, though I knew neither he nor Rune went far. I'd hear their phones or voices occasionally, suggesting one sat across from the door, on a chair placed against the wall, and the other had taken the room just to the left of my office.

The one empty because the woman who had worked there had been murdered.

At least no one was uprooted for my safety, I guessed.

Ten minutes later, the phone on my desk rang. I hit the intercom button. "Yes?"

"Hello, Ms. Syler, Mr. Harrington is here to see you."

I glared at the clock on the wall, at how he'd shown twenty minutes early. People in the regular world thought early was good, but those of us with full schedules knew early could fuck a day over as easily as late could.

"Thank you, send him in."

The intercom went dead as I gathered up the paperwork, clearing the private items from the desk.

The door opened, but rather than the man I was to meet, Colton walked in. He gestured for me to follow.

"I have a meeting," I said as I rose to my feet.

"Yeah, I know, but you aren't taking it here."

"Why not?"

"It's safer to use the conference room. That way, no one who isn't here all the time knows which office is yours. It also gives us better visibility and keeps him farther away from you. This room isn't big enough."

"I'm sure he was patted down before he entered," I reminded Colton. "I don't need you to be paranoid."

"And I don't need you to take another bullet. You either do these meetings *my* way or you don't do them at all. And don't even think about complaining to Kyler. He trusts us to keep you safe."

I pressed my lips together, sealing in all the things I wanted to say.

Like he was an idiot. Like I didn't *need* his protection, and his presence was the only reason I'd been hurt in the first place. If I hadn't had them on my ass, I'd have been properly armed when those men had broken in, and I wouldn't have had an issue.

However, the set of his shoulders said he wasn't budging, and if I pushed much farther, I'd end up on his bad side.

And not in the good way. Not in the way that had me bent over the desk with his cock pounding into me.

Instead, I'd end up back in their house, locked up like some damsel in a tower.

I gathered the papers I needed — and yes, the slam of the desk drawer was probably overkill — before I followed him.

We went down the hallway, to the far end, and took a left. The conference room wasn't the one I'd nearly had the life choked out of me in, thankfully. I would have struggled to focus there. Instead, this was brightly lit, with large windows across one side. The blinds were drawn, and even a glance in the direction of the cord got a sharp jerk of Colton's head in response.

It seemed opening them was a safety concern, and he wasn't budging on those.

I didn't need to wonder where Rune was, since he opened the door and walked in a moment before the man I was set to meet did.

Liam Harrington was forty-eight, a wealthy and well-connected land developer, and the person standing between me and a large parcel of acreage Kyler needed for a project. I'd done my research, knew what it was worth, what Liam planned to do with it and the best plan for obtaining it.

It was moments like these I almost forgot that this was just a cover, that while I did actually handle real estate transactions, it was only to achieve my real goals. For me, it was people reading. Whatever business I was in, it rarely came down to the specifics, to the regulations or the details. It was all about people. Understand what they wanted, and I could always get what I wanted.

His gaze drifted up and down my body, the slow perusal of a man who thought he'd hit the jackpot.

When he finally met my gaze, his grin was nothing short of salacious.

Which would make this all even easier. Men thinking with their cocks were a breeze to manipulate. When their blood traveled south, it made convincing them of anything so much easier.

"Ms. Syler," he said, sticking his hand out.

I reached out, ignoring Rune's sharp glare from the side. "Mr. Harrington."

"Call me Liam." He brought my knuckles to his lips and pressed a kiss there rather than shaking my hand, and I just barely held in the gag.

Still, being underestimated had its advantages. No one feared a creature until they saw its teeth.

"Liam," I said, then gestured at a seat at the conference table. "Please, sit. Thank you for meeting on such short notice."

"Well, it was hard to say no when I saw what you sent over. That's an interesting proposal."

"It's a good proposal," I corrected him. "You haven't been able to unload that property in almost two years, and I'm offering a fair price."

"You're offering less than it's worth," he countered.

"Something is only worth what someone else will pay for it and given you've yet to find a buyer or the right project, I'm going to guess you're overestimating the worth of it."

He huffed a laugh, as if he thought my attempts were adorable. "I've got a few things in the works, things that are a lot more promising than what you're offering."

I waved off his statement. "I'm sure you've heard the saying a bird in the hand is worth two in the bush. Whatever you think you could possibly do with it months or years from now can't stand against what you can get for it today. We both know how tricky those projects are. The wrong inspector, the wrong city council member riled up, and all those plans come crumbling down. Are you really willing to turn your nose up at an easy cash offer? Besides, all that fresh capital could be put into new projects for you, could start making you more money now instead of a few years down the line."

Liam sat back as his gaze drifted from my face to my chest, telling me he'd tuned out my words.

If he'd ever heard them at all…

I got the feeling that the second he'd seen me he'd pegged me as a conquest, as someone to bed and otherwise ignore. Not only was he *not* planning on selling me the property, but he was no longer going to even consider it.

It didn't annoy me, because annoyance was rarely useful. Instead, I went with it, ready to use it to my advantage.

I leaned forward, making sure the action created cleavage where I had little of it. "My boss is awfully insistent I make this work. If I don't, I'm not sure where that leaves me." A quick glance to my side revealed Rune rolling his eyes like a teenaged girl at my flirting.

Liam laughed, spreading his legs a little as he leaned back in his seat. It was one of those stupid power moves men liked to do, as though anyone thought their dick was large enough to require man-spreading. "Well, darling, I wouldn't worry about that. You seem like the sort of girl who can get whatever she wants." His gaze dropped meaningfully to my thighs.

"I wish," I said, uncrossing and recrossing my legs to keep his attention there. "I'm new in town and I really need this job to work out."

He leaned in, setting his hand on my knee. "You know, even when things don't go the way you expect, they still can work out."

The weight of his hand was, at the worst, an annoyance. It didn't frighten me, didn't sicken me, but did absolutely nothing to wake up my libido, either. That was probably a good thing, though, since I had zero desire to want this arrogant asshole. I wasn't sure how I'd react if I ended up hot and bothered from this blowhard...

Still, I painted on my most seductive smile. "If we could get this handled, I'd be so thankful."

Thankful meaning — *maybe I'll suck your dick.*

I mean, I wouldn't, but all I needed was to make him think it was possible. That was what so much of negotiating was — making the other person thing they *could* get something, whether or not it was possible.

His smile spread, as if he'd already stripped my panties off. "I bet you would..."

Bingo.

"Let me get the papers for you to look over. If we could figure it out, I'd feel so much better."

I rose, then *accidentally* dropped one of my pens to the floor. It sure as hell wasn't an accident when I bent forward — outside of his reach because I doubted I'd be so nice if he actually groped me.

A groan from behind me screamed all the things Liam was thinking. *Perfect.* The more distracted he was by my ass, the better odds I could maneuver him exactly where I wanted.

I picked up the pen I'd dropped and laughed, an almost painful *'what a silly, adorable idiot I am'* sound. One more smile sent Liam's way before clutching the papers to my chest and walking out of the conference room, into the small room to the back. It had a window into the conference room as well, but the drawn blinds made it private.

I didn't really need any papers — everything was in the folder — but giving someone a minute to think about it would make them less reluctant. I wanted him to sit there with his erection, let that ache settle so his need seemed even larger than it had before.

The door closed behind me, and I didn't need to turn around to know who it was.

Rune's huge frame was easy to pick up, even in my peripheral vision. Of course, that wasn't what drove home who it was.

Instead, it was when I found myself shoved up against the wall, just beside the window that separated this space from the conference room, and Rune's rumbled voice slid through me as he pinned me there.

"I don't think I like him looking at you like that," he all but growled.

"Like what?"

"Like he owns you." Rune slid the hand not holding me against the wall down my front. "Because he fucking doesn't. If anyone owns you, it's *us*."

I had a feeling Rune was about to try to teach me that, and I had to admit...

I was pretty sure I'd enjoy his lesson.

Rune

How a woman could drive me *this* mad, I had no idea. I'd fucked strippers in the past who had gone off with someone else after wiping off — I'd never given a damn about jealousy before.

So why was it that seeing that asshole's hand on Nem's knee, watching him eye-fuck her in front of me, had me ready to slit his throat for the fun of it?

Because she's mine, damn it.

Maybe because I'd never had anything else worth being possessive over, I didn't recognize the feeling. Yet, that was exactly what this was.

I couldn't stop myself, not when I'd followed her into the small room off the main space, when I'd shut the door and took one look at her red hair, at the way her ass looked in that skirt.

Fuck me.

Or fuck her, in this case…

I grabbed the bottom edge of her skirt and pulled— not hard enough to rip it, but enough to take the edge off my aggression. I rucked the fabric up until I could reach beneath it.

Nem placed her hands on the wall, and I was ready for her to swing her head backward, to try and nail me in the face for the insult. I'd take a broken nose to get what I wanted, to calm the aggression inside me that demanded I claim her. I only fell deeper into whatever trance she had me in when she shoved her hips backward like an offer, however.

She was hard to read, but clearly she felt the same pull I did.

"Fuck, yes," I groaned into her ear as I ran my fingers over her lace-covered pussy. She was fire itself, and I didn't mind getting burned.

Instead of teasing, I hooked my fingers beneath the crotch of her panties and bypassed them, seeking the heat of her tight cunt. It only took one quick stroke along her pussy to gather wetness before I focused on her clit.

It was already hard, already begging for my attention.

Nem inched her feet out to make more room for me, but I didn't feel like giving her any chance to get herself in trouble. I left my hand on the back of her neck, keeping her pinned against the wall.

A few rough strokes of her clit—probably too hard to enjoy entirely—and I plunged two of my fingers into her drenched, waiting cunt.

"I don't like him touching you," I whispered, not giving a damn about what I said. Normally, I watched my words, but her little act out there had driven me well past the edge of sanity. "And I really don't fucking like you playing along."

"Maybe I wasn't playing," she said, though her words were cut short when I fucked into her especially hard. Her shaky moan told me she didn't mind it at all. Then again, no matter how Nem played at being sweet when around these other men, I'd seen she was more than able to hold her own.

"*Right.*" I rotated my wrist, making sure she felt how thick my fingers were inside her. She was already wound up, already rocking her hips back in the tiny amount of space she had to move. "You want to pretend like that? Because the way I see it, you're here, just about fucking yourself on my fingers. You ain't in there with him, and that says it all."

"Last I checked, I didn't ask you to follow me."

"Oh, you did, just not with those lying lips of yours." I groaned at the way her cunt gripped my fingers, the tight squeeze telling me how close she was. "Fuck, the way you heat up is beautiful. Your body is begging for it, ain't it? Bet you've been wet all day, just waiting until one of us takes care of you."

Her face was turned, her cheek against the wall, and it let me see as those red lips of hers parted on a gasp.

Fuck, she was pretty like this. Desperate and disheveled even though her makeup was still perfect. That was what I enjoyed about her so much, the extremes.

The woman was wicked smart but seemed to be getting herself into a situation too big for her to handle. She was stubborn but when she surrendered, she did it so beautifully. So, I had her skirt raised up, my fingers deep inside her sweet pussy, her cheek pressed against the wall, her white blouse and perfect red lipstick seemed untouched.

And it was one hell of a sight. My cock didn't just ache, it *hurt*. I wanted to slide into her, to take advantage of her sexy body, but there just wasn't time for everything I wanted.

So instead, I'd remind her that she didn't need to be making eyes at some fucking stranger, that she didn't need to let some man put his hands on her. Whether or not she liked it, whether or not she wanted it, we had a connection, and I had no issue making that clear all over again.

She shivered, a delicious sound leaving her — thin and as close to a plea as I'd bet she could manage. Her hands were pressed against the wall, and she curled her fingers in as if fighting me.

She thought she'd resist? That she wouldn't come? The thought was almost enough to make me laugh. She was already so close, already treading along that sharp edge, so it wouldn't take much to shove her over and watch her freefall.

And what a fucking sight she'd make when she did. How much she kept hidden, how much she tried to control was never as obvious as when she came, as when all that snapped and I got a look at the woman beneath it.

That was what I'd meant in the elevator, about the real her, about getting a glimpse of it when we got her to this point.

"You'll come," I promised her, pressing harder where my hand was on the back of her neck, a reminder she wasn't going anywhere until I allowed it. "I don't give a fuck if you think you can resist—you can't. You're going to come all over my fingers, then you'll walk the fuck back in there sensitive, with your panties drenched, and you'll finish that fucking meeting knowing I was the one who did it to you."

Whether it was my words or my fingers that ended up doing it, I had no idea. It didn't really matter. She came—*hard*. She arched against my hold, the vice-grip of her cunt enough to draw another groan from me as I pretended it was my cock there.

Her lips parted, and the sounds she made were heavenly. She sagged against the wall, against my hold, as her cunt pulsed around my fingers, my reluctance to let her go meaning I hadn't pulled 'em free yet.

I twisted my hand, rewarded with a sharp gasp from her, before I pulled out. I leaned in, pressing my body against hers, letting her feel just how hard I was. "This isn't close to over, Nem. Soon as I get you alone?"

I left the statement open, let her put in whatever the fuck she wanted there, mostly because no matter how depraved the things she came up with were...

I was damn sure I could do better.

Nem

Walking back into the conference room exactly as Rune said I would chafed in a way that was even more uncomfortable than my wet panties against my sensitive clit. I'd pulled down my skirt, swiped a finger beneath my eyes to ensure I hadn't smeared my liner, then given Rune one hell of a glare.

At the very least, a glance at his crotch said he'd be far less comfortable in there than I would.

Liam wore the same smile he had before, oblivious to what had just happened. It told me he had no idea what a satisfied woman looked like, probably because he'd never left a girl in that state before.

I tried to regain the cool composure I'd had before, tried to quiet the way Rune had broken that leash on my feelings the way he always did. My cheeks were warm, no doubt flushed, and my breathing hadn't gotten back to normal.

Still, I threw myself into the task, into what needed to get done. No better way to distract myself than with a puzzle, than a problem, and acquiring this property served well enough.

I spread out the files on the table this time, pretending I'd gotten new things from the back. "This is a good deal," I reiterated.

Liam stood to look over the papers, standing far too close.

I turned to see Rune and Colten together, Rune speaking softly, Colton's eyes locked on me. The intensity made me shiver, a reminder that while I might have been satisfied, *neither* man was. That meant they had at least two more goes in them.

"Ms. Syler," Liam said, drawing me back, making me realize I'd missed whatever he'd said.

"Sorry," I answered quickly, trying to ignore the men in the corner of the room.

"I just don't see how this would make good business sense for me. The last thing I want is a reputation as a man who gives in to women, no matter how pretty their lips might be." He set a hand on my hip, stepping in closer. "I'm sure you know what a reputation does for a person. A girl like you, you've got quite the reputation, I'm sure."

Of course he figured I was where I was because I'd fucked my way there. He couldn't fathom a woman gained power any other way.

The memory of Rune's fingers deep inside me minutes before hit me, my body still haywire from the orgasm he'd ripped from me.

It made the weight of Liam's hand worse. Before, it had just been data points, but now, after Rune, my body wanted to reject any touch of Liam's. It was like how, after brushing my teeth, orange juice was beyond repulsive.

I shifted, trying to unsettle his hand from me. "This is the smart choice."

Over his shoulder, I locked gazes with Colton, so much promise there. Except, it wasn't just the look. That I could have dealt with, could have managed to rein back in my feelings, quiet the flames they sparked to life inside me.

What broke me was when he grasped Rune's hand and lifted it, then took the fingers that had been inside my pussy a minute before into his mouth. He licked them clean, his gaze never straying from mine, as if he wanted to make sure I saw just how hungry he was for a taste of me.

That shattered my ability to play the game I needed to with Liam, made it so I couldn't stay detached.

It meant when Liam touched me again, his hand sliding from my hip back toward my ass, I'd had enough. That thing inside me, the one they'd resurrected, whatever was there, birthed by the flames of death of before, had had enough.

I grasped his wrist and squeezed *hard*. "I'm not a part of this deal," I said, letting my voice go back to normal, to the sharp edge.

I let him see my teeth.

He yanked his hand away and I let him. "What the hell do you think you're doing?"

"Making things clear." I pulled my shoulders back, standing tall as I stared at him. "You're going to sell the property, and at ten percent less than the offer I already gave you because you've wasted my time."

"No fucking chance."

"Oh, yes, you will. See, I've already contacted someone in the city council, and if you don't play ball, they've agreed to zone that property historical. Do that, and it's worth exactly shit. No project will be allowed, no one will touch it with a ten-foot-pole."

He narrowed his eyes. "You're lying."

"You really think I came into this without background? Without doing my damned job? You have exactly one option, not the few you lied about. That project is with Ranstein Industries, but they haven't even secured funding, yet. Fuck knows they don't have the money or time to deal with the complications of a historical zoning issue. A whiff of that, and they'll run in the other direction. No one will touch it."

He narrowed his eyes. Was he finally getting that I wasn't some skirt he could fuck and get what he wanted from? "So I'll hang on to it. Property goes up in value, and I'll unload it later. There's no way I'm going to sell it to you, not now."

I leaned in, meeting his gaze head on. If people like the Quad couldn't make me wilt, if I didn't shirk from people a hell of a lot scarier than this pompous businessman, I wasn't going to give this asshole an inch of space. The way Rune made me feel, the way he could rouse emotions in me that I'd thought gone, ones normally frozen, meant I was only too happy to turn that on Liam.

"A few calls from me and you're done for. It took me an hour to put this together, and if you piss me off, if you push me any further, if you even so much as glance at my tits again, I'll devote the next week to ruining your life. I'll make sure your wife knows about every last girl you've fucked behind her back, then dig into every last backroom deal you've made, bring all that to light. I don't think you'll enjoy a microscope like that on you."

He pressed his lips together into a thin, angry line. "You wouldn't dare."

"Try me."

He pulled his shoulders back, and a flash there in his gaze told me what he wanted. It also told me I wouldn't mind ruining him no matter what he did. It was the look of a man who was used to beating a woman down if he couldn't get them beneath him any other way. The idiot had the stupid idea to actually hit me? I almost wanted him to try it, to give me an excuse.

A hand wrapped around his arm, and I realized I'd forgotten all about Rune and Colton. In that moment, I'd missed that I had them there, that I had back-up.

Rune's voice was as rough as his grip on Liam's arm. "Bad idea."

Liam turned toward Rune, somehow managing not to cower...*yet*. "You heard her threaten me. I don't think Kyler would like—"

"I don't give a fuck what Kyler would like," Colton said. "Even look at her again and you won't need to worry about her threats because I'll kill you and leave you where no one will ever find you."

While Liam hadn't quite believed me, it seemed, he sure as hell took Colton at his word. He nodded, then all but ran from the room, not looking back at all.

"He better agree to the deal," I said.

"After the way he put his hand on you, I plan to pay him a visit anyway," Colton said, crossing his arms.

"I need him to be able to sign, still."

Colton didn't smile, his gaze still locked on the door like a predator who wanted to chase down his prey. "He only needs one hand to do that. I'll leave it intact, at least until he signs."

And as strange as it was, that was damned near a romantic gesture from a man like Colton.

Chapter Eighteen

Nem

I sat up, gasping, my hands flying to my chest. I clutched at where the skin was raised, at the scarring where the bullet that had pierced my chest had gone in. I dug my nails into it, my lungs burning as if I couldn't draw enough air no matter what I did.

I fucking hate nightmares.

There should have been a limit on them, a point where they didn't happen anymore. There was no damn good reason my brain should keep doing these things a decade after the event, that it should make me relive that moment.

And it was always *that* moment I was dragged back to. Sure, I remembered the flames, the way I'd pulled my body across the floor to the secret room in the closet. It wasn't those things that haunted me, though.

It wasn't even the two bullets that had hit me once I'd fallen, the ones that went into my back, near my side.

The part that replayed in my head was the bullet to my chest, seeing the man with his gun out.

I closed my eyes, because blocking it out was pointless. I'd learned that the best option was to let the memory swarm over me, because the more I tried to fight it, the more it clawed at me.

Geoffrey had lifted his gun first, after shooting my mother, after tearing the necklace she'd always worn from her. I hadn't cried, hadn't screamed. It wasn't bravery, but rather an inability to process what was happening. My perfect little world had cracked apart before my eyes.

He'd pointed his gun toward me, then frozen.

Carlos had come into the room. *"We need to get going."*

Geoffrey had frowned, then looked over at him. *"She's just a kid, man."*

"She's not just a kid – she's seventeen. Get it over with."

Geoffrey had shaken his head. *"Fuck, look at her. I can't kill a kid."*

"You knew the job. We need to get going."

The man's arm had trembled before he dropped it. *"Can't we just tie her up? The flames'll take care of her."*

"For fuck's sake," Carlos had muttered, and I hadn't had time to consider what he meant before he'd pulled his pistol from the holster at the small of his back and pulled the trigger.

Phantom pain still radiated through my chest, well after the actual wound had healed.

Sleep for the night seemed a total loss. I didn't dare close my eyes again because I feared I'd end up right back there again.

Nightmares didn't happen that often. I'd moved past that, past the trauma.

No, that wasn't quite right. I hadn't moved past it, hadn't processed it, it had just seemed to slip away. It was as though, once I'd woken back up, once I'd been on the other side of it, it had happened to someone else. Only the dreams pulled me back, bridged Kelsey and Nem, the past and the present. It was probably being right back in the middle of this entire world that brought the nightmares back.

It meant the quicker I got through this all, the better. A person should only need to experience their own death once.

I pulled on a pair of thick socks before heading out of the room. Fresh air and a cool breeze could clear away the memories and the images.

Carlos was always the face that plagued me. Maybe it was because he had been the one to pull the trigger, the one who hadn't given a damn about me.

That was the worst part...

Geoffrey had cared about pulling that trigger. He'd hesitated. Sure, he'd murdered my mother, and he'd wanted to leave me to burn to death in a fire, but at least he'd seen me as a person. For Carlos, I hadn't been worth even a thought.

He hadn't killed me because he'd been angry or because he hated me. He hadn't given a damn. Pulling the trigger was just another step in his day, something inconsequential on his daily to-do list to check off.

That was what really got to me — how little the worst day of my life meant to him.

I doubted he'd ever thought of it again, that it was of so little importance to him, it didn't keep him up at night.

Which was altogether unfair. I shouldn't be the one who had to suffer with nightmares. It made me even more sure that killing Carlos was the right choice. Maybe, with him dead, I'd sleep better. Maybe by wiping him off the face of the planet I could clear him from my mind, as well.

The plan for him would take time, the steps more complicated and my shadows further causing problems. I'd set up a good reason for him to leave, though it was still a good week and a half away. He'd get a notice about an error at his bank that he needed to deal with in person.

If there was one thing that could get even a man as paranoid as Carlos out of his compound, it would be his money.

I used the plan like a mantra, reassuring myself that Carlos didn't have much time left.

As I exited the back French doors, the blue glow of a screen and a familiar face made me pause. Bray sat outside, his laptop perched on his thighs. He lifted his gaze to mine.

Sure, hatred from him wasn't uncommon—he'd made his feelings clear enough—but at the moment? With my nightmare so damn close?

I sighed and went to go back inside.

"Wait," he said.

I turned back toward him. "I don't have the energy for this fight," I admitted.

He closed the laptop, then set it on the table. "So, let's not fight."

I wrapped my arms around myself to keep from scratching at the scar on my chest, my nightmares always making me aware of it. It was like a dream could tear open the wound again, and I needed to touch the mark to center myself, to ground myself in the present. "We don't do anything but fuck and fight, and even our fucking is exhausting."

Bray tilted his head before patting the spot beside him. "We could both take the night off from that. You don't look like you're any more interested in bickering than I am."

The thought of going back inside turned out to be worse than the risk of doing as he said, so I sat beside him on the outdoor couch. "Why do you work so late?"

"I like the quiet of the evening."

That made me frown.

He lifted his dark eyebrow. "Not a fan of quiet?"

I shook my head. "Not really, no. I've spent a lot of years on my own, and the quiet isn't all it's chalked up to be."

He nodded, leaning back on the couch. "I live with three other men, so quiet isn't something I often have — especially with Dane."

That made me smile despite myself, at how Dane never did shut up. It was as though he thought he might die if he ever stopped talking, as if his heart beat only as long as his mouth was moving.

As much as Bray seemed to thrive with some silence, Dane was allergic to it.

And me? I fit somewhere between it, between the constant noise and the desire for absolute silence.

"Besides," Bray added, as if to try to spur further conversation when it stalled, "I've never slept all that well. I prefer a few short bursts rather than a regular eight hours. Sleep is dangerous, a time when a person is at their most vulnerable. If I could do away with it entirely, I would."

I followed his lead, leaning back and slouching down on the couch. While things with Bray were...tense, at best, it was nice to relax.

Bray and I hadn't ever been as openly close as the others. We weren't affectionate, even when I'd been younger. He was a hard man to read, someone who said little and kept anything important close to his chest. Still, he'd always been there, watching over, and the rare smiles I'd stolen from him had meant the world to me.

Even back then, he'd been more serious, but in the years since?

He'd hardened in a way that felt like a loss.

"So, do you want to explain why you really hate me so much?" I asked when I couldn't help it, a need to understand where his animosity came from.

He let out a long sigh, as if the question were unwelcomed but not unexpected.

Before he could give me a bullshit answer, I interrupted him. "Don't tell me it's just because you don't trust me — we both know that's not all of it. This is personal, and since we have to put up with one another for a while at least, I think I deserve to know why you treat me like I'm trash."

His lips pressed together into a thin line before he rubbed at the inner corners of his eyes, behind his glasses. "You're right. It isn't fair to take it out on you when I haven't even explained it."

I waited when he didn't go on at first. He stared off at the dark sky. Was he getting his thoughts in order? Figuring out what to say?

It was hard to read, hard to know with him.

Finally, he nodded. "You've lived in this world long enough, are comfortable in it enough to know trust isn't something safe to give to many people. My list at this point is just Rune, Colton and Dane. That's it."

"I'm not asking for your trust," I reminded him. "Fuck knows I don't trust you, either."

He let out a snort—as close to a laugh as he was probably capable of anymore. "The thing is, in my experience, women have a habit of worming in past the smarts of normally careful men. You get a woman involved, and suddenly men start making dumb choices."

"From what I've heard, you four have fucked your way through plenty of women. I can't believe you'd manage to bed as many as you have if you treated them all like this."

"Fair enough. You're…different. I don't know why, can't explain it, but it's like when we first met you, you were already half an inch under our skin. That's not normal, not something I've seen often, and it's dangerous." He stretched his back, though that wasn't a shocker. There was no way hunching over a laptop was posture-approved for the spine.

"So, this is all because you sort of like me and that annoys you? What is it? The adult version of pulling a girl's pigtails?"

Bray shook his head. "It isn't that simple—nothing ever is. Look, about nine years ago, there was this woman, Theresa. I wasn't in the best place—fuck, none of us were—and I fell hard for her."

Nine years ago? Math wasn't my strong suit, but that would have placed it just after Caroline's death, after the attack. The idea he'd gone off and found someone so soon after made me grit my teeth and keep in any cutting insult before it could escape.

Not only was it not fair to be mad about that — it wasn't even like we'd been romantic — but I couldn't exactly say much.

And them being in a bad place? I had no idea if that was due to guilt, grief or regret.

"So what happened?" Even without asking, I was pretty sure I knew. Some stories only went in one direction, and the look on his face told me where this one ended up — *heartbreak.*

"She was a dancer at a club — not Diamond's Edge, just some little hole-in-the-wall dive where the drinks were cheap and the lights were low. It was the kind of place someone goes when they don't want to be recognized. Well, I was an idiot, looking for something, and before I even knew it, she'd wormed her way into my life."

"Just yours?"

"The others, we'll take girls together sometimes, but we don't really date the same women. Never works out well — girl gets jealous, or she likes one or two more than the others, and favoritism ends up biting us all in the ass. So, no, Theresa was just mine." He let out a long breath. "Or so I thought. I was stupid, sloppy, desperate for it to be *something*, to convince myself it meant more than it did. About two months in, she was at my place —"

"You didn't live with the Quad?"

"We've always had a place together, but there are times when one of us needs our own space for a while. It was an apartment in the city — small and quiet and close to where the others lived. See, she made me a drink. I didn't think anything of it, we drank together a lot—did a lot of things that were bad for us together—but after I had it, I passed out."

My staggering rush of anger on his behalf surprised me. I rarely felt much anger and feeling it one someone's behalf else was strange. I wanted to track down this girl, to tear her apart for him.

Bray must not have noticed, because he kept talking. In fact, his gaze was locked off in the distance—he probably hadn't looked my way at all, as if I wasn't even there. "I woke up a few hours later, heard her talking with a man. They were trying to get into my safe, wanted the cash they figured was stashed in there and the files I kept backed up there. Theresa, she was talking like I was nothing, just a mark, and that was the point I realized just how stupid I'd been. I'd seen what I wanted to see in her, in us. There were plenty of signs, and if I'd opened my damn eyes for just a minute, I'd have seen her for what she was, but I didn't. I pretended because I wanted to, because I was so pathetically desperate for some bullshit fairy tale that I ignored it all. I was broken and hollow and went looking for something fake because I knew damn well I'd lost what I really wanted."

"What happened?" I asked when he paused.

"Well, they hadn't killed me yet because they wanted the files before they did it, in case anything was password protected. They figured whatever they'd drugged me with would last longer than it did. Guess they weren't as good at dosing as they thought. I pulled myself over to the couch, to where my pistol still was. They were in the other room, and both were high as fuck, so they didn't hear anything. I waited for them to come back and put a bullet in the man's brain."

"And her?"

"I asked her why she'd done it. Stupid and sentimental, I guess. I mean, does why matter? What does it change? Nothing. She talked and begged and lied some more, but none of it changed anything. At the end of the day, she'd done it for the payday, because she'd taken one look at me and wanted to see what she could get from me. Funny thing is, even then, even at the end when I *knew* what she really was, I still had this part of me that thought I could fix it, that figured maybe there was still a way to get the stupid fantasy I'd built up in my head."

"You let her go?"

"No. I put a bullet between her eyes." He turned his head then, locking his gaze on mine. "That's the thing, Nem, it fucking hurt. It *still* hurts. That's why I don't like you, that's why I act the way I do. I killed her even though I'm pretty sure my dumb ass still loved her, and I'd do it again if I had to. I'm pissed at you because I see it coming this time, someone who's lying, who's scheming, and even knowing that, I *still* want you. Doesn't matter, though, because I'll end you if I have to, just like I did her, knowing damn well it's a wound that won't ever heal. So, yeah, I hate you, because looking at you is like looking at an injury I just know is coming. It's like seeing the bullet I'm going to put in you, knowing how fucking much it's going to hurt, but not being able to stop it. You, Nem, are nothing but heartbreak coming."

I wanted to argue, but fuck…he was right. Either he had something to do with what happened to me, in which case I'd kill him, or he didn't, and he'd know by the end who I was and lose me all over again.

Maybe that was the truth, though — life was nothing but heartbreak coming.

* * * *

Arriving at Kyler's house was normal in a way that unsettled me. He'd called to ask me to join him for dinner.

It didn't seem romantic, but I'd misjudged and misunderstood him before, hadn't I?

He acted more like we had some weird, twisted bond between us, like I knew him on a level that others didn't.

Maybe he was right. No matter how much I wanted to deny it or pretend it wasn't true, I sure as hell had learned a lot from him. Some of my worst lessons, some of the ones that had both hurt and benefited me the most had come from him.

He'd taught me the real risks in the world, taught me people couldn't be trusted, taught me family was a lie. I'd watched him for years as a kid, desperate for his attention, and in the end, he'd given me just that.

Still, I didn't like walking into something I couldn't prepare for, something with so many unknowns.

"Be careful," Dane said as Colton pulled the SUV up the driveway toward Kyler's house.

"Always am," I countered.

Dane, who sat in the backseat with me, turned to face me. "I'm not kidding, Nem. Kyler can be charming when he wants to be, can be…persuasive. He knows how to twist facts and what people want to make them think he is the only one who can give it to them. The thing is, at the end of the day, he's only looking out for himself."

"I don't think you get to tell me what a horrible person he is when you do his bidding."

"You don't understand," Dane bit out.

"Oh, I do. Money is money, right? Work for the devil if it gets you a good spot in hell."

Dane narrowed his eyes, that temper of his exciting me. The idea of pushing him enough so he fucked me here, in Kyler's driveway, was far more of a turn-on than it should have been. Sadly, he answered with his words instead of his cock. "We work for him because we're honor-bound. That doesn't mean much to some people, but it does to us."

The idea that Kyler had ever done anything to deserve that sort of loyalty or oath didn't make a bit of sense. For people in our world to be honor-bound, it meant they'd pledged themselves to someone, and that was a rare thing. Even rarer was for it to be from men who actually took that sort of thing seriously.

I shook my head, feeling as if it were yet another answer that spawned more questions than under-standing. "I can take care of myself," I assured him.

"So I've seen. Still, just, be careful. I haven't seen Kyler like this in a long-damned time, and change isn't a good thing when dealing with people like him."

His concern was annoying rather than sweet. It made me feel like a kid all over again, like Dane was telling me how boys only wanted one thing after dragging me home from a date I wasn't supposed to be on. He was underestimating me again, thinking me fragile and easily manipulated.

Idiot.

I steeled my look as I stared back at him. "Trust me—I can handle anything Kyler wants to throw at me."

My confidence fled, however, the moment the front door opened and not just Kyler stepped out but a girl as well.

No, not a girl but a woman…

Kenz.

Chapter Nineteen

Nem

I couldn't breathe, couldn't seem to make my brain wake the fuck up and work.

Kenz was standing right there, beside Kyler, and she was the spitting image of our mother. She had Caroline's long dark hair, the ends curling. She had her dark eyes, with a dusting of freckles over her nose. She wore a pair of high-cut shorts and a crop top, making her seem even older than her actual age of eighteen.

It was my first time seeing her since that morning, when we'd sat at the kitchen table and talked about her appointment. The moment hit me in the stomach, made me recognize just how long had passed.

Time had been an idea, something without concrete form. The years had been just numbers. Now it was the inches she'd grown, the wariness in her gaze, the teenage rebellion she wore.

I'd lost so much time…

And I wasn't getting any of it back, either. The point of this all wasn't to get time back, or even to get her back, but to free her. It was to give her the life I never got, the one she deserved, the one Kyler would steal from her one way or another.

"Nem?" Colton's voice had an edge that implied it wasn't the first time he'd said it.

It shook me awake, made me want to curse myself for my lack of focus. Still, seeing Kenz was the last thing I'd expected. I'd known she'd stay at the mountain property I'd obtained for Kyler, but I hadn't thought I would see her before then.

I certainly hadn't expected to sit down with her like some twisted family dinner.

The SUV behind us, the one that had Rune and Bray, pulled up to the left of ours, yet another reminder to stay on track.

Colton got out of the driver's seat, then opened my door. I slid out, with Dane getting out on his side, and Bray and Rune leaving their vehicle.

I turned toward Kyler and Kenz, after patching up my defenses against the pointless sentimentality. I ran through my list again, letting it center me.

Kill Carlos.

Save Kenz

Kill Kyler.

I clung to the repetition of my plan, let it strengthen me.

Dane didn't approach me, instead going toward Kenz. She offered him a smile that made my stomach drop, one that showed how fond she was of him and how much she'd missed him.

She threw her arms around Dane, and he hugged her back. It was sweet, like seeing an older brother at a holiday dinner.

"It's been too long, kid," Dane said before letting her go.

She shoved his shoulder. "Well, *you* never visit."

He gave her a smile, one that looked damn sincere. "Sorry," he said without elaborating.

He didn't really need to, though. Reading between those lines was easy. The sharp look from Kyler and my knowledge that he'd never approved of how the Quad had been intertwined with our lives said it all. No doubt, he'd kept Kenz away from them on purpose.

So what had changed? Was it just the stress I'd put on him by killing off the people he'd hired? Did he feel having her closer was safer, even if it meant having the Quad around her?

And why have her meet me at all?

Too many questions and not enough answers made me uneasy.

Rune came up for a hug from Kenz next, then Colton. Even Bray, who had shown nothing but disdain for me so far, went in for a hug. In fact, he held Kenz longer than the others, as if he struggled to let her go.

It was strange, like a peek into something I shouldn't see, like a private moment I shouldn't have been privy to.

Kyler approached me, moving his gaze from Kenz and the men. "I'm so glad you came," he said.

I offered him a smile, letting the nerves show. He'd no doubt attribute them to nerves about dinner rather than my being unsettled by seeing Kenz. "Of course. It's been a long time since I've had a nice dinner at a home like this."

"I understand that. It seems like I work so much, it's pretty rare for me, too." Kyler turned, holding his hand out. "Mackenzie, I'd like you to meet Nem."

Kenz watched me suspiciously, the sort of edge a girl her age shouldn't have to use when meeting people with her family. It took me back to when I'd been her age, to the way I'd learned each person I met might just be an enemy I hadn't known about.

I gave her the kindest smile I could manage. "Nice to meet you, Mackenzie."

She nodded, then returned a smile after a moment. "I like your hair."

I took a piece between my fingers, as if I'd forgotten all about it. "It's a lot of work to keep it this color, but I learned a long time ago, what's the point in blending in?"

Her smile widened, and that old ache started up in my chest at how easily I'd won her over. Even with that hesitancy, she clearly wasn't safe. She trusted too easily.

But she *should* trust easily. She deserved a life where she didn't have to question every person, where she had to wonder about their motives. A meeting like this, a dinner like this, should have been commonplace and relaxing.

And she's going to get the life she deserves, because I'll make sure of it.

The men took off quickly, never making it past the front door of the house. Not that they left—they headed for the casita that housed security for Kyler and the property. It gave them a place to go and not be underfoot, but kept them close enough in case they were needed.

Which left Kyler, Kenz and me alone.

Talk about awkwardness…

It was like the little reunion no one had wanted. Even to the most dysfunctional of families, no one could have mistaken our fucked-up get-together as anything close to a happy family.

I kept that off my face, however, struggled to play the part despite the change. Dane's words came back to me, ones I'd heard Jarrod echo in the past — *change is never good.*

What did Kyler want? Why had he invited me? Was Kenz being there just a coincidence, like he needed a place for her since the mountainside mansion wouldn't be ready for another week or two?

I had no answers for any of that, which was the most frustrating part of it all. It was impossible to formulate a plan without having enough information, and I had fuck all.

No one spoke while we went through the house and into the formal dining room. A table large enough for eight sat there, with three spots at one end made up. One for Kyler — the head of the table, again — and one to each side of it for Kenz and I. Kyler gestured Kenz toward one, then pulled the other chair out for me.

Once seated, he poured wine in his and my glass.

"None for me?" Kenz asked, a playfulness that stopped me short. Then again, as much as I might hate Kyler, he *was* her father — and the only family she had left.

"No." Kyler set the wine bottle down between his spot and mine. "You're too young."

She rolled her eyes before picking up her wineglass full of what must have been sparkling cider and took a sip.

I tried to recall feeling like that, being a child. It felt so long ago, like it hadn't even been me.

It wasn't really, though. It had been a different girl, the one who had died on the ground in the backyard of

Jayce Carter

that house. I wondered for a moment just what it would have been like to have a sister, a real one, to have grown up together. I wanted to give Kenz advice, to laugh over the things our parents did that stressed us out, to have her call me when something upset her.

That wasn't the life either of us got to live, though, and wishing for impossible things was a waste of time. It wasn't like we were headed for that sort of familiar bliss.

I took a deep breath, then slid into the role I needed to play. Sweet, trustworthy, smart but not smart enough to be a risk. "So what grade are you in?" I asked Kenz.

"I would be a senior, but I don't go to a regular school. I move too often for that."

"You were also kicked out of the last two boarding schools I put you in," Kyler added.

She ignored him, keeping her gaze on me. "We had differences of opinions about the proper behavior for a lady. Instead, I did an accelerated course last year and got my diploma. Next year, I'll start college courses online."

"What do you want to study?"

She nibbled her bottom lip, something odd and wholly her. Lord knew our mother had never done that, never showed an ounce of uncertainty. "I'm not sure. I think I want to go for an art degree."

That one surprised me.

Kyler let out a snort. "Art is hardly a useful skill."

"Say that the next time you spend a hundred thousand on a painting or when you pay an interior designer to decorate your house."

He gave her a look I'd seen many times in men. He was used to the world bending to him, to people cowering for him, and yet his own daughter seemed to counter what he said without worry. "It doesn't matter, anyway. You can see, when next school year comes around, what your options are."

The words didn't make sense to me, but I had a feeling I lacked an important context clue when Kenz deflated, when she curled her shoulders in and dropped her gaze to her plate.

It ended the topic, and there was no good way to start it up again without drawing suspicion.

It was a good break for the conversation anyway, since two people came in, plates balanced on their arms. They passed out the food, the scent of it heavenly.

"I know you mentioned a home-cooked meal," Kyler said, "but I don't cook much. I figured a chef cooking it in my home was a good compromise."

"It looks wonderful." I didn't even have to lie about that as I stared at the perfectly cooked grilled chicken breast and the salad beside it. "I really appreciate the invitation, but are you sure I'm not imposing? It sounds like you don't get to see your daughter much—I don't want to get in the way of your time."

Kenz made a soft sound beneath her breath that didn't take a code-breaker to decipher.

They didn't spend time together, so there wasn't anything to impose onto.

Kyler didn't say anything to Kenz, as if by ignoring her he could hold on to the perfect little lie he liked to sell the world about his life. It was funny because anyone who had kids—especially teenagers—knew life was always imperfect with them around. "You aren't imposing at all. In fact, I wanted to have this dinner so you could meet Mackenzie, and to discuss plans for the house."

I cast my gaze Kenz's direction. "She knows about it?"

He nodded. "I had her security detail show it to her last night before they came in. She says it's perfect."

"That isn't what I said," Kenz snapped.

Kyler gave her a sharp look. "Don't be rude."

"Then don't lie."

"If there's a problem with it, I can fix it," I offered. "I still have plenty of people able to make changes quickly, and it shouldn't affect the timeline at all."

Kenz pushed her chair backward, the feet scraping against the wooden floor. "There's nothing you can do about it unless you can talk sense into my father."

"Mackenzie Mercy Williams," Kyler said, the use of her middle name the universal *'I'm done with your shit'* sign. "You will not embarrass yourself or me in front of guests."

She rose. "Then I'll leave you alone, which is what you really want anyway." Kenz stormed away from the table, and a minute later, the slam of a door upstairs told me she wasn't done making her point known.

Kyler sighed. "I'm sorry about that."

"Kids will be kids." I went for noncommittal. "I'm serious, though—I can still change anything she doesn't like."

He shook his head, leaning back in his seat. "There isn't anything that you can do that will change her opinion. She's unhappy about things that are set already."

"With enough money and contacts, everything can be changed."

"Mackenzie's still young. She's still in that age where she has this fantasy about what life is. She wants to go off to college, study art, travel the world without a care. She's a dreamer, and I have no idea where she got that from. Her mother was as practical as they came, and I'm like that too."

"Are you?" I thought back to his story, to how he'd grown up. "You saw the life you wanted, and even if no one else thought it was possible, you achieved it. It seems like you're a bit of a dreamer yourself."

He tilted his head, as though the idea had never occurred to him before. "Maybe," he admitted softly. "The thing is, Mackenzie doesn't get to just do whatever she wants. She has obligations and a name to live up to. She's always known this, but now that it's time to follow through, she's reluctant."

Obligations sounded like a bad word when it left Kyler's lips.

"What sort of obligations?"

"It's become clear recently that some things I had thought were settled aren't. I need to make some assurances, make hard choices that will ensure the safety of my line and my name. Mackenzie has always known what would be expected of her as my daughter, but she thought it meant down the line. It's happened sooner than any of us thought."

"What has happened?" A sinking in my stomach came over me, like looking over the edge of a gorge just before walking across a rickety bridge.

"That house you're working on? It isn't just for her to live in. It's going to be a wedding gift."

"Wedding gift?" I knew it was stupid to just repeat his words, but I couldn't seem to make sense of them.

Kyler nodded. "The daughter of a man in my position offers one thing — a potential alliance. I seem to need it sooner than I'd expected, so in a few weeks, whether she likes it or not, Mackenzie will be marrying a business associate of mine. It'll secure an agreement between the two of us, and Mackenzie will have a safe future."

The floor went out from beneath me, and I struggled to keep my face from showing it all. Worse, the words left my mouth before I could censor them. "But she's so young. She's still a kid."

"I wasn't much older when I married her mother. She's naive, too childish for her age. She'll complain, she'll slam some doors, but she'll do what she needs to when the time comes because she's a Williams, because she knows her obligations. I hadn't expected this to happen so quickly either, but things change. We all have to do what we need to do, regardless of how we feel about it."

And right then, I knew the *change* he was talking about. It had been me, my actions, the people on my list I'd killed. I'd applied the pressure, forced his hand, but I hadn't expected it would put Kenz in danger.

I'd done all of this for her, but I might have ended up doing the one thing I was trying to save her from— trapping her.

* * * *

Even the music at the Diamond's Edge didn't take away my frustration or dull the self-hatred that had grown inside me all night.

Dinner hadn't last long after Kenz had stormed out, which was good because I wasn't sure just how long I could keep my composure.

I did this.

I had pushed Kyler, had played a game without seeing all the possible outcomes. Never had I considered Kyler's play would be to marry Kenz off.

Now, on the other side of such a choice, I wondered how I could have missed it.

He felt unsure, insecure, unsafe. What better way to put him back on steady ground than to play the biggest chip he had?

His daughter, the last known member of the Hester bloodline.

She'd make quite the prize to the man who could give Kyler what he wanted.

Fuck it being more difficult to get her if she were in the clutches of another family, if she were moved God-knows where, but the thought of what she would suffer in the meantime had me tightening my hand around the glass until it broke.

I didn't curse, even when whiskey touched the new slice in my palm from the glass.

"That whiskey was too good for spilling," Valeria said before placing a new glass in front of me. "Alcohol that top shelf should be for drinking."

"Or for setting your enemies on fire," I countered before picking up the new drink and taking two large gulps. Blood smeared the glass, like some abstract piece of art where people argued the meaning of.

She smiled, as if the thought of lighting people on fire pleased her. "Fair enough. If you have anyone worthy of that honor, let me know, and I'll donate a bottle to the cause."

From the corner of my eye, I spotted Rune, his gaze locked on me. They were all there, sitting at a table with a perfect view of me at the bar. I'd made it clear in no uncertain terms that I didn't want to talk to *any* of them.

Maybe they chalked it up to a bad dinner, or to my general tendency to be a raging bitch, but whatever it was, they'd listened.

"So what is it that has you drinking like this?" Valeria asked.

I stared into the glass. People talked about trying to find answers at the bottom of liquor bottles, but I'd never really understood the saying until now.

It wasn't answers I was looking for—just a way to numb the answers I knew too well. That coldness I'd lived with for so long, it had thawed beneath the news about Kenz. I couldn't find the calm, the level-headedness I usually relied on.

Instead, it was only rage. It was a fire that burned inside me, scorching through me, and I had no idea how to put it out. The men woke it in me, but only for the smallest moments.

This time, it wouldn't go away. It burned me, licking at my insides, consuming me. I didn't feel so dead all of a sudden—I felt far too alive.

"I work so damn hard, plan everything, and it all goes to shit so fast."

Valeria sat on the stool beside me, a water bottle in her hand. Did she ever drink? She struck me as the sort of woman always in control. "Plans that go right are a fluke, Nem, not the rule."

"What do you do when it just keeps going wrong? When other people are going to pay the price because I wasn't smart enough, wasn't quick enough, didn't plan enough?"

"You say pay the price like there is a price, but we both know that's not how life works. We're all fucked, and life is the one with the strap-on. Everyone gets their teeth knocked in now and then, and all we can do is pick ourselves up and get ready for the next round."

I peered around the club, then shook my head. "I'm not talking about petty little problems, about bar fights and hookers who quit."

If I hadn't been drunk, I might have realized that speaking to Valeria like that was a bad idea. She had a reputation for a reason, and while few seemed to know the full story that bought her such fear and respect, it didn't mean it was smart to test it.

However, Valeria was also the closest thing I had to a friend. The words poured from me, angry and wanting to put the blame anywhere but where it belonged — on my shoulders.

"This place wasn't always mine, you know. I started here like most of the girls — from the bottom. Trust me, I've dealt with plans, and I've seen them go by the wayside, and I've taken the blows I've had to to get where I need to be."

I twisted to catch her gaze, to study her eyes, and found the truth in them. It was a hardness that grew in some people, proof of what they'd endured, what they'd survived. It felt like a scar, something I could spot in a person's eyes, and there wasn't any way to fake it.

Valeria knew exactly what I was talking about.

"And how do you do that?" I asked, my voice almost a plea. "How do you pick yourself up when everything you do makes it worse, when you can't see a way forward?"

She leaned her elbow on the bar. "First? I'd let your shadows know you need to use the restroom, and that I've said you can use my private one next to my office. Then I'd use the adjoining door to my office, and skip

Jayce Carter

out using the door to the alleyway from my office. There's a driver outside who will take you wherever you want."

I frowned. "Then what?"

She met my gaze, steady and terrifying. "Then do exactly what you know you need to. See, we don't get stuck because we're stupid, because we're weak, because we're not as good. We don't even get stuck because we don't know what we need to do. People like us? We stumble because we try to be something we're not. We try to tame ourselves, to put ourselves in the boxes we think we should be in, and we end up tangled and trapped. So, you want to get out of whatever mess you've dug yourself into?" She gestured toward the waitress who handed her a bottle of the whiskey I'd been drinking. It hit the bar with a heavy thud as she set it down in front of me. "I'll donate a bottle for you to use."

And for the first time since I'd come back, since I'd thrown myself into this world again, I felt like I had my feet beneath me.

Fuck the plan.

Colton

"She's going to need to be carried home." I leaned against the wall outside of the private bathroom Nem had gone into. The girl had put away more alcohol than she should have, given her size, and I'd seen the bottle of whiskey Valeria, the club owner, had given her.

"Hey, drunken sex doesn't sound so bad," Dane said from his spot, across the hallway, against the opposite wall.

296

"I'm not into getting thrown up on." I crossed my arms. "She's past the fun stage of inebriation."

"What's wrong with her?" Bray asked, the question odd from the quiet one of our group. Bray rarely spoke much, and especially not without prompting.

"I'm going to bet it would take a very, very long list and a team of psychiatrists to answer that question," Dane said.

"I'm serious. After dinner, something was different."

Rune shifted, leaning beside Bray, his gaze on the floor. "You don't think Kyler did anything, do you?"

That made me draw my hands into fists at the very idea. Kyler was an asshole, but he wasn't *that* kind of asshole.

And if he was? If he'd hurt Nem in some way? I wasn't sure my oath would mean a whole lot. Besides, my honor hadn't ever been bound to *him*.

Bray shook his head. "No. It wasn't upset like that. It was...anger? Fear?" He looked in Dane's direction, as if asking for help.

Dane shrugged. "I can't read her worth shit."

I muttered a curse. It was just our luck that the one fucking person Dane couldn't read was the one we needed read. Dane would spend his days picking us apart, picking every innocent bystander apart, but the one time it would have been useful, he had nothing.

"Could also try to fuck the answers out of her," Rune offered, a curl of his lips saying he was hoping for just that.

"We've done that before and it didn't help," I reminded him.

"Be worth trying. Even if it doesn't work, it'd be a good way to spend the night. Fuck knows that girl does angry sex right."

"Stop thinking with your dick," Bray said. "There's something wrong with her, like her safety is off all of a sudden, and I don't know about you three, but I don't want to get shot."

I couldn't deny what he said. In the car ride here, when she'd all but demanded to come to the club despite the objections and worries over safety, it wasn't hard to see some switch had flipped in her.

Those eyes of hers which were always calculated were...simple. I couldn't read them still, but they lacked the purpose they'd had before. She'd seemed adrift.

I recalled how she'd broken the glass at the bar just before Valeria had stepped in.

The woman who owned the club had first come over to us, made sure we had drinks before asking about Nem.

Not that I'd tell her anything. I learned long before never to give anything away that might bite me in the ass, and Valeria was the sort of woman who would take a bite. She'd said she'd talk to Nem, that she'd offer her personal restroom so the girl would have a private place to clean up.

Or get sick, which was the more likely purpose.

Dane knocked his fist against the door. "You done yet, Nem? I've got some mints to get rid of that puke taste."

Smooth. Funny that someone so talented in manipulating people could also have no tact.

No answer came back. It was as if we all realized at the same moment that something could be wrong. Had she passed out? Hit her head? She was in a bathroom with no windows and only a janitor's closet—we'd checked first.

Dane twisted and knocked harder—*still nothing.*

Patience wasn't one of our virtues, which meant the next attempt was Rune using his booted foot to kick open the restroom door. Inside, we found it empty, the closet door ajar.

I rushed in, then peered into the small closet. At the back, the brooms that had rested against the wall were moved, revealing a doorhandle I hadn't seen upon first look. Through that door...Valeria's office and still no Nem.

An unfamiliar panic gripped my chest. *Where is she? What the fuck is she thinking?*

Dane probably had the same questions before he left the office—through the main door, and a minute later, Valeria walked in, him behind her.

And even I had to be impressed with the way she moved. She was surrounded by four men that people far scarier than her feared, by men who had no issue putting anyone in the ground who crossed us, but she didn't show the slightest bit of fear.

Her arms weren't crossed, no sign of defensiveness. No guilt, but no confusion either.

The bitch knew exactly what had happened. Hell, their little chit-chat at the bar had turned sinister.

"Where is she?" Rune asked.

Valeria shrugged, her thin shoulders odd against the backbone she showed. She and Nem really were two peas in a pod, weren't they? "I didn't ask."

"What did she say?"

"Nothing important, nothing that could help you find her."

"There are people out there who would happily see her dead. Why the fuck would she run away?"

"Because her life doesn't revolve around you?" Valeria did a head-to-toe perusal of each of us, and her lifted eyebrow said she found us lacking. "Believe it or not, your cocks aren't worth a woman giving up her life for. Nem needed space."

I moved forward until I was just in front of her, trying to use my size and reputation like a weapon. "Do you really want to play this game with us?"

Valeria lifted her chin, staring me down. "I don't play games. Now, this is my private office, and I don't recall inviting any of you in. I suggest you leave while you still have that option."

Her dismissal burned. She was the only target I had for the fear rushing through me, for the unanswered questions, the only lead I had for where exactly Nem had run off to. Instead of giving even a moment of thought to me, to the other men, Valeria treated us as though we were nothing more than kids going door to door to sell candy bars.

"If she's hurt…" I left the statement unfinished, partly because people could fill in their own horror, but also because I couldn't bring myself to think about that, to even consider what I'd do if something happened to Nem.

Which was beyond strange. She'd been a part of my life for such a short time—and she'd been a fucking pain the ass mostly—yet the thought of her being hurt, of losing her, seemed impossible. How the fuck could she matter to me this much, and why hadn't I realized it before now?

Dane shook his head and had his phone out as he exited the office, no doubt throwing himself into work mode. We needed to try and track her down—her phone, cabs, ride shares, bank accounts—it all needed to be sifted through to figure out where she'd gone. Rune followed, rolling his shoulders then his neck as if prepared to do whatever it took, beat information out of whoever he needed to.

I offered Valeria one last glare before following.

Bray remained behind, and his voice was quiet but dangerous. "Watch yourself, Valeria—I thought you learned before that sticking your nose in places you shouldn't will get it bitten off."

I turned to watch the exchange. To her credit, Valeria didn't wither beneath the words, though a tic in her jaw said she knew what he meant. "Watch yourself, Bray. You might have caught more than you can handle with that one, and I'll enjoy my front row seat to watch her castrate you all."

Bray returned the hard look, neither willing to back down.

Which was fine by me. They could play their games, roll around in their bullshit.

I didn't give a fuck about anyone else right now.

I needed to find Nem, because that girl was about to find out why so many people feared us and just how dangerous we really were.

Chapter Twenty

Nem

As it turned out, alcohol worked nearly as well as pain pills when it came to numbing the ache in my shoulder. I'd been only slightly buzzed when I'd left the club, but after having Valeria's driver drop me off in front of my target's house, I'd downed more of the whiskey. I was comfortably plastered, now.

I lifted the pistol in my hand and squeezed the trigger, a bullet flying through one of the guards in the large house. Normally, alcohol would have dulled my reflexes, but maybe anger and adrenaline had helped stave off that response.

Or maybe I'd waited so long for this moment that nothing could stop me, like something driven by fate.

Carlos was upstairs.

The plan that would have taken effect next week, the well-crafted sequence of events that would have left him vulnerable to attack had been too far away. It didn't matter how perfectly planned it had been, how easy — the fire raging inside me refused to wait. Anger had shoved all that work aside and demanded I do something *now*.

That something turned out to be cutting the power to his house at the breaker box, using a jammer to prevent any calls for back-up or help, and bringing enough bullets to finish this.

Plans were great, had gotten me pretty far, but Valeria had reminded me that I wasn't just a plot. I was vengeance made flesh, a corpse driven only by the need to set right the things Kyler had done. Maybe I kept failing because I'd forgotten that, because I'd tried to be Jarrod and Kyler and the Quad instead of myself.

A quick stop at my storage place had given me access to everything I could have wanted. The most important thing was my 9mm along with prefilled magazines for quick reloads.

Thankfully, it seemed as paranoid as Carlos was, his actual security force was bare bones. Maybe he'd realized that, being past his prime, the number of people willing to come after him now weren't all that high.

Of course, it only has to be the one…

I walked in without knowing exactly what was there. It made me feel alive, forced me to focus only on the moment. I wasn't just following a list, not just a group of steps. I embraced that feeling, the electricity running through me, the way every step rooted me in the now, in what I was doing.

I didn't think about Kenz or the Quad or Kyler — nothing but Carlos.

I felt like a dog with a scent, the rest of the world fading away so all I had to do was follow this trail, was take down my prey at the end.

The bodies left behind, the questions, the mess, none of it fucking mattered.

What mattered was that Carlos had put three bullets in me ten years ago and never paid for it. He never got what was coming to him over it. He'd helped plan the whole damn thing, had picked the men, had set it all up, and now he thought he got to retire? He thought he could fade into the background and never get his due?

Fuck that.

I was far from some avenging angel, but my chosen name, the one I'd picked when I'd clawed myself from the edge of death, when I'd put myself back together, I'd picked it for a fucking reason.

Nem.

Short for Nemesis, an old goddess known for enacting retribution, especially against those who showed arrogance.

It had seemed perfect, a reminder of what I needed to do, of how I wouldn't let anything stop me, of who I was now. Just like the Nemesis of mythology, I had nothing except that need to bring vengeance to those who deserved it.

Carlos had thought me dead and gone, just ash on the floor of an old house that didn't matter anymore. He thought he'd finished me off, that he got away with it all.

He was wrong.

I made my way through the darkness, listening carefully for the creak of steps, for the heavy breathing from untrained men. They gave themselves away too easily, calling themselves security forces when they were just muscle without skill.

Counting didn't even matter. Their stories didn't matter, their histories or their names. They'd taken the job to protect a vile man, and if they wanted to take a bullet for him, I'd give them just that.

Before I knew it, no more sounds filled the house. Blessed silence. Five bodies were spread throughout the space, none of them having even gotten a shot off.

I took the stairs slowly, my steps silent, my ears tuned for anything.

At the top, a line of doors, all open, except the one at the end.

Carlos lived alone, which meant he had to be there, just beyond that door, hiding there like a coward.

Wetness made my face itch, and I knew red painted my skin. Splatter was no joke, and I hadn't been careful. Blood didn't bother me, especially when the people losing it deserved what they got. I'd lived my new life in blood, from the start, when I'd bled out, to what I'd lost when training, to what I'd spilled when I needed to. I'd happily bathe in it if it got me what I wanted.

At the far end of the hall, I pressed my back to the side of the door, then twisted the handle and let it creak open.

The loud bang of a gunshot, then a curse. *Carlos*. I'd recognize that voice anywhere, even after so many years. The shot also let me know he was on edge, because no one in control of themselves would have fired wildly at a door without seeing a target.

It was funny to think that the man who had haunted my nightmares, the one who had tried to kill me, now seemed like little more than a frightened child.

"James?" Carlos called into the darkness, his voice like a plea, as if he were praying it was one of his security force. "Someone answer me! What the fuck is going on?"

I kept still, waiting for the right moment to move. It came when he walked out, his pistol held far in front of him, his gaze locked on the stairs. Whether time or age or just a lack of practice made him clumsy, I had no idea. In fact, maybe he'd always been this incompetent, and I just hadn't known before. Maybe I'd been the one to turn him into a monster in my memory.

It was strange to think that, to wonder if he'd never been as scary as I'd made him out to be, if I'd pushed myself so hard, formed myself into a weapon, only to find out he had never been the man who had plagued my nightmares.

I swung my gun down, striking his wrist with the butt of it. His weapon slipped from his grasp, and a quick kick sent it skidding down the hall. I twisted, bringing my elbow into his face, fast enough he couldn't brace for it—especially due to the dark.

Carlos stumbled backward, into his room, and I followed, training my pistol back on him.

He fell, tripping over his own damned feet, and landed on his ass. He cradled his face in his hands and stared up at me. I said nothing as his eyes adjusted, as the light that filtered in through the window let him see me. "Who the fuck are you?" he asked, his voice muffled by his hands.

It didn't surprise me that he had no idea who I was. In fact, even if I looked exactly as I had back then, I doubted he would have remembered me.

I didn't matter to him. I hadn't that night, and I still didn't.

Well…I guess I do at the moment. There was something almost as intoxicating as the whiskey about that, about the fact I was finally important to him.

"Ten years ago," I said as I stared down at him. "Ten years ago, you took a job."

"I've taken a lot of fucking jobs. You'll need to be a lot more specific."

"Kyler Williams hired you to kill his wife and daughter."

That seemed to get his attention. It wasn't fear on his face, though. He didn't show any signs of guilt at the reminder, just an understanding, as if sure, he recalled that. "Yeah, so?"

"So? That's all you have to say about it?"

"I've lived a long time, and that ain't the worst thing I've ever done. He paid me well. We didn't let either of 'em linger. I call that a clean job."

"Clean?" I crouched, far enough away he couldn't reach me even if he kicked or lunged. "How much did Kyler pay you for that?"

"More than enough."

"And did he ever tell you why you were doing it?"

Carlos huffed, a bubbling sound accompanying it due to the blood. "I don't ask questions like that. Ain't my business why people want things done — it's my job to get 'em done. I did hear that his whore of a wife had passed off a kid as his who wasn't. If that was true, far as I say, she got what was coming to her."

I smiled. That coldness hadn't returned, but it was as though the fire inside me, the anger, burned so strongly that it gave me an odd sense of calm. Maybe surrendering to it was what did that, maybe fighting against the flames caused the panic. "So you killed a woman and her teenaged daughter just because Kyler has some fears of inadequacy?"

"I'm tired of this fucking game. What do you want? A little bitch like you ain't breaking in here for a chat."

"You're right about that. I could have put a bullet in you like I did your pathetic guards. I could have ended you already, like I did Lucky and Shelia and Geoffrey. That wasn't *enough* for you, though. I wanted to talk to you, to see your eyes when you figured out exactly how badly you fucked up, when you realized that shit you thought you'd burned to ash wasn't as gone as you'd figured."

"Quit with the riddles and come out with it, already."

I rose, staring down at him like the trash he was. "You couldn't even do one job right. One teenage girl, and you couldn't kill her." I hooked my fingers into the neckline of my top and pulled, two of the buttons giving way, to reveal the scarring over my heart. "One bullet to the chest, then two more through my back when I hit the floor. Two feet away, and you couldn't manage to finish the job, couldn't put me down."

His eyes widened for a moment. "Bullshit," he spat back. "I saw that place go up in flames."

"Yeah, but what you didn't see was the hidden room in the closet. You didn't see the backyard where I crawled to, bleeding the whole damn way. Bet you wish you'd looked closer now, don't you?"

"You were dead. No one survives that."

"You're right about that. My heart stopped in that backyard, as I bled out. Too bad for you, corpses hold grudges."

"We can work this out," he said after a moment. "I got money. I got a lot of friends who owe me favors."

"The only thing you've got is thirty seconds before I put a bullet into your head. See, I learned something from you—make sure they're fucking dead before you walk away."

He shook his head. "It wasn't personal—it was just money, just a job. I can give you whatever shit you want—"

"Can you give me back my mother? Can you give me back my old life? Can you give me ten fucking years of my life back? Can you change that I'm wrong, now? That what you did twisted me and broke me and turned me into whatever I am now, and I have to live with that forever?"

He gulped hard, as if recognizing for the first time he wasn't getting out of this alive. Still, it seemed he wanted one last-ditch effort. "Look—"

I pulled the trigger, his thirty seconds up, sending a bullet into him.

Not just one, though. Hell no. I squeezed the trigger again and again, glad I'd put in a new magazine on the stairs.

Five bullets later and there was nothing of his face left. It felt good—right. I thought about the ash he'd left my mother as, and it seemed fitting he was left in a similar state. It didn't heal a wound, but damn if it didn't feel like removing a piece of shrapnel that had been stuck in me for years.

A sound behind me made me spin, my gun out.

When I saw who stood, I pulled the trigger, the reaction immediate. The click of my gun reminded me that I'd left all my bullets in Carlos.

It left me weaponless and standing there, having just outed exactly who I was, in front of the Quad. Their expressions, the way their eyes moved over me, dipping to where my shirt still showed the old scar on my chest, all said the same.

They'd heard. They knew exactly who I was and that I'd been lying to them.

Well, fuck...

Want to see more from this author? Here's a taster for you to enjoy!

Nemesis: The Resurrected Queen
Jayce Carter

Excerpt

Nem

Nothing stays a secret forever.

I stood there, covered in blood, facing four men who I was hopelessly bound to, who now knew I'd been lying to them, and who might just kill me for it.

Carlos' body still rested on the floor behind me, and I'd have put a bullet into Rune — mostly because he was the biggest target — if I hadn't run out of ammunition.

Which was part of the reason I couldn't blame them for the seething anger they stared at me with.

"Kelsey?" Dane asked, as if he might have misheard the entire conversation. His gaze didn't stray from my eyes. Was he trying to see the girl he'd known there? Trying to see if he could catch a glimpse and recognize me?

Good luck, buddy. That girl died ten years ago.

I nodded, dropping my arm since the gun was heavy and useless at the moment.

"How?"

"I'm pretty sure you can work that out for yourself." I risked glancing across the four men, not meeting their eyes but searching for a reaction from each. Mostly, they wore shock, as though they had to replay everything that had happened between us to come to terms with the idea that I wasn't who they'd thought I was, that they'd already known me.

Colton took a step toward me, and I took a big jump backward.

He froze, his expression hardening as though he didn't care for the reaction. *Too bad.* Only an idiot would trust them, especially now. They had every reason to kill me, even if they hadn't before.

Still, he didn't argue, didn't try to reassure me. Instead, he glanced around the room, sliding into a familiar 'all business' mode. After a second, he nodded. "We've got work to do. Five bodies downstairs, one up here. There's too much blood and not enough time to clean it properly. Let it look like the hit it was—just make sure no one knows who did it. Let's get rid of any evidence."

"There isn't any," I snapped.

Colton gave me a chilling look, one that reminded me of why I'd backed away earlier. The man was terrifying when he was calm like that. "How about the bloody handprint on the banister? That left a good set of fingerprints. Or perhaps the video footage?"

"There isn't any footage. I made sure the power was off before I got in front of any cameras."

"For this house, sure. You failed to notice that the camera at the neighbor's house watches their RV and also gets a look at the front door of this place. Also, did you bother to find out if he has any universal power supplies hooked up to his camera feeds? This was sloppy, Kelsey, no matter what you want to say."

The criticism sucked, but it wasn't nearly as painful as the way he said my name. That took the breath from my lungs, threatened to connect me back to the girl I'd been, to the life that had been stolen away.

"I can help," I said, rather than trying to argue with him. The reality was that it had been sloppy. It had been impulsive and foolish, and I still had too much alcohol in my system to pretend I was on the best footing.

"Not a chance." Colton looked over at Bray, who still hadn't said a word. "Get her back home with Dane. Rune and I will clean up this mess."

A moment of hope hit me, the idea of getting a moment alone, of figuring out a way to put everything back right again, before I'd managed to royally fuck up the entire plan.

It fled, however, when Colton landed his heavy gaze back on me. "And when we get back? We're going to have one hell of a talk, *Nem.*"

I had a feeling I wasn't going to enjoy the sort of talk he meant...

* * * *

Dane

There were moments when life liked to really kick a man in the balls. I'd experienced plenty of those, when everything lined up perfectly to fuck me over.

And this was sure as hell one of them.

I sat in the backseat of the car beside Nem — *beside Kelsey* — and couldn't get my brain to catch up. Me, who never shut the fuck up, couldn't figure out a single thing to say.

Now that I knew, I wondered how I'd ever missed it. How couldn't I have seen it before?

The same nose, even the same smirk when she didn't want to laugh but couldn't help it, the same damned eyes.

Sure, she'd grown up. The last time I'd seen her, that morning before it all went down, she'd been seventeen, that age when kids thought they were adults and were only too quick to want to prove it. She'd started to fill out a bit, to lose some of that gangly stage girls went through when they got taller but lacked the curves that came with adulthood.

A flash of Nem naked hit me, a memory of just how much I enjoyed those curves coming over me.

How could it be her, though?

A memory from ten years ago, from a night I never wanted to remember, came back to me, aided by the way the streetlights flashed inside the SUV as we passed them...

I couldn't breathe, couldn't think, couldn't do a damn thing beyond putting one foot in front of the other. Getting news when I could do something, that was one thing. Adrenaline hit a person, put them into fight or flight so they could solve the problem.

If I'd gotten the news when I'd been in town, I'd have been at the house within ten minutes, running into the damned flames myself, uncaring that they still roared. I would have happily burned alive in that house if it meant saving Caroline or Kelsey.

Instead, it had taken three hours to get back, and by the time we did?

It was all over.

The fire was out, the house nothing but charred remains, blackened supports and soot.

Caroline was dead. Kyler had called and told us the news. The drive back, not wanting to tell Kenz, had been torture on a level I hadn't known existed. Kyler would tell her—it wasn't our place to do so.

After dropping her off, we'd come to the house. Why? Maybe some stupid vigil, some sentimental desire to stand watch over what we lost.

Kelsey…

As much as Caroline's death hurt, it was nothing compared to Kelsey. She'd been too young, too sweet for this to have happened. It was as if some hollowed-out piece of me remained, something she'd taken with her, had burned away beside her.

I remembered when she'd tried to kiss me just weeks before, her young want, the foolish romantic notions, and how I'd set her aside. It wasn't that I hadn't wanted her…

Fuck, I had.

I'd just cared too damn much to let it happen. She didn't know what she wanted, was too young to have a clue, and I wasn't about to let her keep going with that stupid fascination.

Kelsey had a real life ahead of her, a chance at a family, at a home, at all the things she deserved. She'd get none of that if she pursued the idiotic idea of some romance with me, with my brothers.

She'd get none of that now…

Yet, staring at the ash, the rubble, it wasn't just the loss of her that dug at me. It was the loss of the stupid fantasy I held on to as well.

An idea I kept locked away except for the brief moments it broke free, usually at night just before I fell asleep, when I thought…*what if?* What if she grew up a bit more, figured out her life more, then…

It didn't matter anymore, did it?

She was gone. Gone because someone had targeted her to get back at Kyler, gone because someone had been a coward and killed an unarmed child.

I followed Bray around the house, to the backyard. I didn't need to ask him what he was looking for.

Bray was quiet, but he held hope the rest of us had lost a long time before. "She knew where the safe room was."

"The safe room is ashes," I reminded him. It had been created to hide a person, not to protect them from flames.

Even if she'd made it there, she'd have been trapped inside while she burned. That was a worse thought than her taking a bullet or two.

Still, I let him hold on to the idea. It would get torn free soon enough.

In the backyard, the blackened grass hid signs of anything. I was caught by the patio swing there, the cushions burned, the metal like a skeleton left over. I remembered how Kelsey would sit there in the mornings, watching the sky as the sun rose. I woke early, so I'd usually been the one out there with her.

We didn't talk much, one of the few times I could just be silent, where I could rest. She'd been too fucking good for me, for any of us, for the whole damned world we lived in. She'd given me a sense of calm I'd never found in any other place.

I pulled my gaze from it, trying to bury my reactions, trying to take the pain that shot through me and shove it down beneath everything else before it consumed me.

On the back wall, where the safe room had been, was…nothing. The fire had eaten it away, leaving no evidence there had been a hidden space there at all.

Bray dropped to his knees, placing his hand on the foundation there, in the ash that was the only thing left. He hung his head forward, his eyes closed.

I got that feeling, the pain, but I didn't let it take over.

Instead, I turned to find Colton coming around the corner, Rune on his heels, their matching expressions hard.

"Anything?" I asked, even though I knew the answer. What was I hoping for? For him to explain how it hadn't really happened? That it was all a big mistake?

Colton shook his head, a quick jerk that screamed anger. "It was Cantor Lorris."

"You sure?"

"Kyler gave me the name. The body they found out front, just outside of the fire, is Cantor's second. Seemed to take a slug when they were coming in — guess the security tried to do something."

I struggled to understand it, to believe it. I'd done some horrible shit in my life, all in the name of duty or power or loyalty, but I'd never slaughtered innocents.

Spouses and kids were off-limits — always.

Of course, expecting others to live by my rules would do nothing but cause heartache. The reality was that other people in our world weren't as principled as we were, and this was more proof of it.

"Why kill them and not Kyler?" I asked.

"Kyler got a text message from Caroline this morning, after we left, saying Kelsey wasn't feeling well and asking him to come home."

A frown touched my features. "Caroline wouldn't ever do that..." Caroline was tough and independent. She wouldn't call for help over something as trivial as Kelsey not feeling well, and she sure as hell wouldn't have called Kyler home.

"Exactly. Near as I can figure, they broke in around nine in the morning and must have taken Caroline's cell and sent the text message. They were probably hoping Kyler would speed home and they'd get him too — take out the whole family in one swoop. Hell, I bet they thought Kenz was there, too."

"And when Kyler no doubt answered that he was busy, they decided to cut their losses," I added.

"Looks like being a selfish fucker saved Kyler's ass again." Rune didn't look at anyone else, his voice a mess of fury, as if he were just looking for a target for all that aggression.

"So what now?" I asked though we all knew the answer. It had been our job to take care of Caroline and Kelsey, to protect them, and we'd failed. We hadn't seen this coming, hadn't been able to stop it, and now two of the only people in the whole fucking world who mattered to us were gone.

Colton answered, a darkness in his voice that reminded me of how dangerous the man was. The rest of us, we could kill — would kill — if we needed to. Colton specialized in it, enjoyed it, relished the part of him that took life with such skill. "We didn't save them, but we'll fucking make sure the people who did this suffer for it."

And that was a plan that I could get behind...

Nem twisted her head, her familiar eyes locking with mine and pulling me back to the present.

All that pain, all that fear, all that guilt I'd carried all this time, and she'd never been dead at all. Where had she been? Why hadn't she *told* us she was okay?

I wanted to wrap my hand around her neck and demand answers, to force her to let me into her head and figure out what exactly she'd gotten herself into. Where had she been for ten fucking years? What had she been doing? Who else knew the truth?

I knew better, though. She was even more stubborn than she'd been before, and now wasn't the time.

So I sat back, tearing my gaze from her even if that was the last thing I wanted. Some part of my brain screamed to not look away, to stare at her, to memorize every detail. I wanted to strip her down, now that I knew the truth, and kiss each freckle on her lying body, to nip each one and bask in having her back.

There would be time for that later, though. The reality was that even knowing it was her didn't really answer shit. It only gave me more questions, more uncertainty.

Nem was a bomb, and if I went poking around with it, it might just blow up in my face. It meant I had to play the game, still, and if there was one thing I knew for sure...

I needed all four of us if we had any hope of untangling the disaster of a woman beside me, because she was too fucking dangerous for any of us to face on our own.

* * * *

Nem

The shower was hot, but even as it turned my skin red, it didn't sear away the memories, the questions, the doubts.

Back at the men's home, I'd retreated to the bathroom to wash the blood off. Bray had taken my clothes, and I hadn't even fought him on it. I loved the outfit, but it was covered in blood. The safest choice was to dispose of it—probably by burning it.

Red ran down the drain, from both the dye that leached from my hair and the blood that I washed off. Most of it had dried, so I used a washcloth to scrub it clean.

And yet, even with all the unknowns, even with the frustration about Kenz, about Kyler, none of that was in the shower with me. Instead, it was *them*.

Would I walk down that hallway and find a bullet with my name on it?

No, that would be too impersonal, and by the looks on their faces, they were feeling rather personal about this.

I tipped my head back, letting water run through my hair, trying to block out the memories that threatened to consume me.

It was like suddenly, now that they knew who I was, I struggled to keep a wall between who I had been and who I was now. They'd shattered that separator, and I had no idea how to build it up again.

I felt like *her* again, like the young girl who was too stupid to see the world for what it was.

You aren't her anymore! You've grown up, gotten stronger, smarter.

If they thought for a second that I'd be an easy target, they had no clue who they were dealing with.

That was the point, though, wasn't it? They didn't know. They'd seen a glimpse, one I'd chosen to show them, but they didn't have a clue how deep my hatred ran, how determined I was, how strong I'd gotten by sheer willpower. They hadn't seen me crawl out of the burning building, hadn't seen the blood trailing me, hadn't watched as I'd built myself into what I was now.

I turned off the water and squeezed my hair to try to get all the water out I could. I wrapped a towel around me before pulling open drawers quietly, searching.

Finally, below the sink, I found it. They'd taken my gun—another fair thing to do, but I didn't care for being unarmed—however it was nearly impossible to keep a determined person from finding a weapon.

A button-up shirt sat on the counter, along with a pair of underwear. I slid on the outfit, then tucked the straight-edge razor I'd found beneath the sink into the waistband.

If they wanted a fight, I had no problem giving them one.

After getting dressed and procrastinating as long as I could, I found myself in front of the four men who I couldn't read.

Well, Rune and Colton looked tired. Then again, cleanup work wasn't the easiest or most fun part of a job. Guilt tugged at me, but I refused to let it get a foothold. I hadn't asked them to clean up my mess, to take care of me.

At least some of their anger had seemed to dissipate. Maybe it was like disasters. Hysterical screaming could only last for so long before people accepted things as the new normal. The men had gone through their shock, and that sort of emotional level couldn't be kept up for long.

Rune and Dane sat on the large couch, while Bray had pulled in a chair from the kitchen and Colton remained on his feet, leaning against the bookshelf. Colton always did that, was always silently watching from the outside.

One more seat rested in the room, a chair in the center that made it clear it was for me. I almost laughed as I remembered times they'd done this before, when they'd tried to scare me into admitting where I'd snuck out to the night before.

It hadn't worked on a sixteen-year-old girl. Did they really think it would now?

Still, I took the spot meant for me, ignoring how little I wore. That was another purposeful step, no doubt. During an interrogation, a person wanted to highlight the difference in power. Make the suspect uncomfortable, make it clear they weren't in charge, remind them how little control they had.

If they thought giving me one of their button-up shirts was going to do that, they were sadly mistaken. We could have done this with me naked, and I'd still have been fine.

The alcohol had faded away, leaving a headache behind but putting me on solid ground for going toe-to-toe with them.

"What happened?" Rune asked, surprising me by speaking.

They normally let Dane do the talking.

"When?" I asked, going for casual, as if none of this mattered all that much to me.

"You were at the house with Caroline when men arrived, judging by what we heard. How did you escape?" Rune spoke as though my mouthing off didn't bother him, as if he couldn't be shaken.

Still, interrogations were a matter of giving the right information while keeping the wrong to myself. "Carlos thought I was dead. He figured the three bullets he put into me would take care of the job. Shelia had taken Caroline's phone, so she couldn't call anyone, and Geoffrey shot my mother. Lucky poured gasoline around the house and lit a match. While everything burned down around me, I dragged myself to the safe room in the closet."

"The safe room was destroyed," Bray said, his tone still untrusting.

"I kicked the vent cover off and crawled out."

"That vent was tiny."

I let out a soft laugh, recalling how I'd pulled myself through, how the smoke had made me cough as I'd struggled — or maybe it had been the blood in my lungs. "I got cut up trying, but I managed it. Seems like when the world is burning around you, you're capable of some surprising things."

Colton spoke up from his spot. "You had three bullet wounds, Nem. You couldn't have walked anywhere, didn't take any of the cars. How did you get out of the backyard?"

It was hard to think about, to force myself back to that night, to the fear and the pain. I did it, though, making myself reach for what had happened. "I got to the bushes before I collapsed. The men who did it didn't stick around — fires attract a quick response. Someone showed up who helped me."

"Who?"

I shook my head. "You don't get everything in my head. All I'll say is that it was a friend, and I'd be dead without them."

Dane pressed his lips together, as if the answer was unsatisfactory, but he knew better than to push. "Why didn't you tell anyone you were alive? Why pretend you were dead? Why let us all think Cantor's men had killed you?"

"It wasn't Cantor."

"Of course, it was." Dane spoke with such certainty, but that wasn't the only thing I heard. Even after a decade, it was the anger that shone through. "He tried to trick Kyler into showing up so he could take out the entire family. When we caught up with him, he was on the run. Not much more proof needed."

"He was fleeing because anyone who had you four after them would run. I lived through it. I took out every fucking person involved except the one who planned it. I know exactly what happened, know who was behind it, and trust me, it wasn't Cantor."

"So who was it?"

I met Dane's gaze head-on. "You want to know why I didn't come back? Why I let everyone think I was dead? Because Kyler set up the hit. He hired those men to kill my mother and me, and I had no goddamned idea if you four were in on it or not."

And that sure managed to shut them up.

About the Author

Jayce Carter lives in Southern California with her husband and two spawns. She originally wanted to take over the world but realized that would require wearing pants. This led her to choosing writing, a completely pants-free occupation. She has a fear of heights yet rock climbs for fun and enjoys making up excuses for not going out and socializing.

Jayce loves to hear from readers. You can find her contact information, website details and author profile page at https://www.totallybound.com

Home of Erotic Romance

Sign up for our newsletter and find out about all our romance book releases, eBook sales and promotions, sneak peeks and FREE romance books!